HEARTS
of
FIRE
and
SNOW

Also by David Bowles and Guadalupe García McCall

Secret of the Moon Conch

HEARTS
of
FIRE
and
SNOW

DAVID BOWLES
GUADALUPE GARCÍA McCALL

BLOOMSBURY

NEW YORK LONDON OXFORD NEW DELHI SYDNEY

BLOOMSBURY YA
Bloomsbury Publishing Inc., part of Bloomsbury Publishing Plc
1385 Broadway, New York, NY 10018

BLOOMSBURY and the Diana logo are trademarks of Bloomsbury Publishing Plc

First published in the United States of America in June 2024 by Bloomsbury YA

Bloomsbury books may be purchased for business or promotional use.
For information on bulk purchases please contact Macmillan Corporate and
Premium Sales Department at specialmarkets@macmillan.com

Library of Congress Cataloging-in-Publication Data
available upon request
ISBN 978-1-5476-1004-4 (hardcover) • ISBN 978-1-5476-1005-1 (e-book)

Book design by Jeanette Levy
Typeset by Westchester Publishing Services
Printed and bound in the U.S.A.
2 4 6 8 10 9 7 5 3 1

To find out more about our authors and books visit
www.bloomsbury.com and sign up for our newsletters.

*To Jesse, for standing watch over
those I love the most.* —*Tu suegro, David*

*To my Mami and Papi in heaven, los tengo
siempre en mi corazón!* —*Lupita*

HEARTS
of
FIRE
and
SNOW

PROLOGUE

When the Great Gods of Chaos at last choose to pluck the princess from paradise and send her back, we—the Goddesses of Fate—sense the devious plan and set in motion our own.

Long ago, we had snarled the souls of her family and enemy together. Now we hook that skein to her destiny, and they go spiraling into the world, whatever memories they retain fading.

Chaos craves their punishment, hungers to see them suffer, longs to see them act out the bloody tragedy once more, wants to gloat as they repeat the mistakes of the past. Not us. Our hungers are unique. We shall devour their faults, their pain, their shame.

We await the signs that will help us find them. Two generations ago, the volcano of our beloved warrior—who has kept his magma and steam calm for nearly a century—erupted in the midst of his regenerative sleep. In the aftermath, we discovered that one of the two dead and icy volcanoes was now tethered to a human soul.

Somewhere in the United States. Reno, Nevada.

Enough of our children's children inhabit the city for us to keep a tenuous watch over this web of broken hearts we helped to create. The ones we believe we recognize, at least.

Twelve years later, we sense her at last—another human soul, suddenly linked to a snowy silhouette. A girl of seventeen winters, icy pride rippling through her being.

Nearby. In the city they call Mexico.

Ecstatic, the oldest of us goes to the volcano to awaken the deathless from his long sleep a little early. There, in that vast chamber near rivers of molten rock, Eldest Sister speaks.

"Majestic child, long-suffering warrior, the debt has been paid. Your deathless vigil of a thousand years is coming to an end. The maiden has at last returned. Rise now and bring her to us so that you both may meet your destiny."

The ancient warrior leaps to his feet, hot heart roiling. The volcano responds, magma surging from below as the ancient rock shudders all around. With a voice unused for fifty-two years, he croaks a single word.

"Where?"

Before we can answer, his eyes go wide, and he clutches at his head.

An awful scream tears from his lips, and he collapses to the bare rock.

"No! Too much! I remember it all, every second, and it burns! IT BURNS!"

His cries echo through the caverns, and the volcano shudders violently in response. Gouts of magma surge from the depths, bursting through the caldera.

Elder Sister has no choice. She touches his forehead, pushing him back into hibernation. Then, sobbing, she begins to make his memories fade, calming the eruptions to intermittent hiccups of smoke and ash.

Then she takes the younger two with her to that distant land, to prepare the way should he ever awaken on his own.

And I stay behind to watch over him.

As I have done for centuries.

Waiting to set things right.

CHAPTER

1

When I open my eyes, I don't know who I am.

Even the room I'm in seems unfamiliar. I sit up in a huge bed, pulling aside sheets so soft they feel like warm clouds. The space is the size of a small apartment, which makes me wonder if I'm in some studio loft in a big city. But how can I know about apartments and cities if I can't remember my own name?

I walk around, hoping that some object will trigger memories. Instead, I just feel confused. There's a black rectangle on one wall that may be a television set, though it also feels different from any I've ever seen. Another screen sits on a desk, and all that comes to mind is the computer in Mr. Spock's quarters on that science fiction program. What was it called? *Star Trek*. Annoying that the title comes so easily.

There's a sofa and a few other chairs. Full bookshelves. A dresser with photographs displayed. I inspect them while checking the mirror hanging on the wall behind them. Both reflection and snapshots show a teenager, perhaps seventeen or eighteen, with dark skin, black hair and eyes, handsome features. Indigenous, my selective mind suggests. Perhaps Nahua, from the highlands near Mexico City.

Then I look more closely at the photos. Something's off. It's hard to explain how I know, but the boy in those images is *not* the same one staring back at me from the mirror. The resemblance is *very* close, as if a talented surgeon or scientist took someone with a similar build and background and tweaked his features to look like . . . mine.

Muffled conversation comes from beyond the closed door. I'm only wearing boxers, so I open the drawers and find a T-shirt to pull over my well-muscled torso. There are no pants in the dresser, but a huge walk-in closet nearby gives me lots of options. I pick some jeans at random and a pair of soft leather loafers.

Once I'm dressed, I take a moment to look out the window that fills most of one wall. Though something feels odd about the skyline, I recognize the metropolis as Mexico City. On the horizon rise the slopes of the two volcanoes, Popocatepetl and Iztaccihuatl. The sight of their snow-capped peaks brings an ache to my chest, so I close the blinds and turn away, gasping.

Wanting answers, I open the door and step into a second-story hall with a railing that leads to staircases at either end. The voices are clearer. They are speaking in both Spanish and Nahuatl, two languages that I apparently understand, as I can follow the mysterious conversation easily.

"But it's been four months!" a man is protesting. A quaver in his voice suggests old age. "With all due respect, Blessed One, we believed you Four would have resolved the problem by now."

"There's no use pushing him to awaken," replies the voice of a woman, maybe younger. "He would just shut down and fall into a coma again. The other three are monitoring the situation in Nevada closely. The candidates aren't going anywhere. There's time for him to emerge from this state when his mind's ready."

Another woman, older, interjects. "When we were still children, His Majesty explained the cycle of regeneration. Nothing like this has ever happened before. You say it's the work of Chaos, but why now, when his plea to heaven has finally been granted?"

"Granted begrudgingly, believe me. Think of this setback as a final trial. To find her, he has to find himself."

I lean over the railing. An elderly couple, elegantly dressed, is sitting on a sofa while a middle-aged woman in a maid's uniform stands in front of them. All three appear to be Indigenous Nahua, like my reflection.

The maid looks up and smiles.

My heart fills with peace and contentment. I know her. She loves me, and that love is precious, somehow. Meaningful.

I get the feeling she's stood by my side through very hard times.

"Goyo!" she exclaims with delight, tears of relief sparkling in her eyes. "You're awake at last. Stay there—I'll help you down."

More quickly than a woman of her age normally moves, she runs up the stairs, but I wave her away. "I feel fine. Perfectly steady and strong."

"Okay, then," she says, giving me a thumbs-up. "Follow me, boy. There's much to discuss."

I descend the stairs behind her. The older couple is now standing, eyes wide. The man must be in his seventies, wearing a tailored suit, while the woman may be fifty-something. Perhaps a little older, her dark hair pulled back by a diamond-studded net of silver.

I realize I know their names.

"Roberto Chan Texis," I say as I reach the last stair. "Dolores Ihpotok de Chan."

Mr. Chan hurries to my side, taking my hand in his. The nails are carefully manicured, the skin soft though heavily wrinkled with age. "Do you remember, then?"

With a sigh, I shake my head. "Not really. I can't recall my name. I don't know who I am. It's like someone emptied my head of all the memories of my life. There's knowledge in there still, but disconnected from *me*, if that makes sense."

The three adults look at one another, disappointed and saddened at this news. Dolores smooths the rich fabric of her dress in a nervous gesture.

The maid wipes a tear from her cheek. Her short hair—black shot through with gray—bobs as she nods. "It's okay. We knew this might happen. Plan B, my children."

Taking a deep breath, she looks into my eyes.

"Your name is Gregorio Chan. These are your parents."

I glance at the couple. My heart tells me that her statement is both true and false.

"I was adopted, wasn't I?"

Dolores . . . my mother . . . covers her mouth with a shaking hand.

"It's more complicated than adoption," the maid responds, "but . . . yes. Your father is the CEO of Grupo Tolchan, one of the biggest conglomerates on the globe. You're its heir. But you've been out of the public eye for a long time. At a boarding school in Switzerland. Till four months ago."

She picks up a newspaper from the coffee table and hands it to me.

The tabloid is in German, *20 Minuten*. The date is May 22, 2023.

I have no problem reading the headline, which means I know at least three languages.

CORPORATE HEIR IN COMA AFTER SKIING ACCIDENT.

Below it is an image of me. Except it isn't me. It's the boy from the photographs in my room.

For the moment, I don't mention the weird discrepancy.

"You've been in a coma for four months . . . son." It's clear that Roberto is not used to calling me that. And I know instinctively that my coma has nothing to do with skiing.

"You three aren't being completely honest with me," I say.

The maid gives a wobbly, almost sarcastic nod.

"You're not wrong, Goyo," she confirms, using the common Spanish nickname for guys named Gregorio. "But you're going to have to trust us. We can't tell you everything."

I think about what I overheard moments ago. "Because I might 'shut down again,' right?"

Dolores, my mother, gives a little groan. "You have to remember on your own, no matter how long it takes."

I look at the maid. A name pops into my head. "Teicuihtzin?"

It means "beloved younger sister" in Nahuatl. A strange name for a middle-aged woman.

Her smile grows wistful. "Yes, my child. But you must call me Teresa. Teresa Segundo. That will be my name in our new home."

"New home?" I ask, confused. "I don't even recognize this one."

My father squeezes my hand. "We're . . . sending you to study abroad again. But this time to the United States. Reno, Nevada."

I raise an eyebrow as I turn my head to stare at him.

"You're transferring me from Le Rosey School in Switzerland to a private academy in *Reno*?"

Teresa laughs. "Oh, it's worse than that, Goyo. Not a private academy. A public high school. In a decent neighborhood, sure. Attended by snobs galore. But an honest-to-goodness, apple pie and football institution in the land of the free and the home of the brave, etcetera."

She has switched to English, which I also understand with ease.

"Why?" I ask in the same language.

"Because there's someone there you have to find," she explains, suddenly serious. "No one else but you can do it. We know she's there, but we don't know who she is."

I can't help but give a weak laugh of despair. "You realize that makes literally no sense, right?"

Teresa's face softens. "Yes. But know this, my dearest boy: you have loved her for a very long time, have searched for her everywhere. You need her, and she needs you. What we're about to do is unprecedented and perilous. You may wish your memories were still erased before we're through. But on the other side of the trials, you'll be whole, all of you, the girl you love and all the rest."

I understand nothing. But deep in my heart, I feel she is telling the truth, and my pulse quickens.

"Well," I say with a shrug, "I'd better pack."

Teresa giggles, a sound so surprising in the mouth of a woman of her age that I can't help but roll my eyes and grin.

"Oh, our things have been waiting in the cargo hold of your father's private jet for months. Say your goodbyes. We leave within the hour."

CHAPTER

2

I close my eyes, take a deep breath, and lock it away in my lungs, letting it feed my body, my mind, my heart. Nothing feels more natural than standing on a precipice on a crisp, cold day. Mount Rose has the best slopes, especially on snowy mornings like today. The Reno + Sparks Chamber of Commerce couldn't have picked a better place to hold their first annual Winter Wonderland Fundraiser.

"Damn it!" my boyfriend, Jackson Caldera, the handsomest most valuable player at Galena High School, curses under his breath. Instinctively, I turn back to check on him. He's bent over, dark blond hair swirling around his proud forehead, as he fiddles with his left ski boot.

"Still not latching on right?" I ask, because I want to make sure he's safe before we go any farther.

"Agh." Jackson tugs on the strap.

"We can go back," I tell him. "Get you another pair. My padrino's not going to use his. I'm pretty sure we're just giving them a ride again, so you might as well take them."

"It's my stupid sock. I can feel it slipping around. Don't worry about it. I'm sure it'll sort itself out," he says. Then he straightens up and gets going, squeezing my shoulder as he walks past me.

"I'm sure you'll forget all about it once we're going downhill," I say, teasing him, because I've been around Jackson long enough to know just how much he hates going down these slopes. Football, not skiing, is his thing.

As for me, this is my "mole." Skiing, swerving, sliding down sunlit white-capped mountaintops—that's my poetry, my music, my inspiration. Unfortunately, it's a passion no one else in my life seems to share, not my friends Tina or Sofía; not Jackson; and especially not my padrino, Rafael Montes, who's been my sole guardian since I was five.

"Here we go," Jackson says, stepping up to the green marker on the beginner's slope.

"Ah, no," I say, signaling for him to move on.

"Fine," he says and keeps going, reluctantly stepping up to the blue marker for the intermediate slope. "But only this once."

"Jackson? Blanca?" Jackson's parents, Ted Caldera, owner and CEO of Caldera Resorts, and Anja Olsson, a statuesque Swedish woman whose old-world money funded the family business, walk quickly to us.

"Mom. Dad. What are you doing all the way up here?" Jackson's stilted tone of voice tells me everything I need to know.

"Well, we can't take the bunny slope if we want to make a good showing, can we?" Jackson's father says, referring to the fact that all winnings, aka matched donations, will be displayed on the leader board as the event progresses, making all our efforts public knowledge.

"We're putting our best feet forward to make sure the Reno Children's Shelter gets enough funding to last all year," Anja Olsson says, in that breathy, sweet voice of hers. There's something ethereal about her beyond the blond hair, green eyes, and perfect porcelain skin. She's kind and so very open-minded—especially with me when I go on about things I'm passionate about. She just gets me. I like her so much; I want to be her someday.

"Ah, yes, the children. Of course." Jackson practically rolls his eyes as he turns away, directing his gaze to the lodge. He's never been as enthusiastic as his parents about these events.

"Well, you two be careful," Mr. Caldera says, touching his ex-wife's elbow, prompting her to get going now that they've got their skis on.

Anja Olsson smiles at him before she turns to look at us again.

"But not too careful. Life's too short. Be joyful and grateful for these youthful life events. Enjoy each other. Have fun. Celebrate your love," she says. Then she winks and waves her mittened fingertips at us. Smiling radiantly, she secures her goggles on her face and takes off, leading the way down the slope with Mr. Caldera following close behind.

"I love your mom," I say, looking longingly up to the double black marker at the summit a few feet up ahead, because that's where I really want to go.

"Everybody does," Jackson says, smiling smugly. "She's the best."

"Look at them, like synchronized swimmers," I say, as we watch them swish and swoosh elegantly down the slope. "It's hard to believe they're not married anymore. I guess some couples get along better as friends."

"Works for me," Jackson admits. "I have two houses I can crash, one here, one abroad. Best of both worlds. Amenities everywhere I go."

I shake my head, because only Jackson would find ways of making the best of his parents' divorce. I think I was more shaken up than he was by their breakup. Anja was the closest thing I had to a mother before she left Reno five years ago.

"Shall we?" I ask, giving him my most winsome smile, the one that makes him melt because he knows how happy I'll be if he just takes a leap of faith with me.

"Don't even think about it," Jackson says.

"But that's how you get the most bang for your buck," I say, disappointed, because I don't want to do this for me. I'm thinking of the Rural Nevada Ecological Society, the young women's coalition from Carrizo I'm representing today.

"Depending on my maneuvers, I could double, maybe even triple, my score. The higher my number, the higher the proceeds, and those young women could really use the money."

"Maneuvers? You mean stunts, don't you? Nope. Too dangerous," Jackson says, following me up the incline despite his protestations.

"Come on. Not even for your team?" I ask because he's chosen to donate his "winnings" to our school's football team. Not necessarily without a conflict of interest, but still allowable by the city board council in charge of the fundraiser.

"Blanca, please," he begs when he figures I'm not going to back down. "How many of these políticos do you honestly think are going to risk their hides to raise money today?"

"Doesn't matter," I say. "This isn't about them."

"Zero," Jackson says, huffing and scoffing the whole way up. "Nil. Not one. I'm not risking my neck for a few measly bucks. I'd rather write a check."

I know he's right, but I can't help but feel disappointed that he won't join me—on the slopes or in my passion for the causes I believe in.

"Now you're starting to sound like my padrino," I say, poking at the snow on the ground by the double black marker with my right pole, trying to disguise my frustration.

"Don Rafael has it right," Jackson says. "He's not wasting his energy out here. You said it yourself. He doesn't have to get into a pair of skis to make this worth his time. While the rest of us chumps are freezing our butts out here, he's fireside, making big business deals from a cozy chair in the corporate lounge."

"How do you know where he is?" I ask, a little annoyed that Jackson thinks this is not worth my time.

"Because he told me where to find him when I was done playing nice," Jackson says, pushing his blondish hair aside. Then, because I must look betrayed, he puts his hand on his chest and defends himself. "His words, not mine."

I'm upset, but I can't—I won't—let my indignation ruin this for me. I have a job to do. So, instead of getting mad, I challenge him. "What? You scared of a little slip and slide?"

"That's not little," he says, looking down the steep incline. "That's downright dangerous, but it's not that."

"Then what is it?" I ask, sliding the toe of my boot into my ski and pressing down to lock it in.

Jackson huffs, irritated. "Come on, Blanca. You know I can't risk breaking an arm or a leg, or worse, losing an eye like that guy did last year. My future is tied to my looks, and . . ."

"Wait. What?" I ask, horrified, because this is not something I'm used to hearing from him. He might be a bit self-absorbed at times, but he's never been vain. At least, I never picked up on it before. "What do you mean your future is tied to your appearance?"

"I'm just saying, I need to be careful." Jackson looks a bit sheepish as he slips his feet into his skis. "I mean, I don't want to lose out on a career in the NFL, and everything that comes with it. You ever see an ugly dude become a sports broadcaster, much less one with only one eye?"

"Well, no, but I haven't been focused on them either," I say, allowing my disappointment to show in my tone of voice, letting it linger in the unspoken words between us.

Honestly, I wish he wasn't so . . . shallow. I mean, the NFL, sponsorship, celebrity status, I get all that, but a good-looking, physically intact sports broadcaster? Really? I wish he wanted to be more, do more with his life, like helping others who are not as privileged as we are. But he has zero interest in making a difference. That frustrates me, because even though I'm still working on what it means to be me, I know I want to be of service. I wish Jackson and I were on the same wavelength.

Below us, I can see the tiny forms of Jackson's parents skiing down the snowy slope, following each other like two slick seals in action, perfectly in tune with each other in joyful bliss.

"Look at them," I say. "They're so . . ."

"Nuts," Jackson says, laughing as he leans over to plant a wet kiss on my cheek.

Pretending to push my hair out of my face, I wipe the remnants of that kiss away. It feels cold and damp on my skin.

"I was going to say in tune," I tell him, perturbed by his mittened hand lingering on the small of my back. I want to be nice, to laugh at his little joke, because I know that's how he deals with stress. But I can't.

The truth is, I don't find him funny anymore. Most of the time, I'm annoyed by his immaturity, especially his disinterest in issues of social justice. It all points to an aversion to growing up, and I just don't know if I want to stick around, waiting for him to grow up.

I know that's what our parents expect from us. That we'll end up together. Our families joined emotionally and financially. It makes sense to them since our businesses seem to work so well in tandem. But I'm not sure that's going to happen. Not if Jackson doesn't shape up. Soon. Before I lose my patience and dump him altogether.

Jackson nuzzles my cheek. "Hey, why don't we ditch the skis and go find a nice, quiet spot with a fireplace where we can snuggle up together?"

"Stop it. That's not what I came here to do," I tell him, pushing him away from me.

"Sheesh," he says, stepping back and fussing with his hair again. "Talk about snow and ice and everything not so nice. What's with you these days?"

"What are you talking about?"

"You've been cold and distant for months now, and not just to me. That's why everyone started calling you the Ice Princess at school. Ever since you came back from Mexico City, you're different. Moody and introverted. Not fun, like you used to be."

Jackson looks wounded. Despite all my reservations about him, his words move me. I don't want to hurt him. He's the only boy I've ever cared for. The only boy I ever wanted to be with. That's the problem, though. He's still acting like a boy, but I'm growing.

Inside, I can feel myself evolving.

Peering down at the difficult piste below, I remember vividly the day it all started—when things changed for me. I was in Mexico City with my padrino at the end of May. But, as usual, he was too busy to spend time with me, so I hired a guide and went hiking at Iztaccihuatl and Popocatepetl National Park, walking around the park with Tina, who'd never been out of the country her entire life. I took her along because, honestly, her parents could never afford to send her on a trip like that.

The guides, Eli and Norma, a husband-and-wife team with their own tour bus, picked us up at the hotel and gave us the experience of a lifetime.

Tina had a blast, but while she was ooohing and aaahing and taking pictures of absolutely every single thing, I stood at the foot of that beautiful, snowy mountain range, Iztaccihuatl, and had a moment. As Norma and Eli recounted the story of Iztac and Popoca, I felt a deep connection to the mountain they call the Sleeping Woman.

"For those of you who don't know the story," Norma said, pointing at the mountain range across the way. "Popoca was a captain in the emperor's army, in love with his daughter, Lady Iztac. She loved him too. So, when word came that he had died in battle, she was devastated."

"I would be too," Tina said, hoisting her backpack higher up on her shoulder.

"To make things worse," Eli said, "the emperor gave her hand in marriage to Tzinacan, who coveted the kingdom and saw her only as a prize. What she didn't know was that Tzinacan had secretly conspired to have Popoca sent to his death."

Norma pressed on. "So, aggrieved, Lady Iztac chose to hang herself."

"That's . . . horrible," I said, shuddering, because I was suddenly ice cold.

"Then Popoca, who was very much alive, arrived to find her lying dead. He picked her up and walked with her into the highlands, where he begged—no, demanded—that the gods bring her back."

"But instead, they turned them both into volcanoes, one dormant, one active . . . ," I whispered, putting it together, the story with the images I'd seen printed on calendars, circulars, and many other items over my lifetime.

It occurred to me then that the fate of those star-crossed lovers was reminiscent of Shakespeare's Romeo and Juliet, yet much more poignant, much more tragic. At the thought of Iztac losing Popoca to the hands of war because of a jealous lover, my heart constricted in my chest and I began to wonder . . . *What good is love if it can't be protected, cherished, allowed to blossom? Why are we here if not to love each other? Why were we created, given breath and life, if not to help each other grow, prosper, and live rich and meaningful lives?*

Two days later, Popocatepetl started rumbling and actually erupted while we were still nearby, spewing smoke, volcanic ash, and fiery rocks for weeks. That was when it happened, when I began to feel the need for understanding, the need for personal growth, the desire to find what my teachers and every book I've ever read referred to as a calling or life's purpose. But Jackson doesn't think any of it is important—not my research papers on environmental issues and water preservation, not my work with the women's coalition, and certainly not this fundraising ski run.

"Blanca, babe, what's going on? Are you mad now?" Jackson asks, and his voice is back to being sweet. "Come on, babe. Talk to me. Can we at least hug it out?"

"I told you, I'm not here for that," I say.

"Then why are you here?" he asks. "With me?"

Tired of the conversation, I pull my goggles over my face, making sure they're tight around my temples and secure against the bridge of my nose before I bend my knees.

"Honestly?" I ask, right before I push off. "I'm here to show these girls how to be fearless!"

CHAPTER
3

During the flight to Reno, I try to learn more about myself. Teresa refuses to answer most questions, handing me a black rectangle and remarking cryptically, "Google is your friend." The device is a small but powerful computer, equipped with a search engine that can call up anything from in-depth articles to ridiculous speculation by random people who seem to invent half of what they claim to impress their allies and anger their opponents.

The easiest thing to learn about is Grupo Tolchan, my father's business. A century after its founding, it's the sixth-largest conglomerate *in the world*, with a *one-trillion-dollar* market capitalization. Even though I don't recognize the rival companies, I intuit that these figures indicate the total value of all Tolchan's shares.

Okay, so I'm crazy rich.

But what am I *like*, as a person?

I find a few pieces that discuss me, but vaguely, as if the journalist was afraid or had been paid to be superficial. A few minutes of my activities, total, have been filmed over the years. I watch these "video clips" and can tell that they feature my doppelganger, the eerie double-not-twin in those photos in the house I never lived in.

"Great," I say out loud. "Nothing new. Gregorio Chan is a smart but pampered rich kid who has spent the last nine years living and studying at a Swiss institute nicknamed the 'school of kings.' He has been seen in Paris in recent years with two different girls: a model and the daughter of a prime minister. He loves fast, fancy cars and skiing, among other dangerous pastimes. But none of that tells me *who I actually am*, Teresa."

Still wearing her maid's uniform, the middle-aged woman looks away from the desert landscape below and regards me with a wistful grin.

"Just be who you are. Trust your gut. Gregorio Chan is whoever you know yourself to be, not what others have observed. Put the tablet down and *look*, Goyo. We're approaching Reno."

As the private jet banks starboard, I peer out the window. The city is cradled at the foot of the Sierra Nevada, the very edge of the arid Great Basin.

"Just like the Mezquital Valley," Teresa mutters, "and the sprawling urb we once loved. Dry. Dangerous. But beautiful beyond compare."

Her words slice through my mind, and I recoil from the view, grabbing at my temples. "Stop!" I beg, glad as the pain fades that she's chosen to tell me nothing. I can only hope that remembering on my own won't be as agonizing.

When we land, a gray-haired man in chauffeur livery is waiting at the bottom of the ladder beside a black vehicle, a Rolls-Royce Phantom. I'm filled with relief and happiness, though I'm not sure if it's because of the car or the driver, who looks to be about the same age as my father.

"Andrés Stilson Mier," I call out as I descend, the name jumping to my tongue before I can think.

I know him. I . . . *care* about him.

"Greetings, Master Gregorio." He opens the door, giving a curt bow to my companion. "Doña Teresa. Panoltihtzinoh."

The Nahuatl greeting is archaic, I realize, and very formal.

"Howdy right back at you, Stilson," she says, her voice as playful as ever. "You look old."

He waits to reply until we've climbed into the back seat and he is sitting behind the wheel. Pulling on leather gloves, he turns his steel gray eyes—the same color as his thinning hair—upon us in the rear-view mirror.

"Quematzin, Nonantziné," he drawls. *Yes, ma'am, beloved Mother.* A strange way to address a maid. "I was set to retire this year. My replacement was waiting, a great-nephew who just turned eighteen. Now, you and Master Gregorio have dragged me north to this gods-forsaken country."

Teresa raises an eyebrow. "Your teenaged great-nephew is of no use to us. Your experience, knowledge, and skills *are*. We appreciate your staying on a few more months. Goyo's memory will come back soon, and he will find the girl who was lost. Then *all of you* will leave your lonely, laborious pasts behind."

Nodding, he starts the car. "Yes, ma'am. So have I been taught since childhood."

The drive to St. James Village lasts nearly thirty minutes, so I fiddle with my smartphone, which is similar to Teresa's tablet. Once I grasp the basics, the rest is simple. Though I don't know *who* I am, I think I'm the sort of kid who picks up new knowledge fast. At no point during the day have I hesitated. My mind just pushes me forward, confident that I can handle whatever comes.

As we approach the gatehouse, the guard recognizes the Phantom and waves us in, eyes lowered. The road winds through a sparse pine forest, past several large homes, before splitting into a drive that leads to a large estate.

"As your father instructed," Stilson says, "I brokered the purchase of four acres on the shore of Joy Lake. Quite a display of wealth, meant to establish you immediately as the . . . top dog, shall we say?"

Beyond the ornate shrubbery and stone walls sprawls an almost palatial mansion, glittering glass and stark concrete accented by rough timber and red brick.

Before Stilson can open our doors, Teresa jumps out of the Phantom, pointing at the hedge lining the mansion walls.

"Stilson can give you the grand tour in a moment, but first, take a look at these rosebushes!"

I let her pull me along the right wing of the mansion. She points out the varieties of fragrant flowers and explains what she has done to make them blossom bigger and brighter.

"The key was blending the compost the gardener uses with a manure-based fertilizer. Then I dribbled a little refined human sin into that mix and voila! Roses that could win me awards."

I feel a twitch in my mind at the phrase *refined human sin*, but no pain. I'm about to ask her to explain when a car approaches along the drive. We turn to watch a black sedan park behind the Phantom.

"Oh!" Teresa exclaims. "I need to go inside before things get complicated."

"Pardon me?" I ask, but she's already scampered off.

Two women get out of the sedan, both wearing badges around their necks with their photos, names, and titles displayed.

The older of the two is a redheaded woman, in her early forties, judging by the wrinkles at the corners of her eyes and lips. I flick my gaze to the other's face and do a startled double take.

21

What?

She could be Teresa's younger clone. Same broad nose and black eyes set wide in clay-brown skin. Same black hair, only long, in a ponytail, and without any streaks of gray. She appears to be fifteen years younger than Teresa, but otherwise identical.

The older woman speaks.

"Perdón, ¿habla inglés? I'm looking for the owners of this home."

Ah. She thinks I'm one of the servants because of my dark complexion, despite my expensive clothes. I'd laugh at her knee-jerk bigotry if it weren't so annoying.

Out of her line of sight, her junior rolls her eyes.

White people, she mouths at me.

"I'm their son," I reply. "Gregorio Chan. How can I help you, ma'am?"

"Oh, I'm sorry!" She lifts her ID. "I'm District Attorney Christina Flowers. This is Daniela Tercero, one of my lead investigators. Are your parents home?"

"Actually, no. They're back in Mexico. I just turned eighteen, so I'll be living here alone for a while. Tomorrow I plan on enrolling at the local high school. My father thinks it's important for me to finish my studies in your country."

Flowers pulls out a smartphone, using its stylus to jot down some notes.

"Is there anything wrong?" I ask.

"Not exactly," she says, lowering her phone. "It's just that your parents paid the full market price for this enormous house from Montes Realty. Fifteen million dollars."

I nod. "My father is one of the wealthiest men in Mexico. He can afford it, trust me. I'm sure everything was completely legal."

There's laughter in her green eyes as she waves away my

22

indignation. "I'm less concerned about the buyer than the seller. Montes Realty. Could you pass my information on to your parents? I'd be very interested in chatting with your father about his interactions with Rafael Montes."

She extends her business card to me. Behind her, Daniela Tercero mouths, *Criminal activity*, for my benefit.

"You bet, Ms. Flowers," I say as I take the card. "Have a nice day."

I stand by the roses a while longer, watching them drive off.

"Stilson?" I say.

"Yes, Master Gregorio?"

"How are there two of them? Teresa *Segundo*. Daniela *Tercero*. Are they . . . like . . . clones or something?"

Stilson has taken off his bowler, and his gnarled fingers twitch at the brim as he turns it round in his hands. "Ah. I'm worried, sir. I've been instructed not to explain . . . certain elements of your life to you, for fear of negative consequences."

I look back at the mansion. Teresa has left the front door wide open.

A thought comes bubbling to the surface of my mind.

"There's more of them, aren't there? Of her?"

He swallows heavily and seems to consider his options. "Yes, sir. Four. You will encounter all of them soon. They have invested a lot to reunite you and the girl who was lost. It is no surprise they want to be closely involved."

It's the third time one of these old people has spoken of the girl that they want me to find.

I may not remember her, but something stirs inside with her every mention.

Stilson gives me the tour. The mansion is spacious, but I'm not overwhelmed, as if I'm used to even bigger residences. There are eight bedrooms, nine baths, a ballroom with a bar, an Olympic pool and fully equipped gym, a small movie theater. If I ever need to entertain guests or distract visitors, all bases seem covered.

My stomach growls, so we sit down with Teresa to eat an extravagant meal made with fresh ingredients native to Mexico and seasoned with spices that something tells me are rarely found in modern kitchens.

As Teresa serves us, I look at Stilson.

"Tomorrow's my first day at school. Will you be driving me?"

"I thought you might take one of the cars I've acquired, sir. I have saved our trip to the garage for after dinner. I think you'll be pleased."

Nodding, I dig in, grunting appreciatively at the delicious food.

"So tell me, Goyo," Teresa says, watching me eat my fill, "how is your memory?"

I take a sip of water and respond. "When I try to remember, there's just a haze. You and my parents have sent me here to find this *girl who was lost*, but I don't see how."

Teresa puts her hand on mine. "You don't need your memories. Just trust your heart."

"But don't you have a photo of her? Can't you describe her to me?"

"I'm sorry," she tells me. "As impossible as it sounds, we don't know who she is. Just that she's here. Attending the high school."

I take a few more bites. But my mind keeps coming back to the mysterious girl. A rising feeling in the pit of my gut—anxiety or yearning—tells me I need to know more. I remember the rosebushes and Daniela Tercero.

"Look, Teresa, it's clear that you and . . . the others . . . have been in town for a while, watching. Don't you have *any* ideas?"

"Sure," she replies. "We've narrowed it down to two possibilities. So stick close. She will be revealed eventually. You'll have . . . more allies like me helping you there at the school. It shouldn't take too long to make a positive identification."

It's all so vague and mysterious. I groan and push my plate away in frustration.

"Who is this girl, anyway? And who lost her?"

Stilson turns away, lifting a napkin to his face. Teresa just stares at me for a while, silent, a look of sadness and sympathy replacing her usual coy, sarcastic grin.

Then I understand, and sadness surges from some dark crevice of my heart, pricking at my eyes.

"It was me," I croak, overwhelmed. Tears I can't explain run down my face. "I'm the one who lost her, aren't I?"

CHAPTER

4

"What's taking so long?"

Tina Gorena, my best friend since fifth grade, turns off her phone and shoves it into her pocket.

"I don't know." I sigh as I wait for Bernice Bertrand, the owner of BerBer's, the most exclusive jewelry store in Nevada, to come back from the vault. I glance over the glass counters and sigh again.

Everything in the store is beautiful, but the necklace I've picked out for myself for the grand opening of my padrino's latest real estate venture, the Imperial Silver Casino, tops it all. The single strand of Tahitian blue pearls with its large teardrop-shaped sapphire sitting over my heart will complement my flowy, azure cocktail dress perfectly.

"Did they go diving for the pearls themselves? I mean, don't they know who you are? Why would they make the Ice Princess wait this long?"

"Stop it," I tell her, pushing my hair away from my face and flipping it back over my shoulder. "I'm not in the mood."

Tina grins. Her dark brown eyes sparkle as she leans over to push a strand of loose hair behind my ear. "Not in the mood for what?"

"She doesn't like it when you call her 'Ice Princess,'" warns Sofía Cisneros, an exchange student from Mexico and the newest addition to our small circle of friends. She needn't worry. Tina and I have an unusual bond, a quirky friendship that allows us to tease each other about everything. But Sofía doesn't know that, because she's only been part of the group for a few months, since she enrolled at our school so late in May last year.

"I don't care about that," I correct Sofía. "I just want to get out of here. Tomorrow's the first day of school, and I'm ready to get that over with."

"Why? I've never known you to be nervous on the first day of school."

I tap my fingers on the counter and lean over to try to look into the back of the store. But it's no use. I can't see the owner from out here. "I'm not—but I'm ready to get school over with."

Tina frowns. "Are you kidding?" she asks. "It's our senior year! Our last opportunity to be kids!"

I look at her askance. "Kids?"

Tina laughs, a lilting little sound that effervesces out of her jovial lips. "You know—to be wild and free."

I think about what that means. Being a kid for Tina is fun. Unlike me, she has real parents, people who love her unconditionally—warm, sweet people she can call Mami and Papi. Me? I have my padrino, Rafael Montes. As a real estate developer, he's a genius and well respected because he single-handedly changed the landscape of Reno.

But as my godfather and executor of my parents' trust, he is remote and utterly unapproachable. Unfortunately, I can't make a move without him, let alone get a place and live my own life until I'm eighteen. So, yeah. I can't wait for that day to arrive. Two more months.

"Here she comes!" Sofía practically jumps in place as we watch the jeweler come back into the room carrying a large rectangular black velvet box in her hands as if she's presenting it in front of a royal court. Ridiculous.

"Oh my frigging God! Look at that sparkle! Are my eyes bleeding? I think I'm going blind!" Tina says, as Bernice flips the lid of the box to reveal a long, draping necklace that drips with diamonds as she pulls it up, cradles it against her palm, and shows it to me. The gems catch the brightness of the heavy lighting overhead, reflect it back to me gaudily, and I think I'm the one going blind.

"What is that?" I ask, horrified by the ostentatious piece. "Where's the sapphire I picked out?"

Bernice's lips turn up, but her attempt at a smile does nothing to assuage the coldness I feel when she shoves the diamond necklace my way. "Your father selected this piece especially for you, Ms. Montes."

"My father?" The misnomer angers me, so I do what I have always done to manage my emotions when it comes to my padrino and his control issues. I stand still, push back against the rage, and take small, quiet breaths to slow down my heartbeat before I can deal with this.

"Blanca?" Sofía's eyes glitter. My name on her lips is small and cautious, unintrusive. "Are you okay?"

"I am," I tell my friend. Then I step away from the counter and Bernice with the dripping diamonds spilling out of her hands. "Can I see the one I picked, please?"

"But your father . . . he said . . . I'm not sure . . . ," Bernice starts, stammering as she tries to negotiate the situation, because I'm sure she's gotten her *instructions*.

"Padrino," I say, interrupting her with the delicate firmness I use whenever my wishes are being trampled on by those my padrino sends to do his bidding. I can't be mad at her; it's not her fault my will is constantly under attack.

"Pardon?" Bernice asks.

"*Padrino* Rafael," I explain, as I walk away from her, lingering at the end of the counter, pretending to entertain myself with the inferior baubles under the glass. "He is my *padrino*—my guardian—not my parent."

"Oh, I'm sorry," the jeweler says. "It's just that he was so happy when he saw this necklace. Said it was perfect for you. I just, well . . . he refers to you as his daughter. I forget . . ."

"The sapphire?" I divert the conversation back to my needs. "Is it here? Can I see it?"

"Yes, yes, it's here," Bernice says. "I'll get it for you."

Bernice rushes off. She comes back in seconds, still holding the diamond necklace in one hand as she puts a long navy velvet box in front of me. "Here it is—the Royal Teardrop. It's one of a kind. You have great taste."

I take the box and open it. The sapphire is more beautiful than I expected.

"OMGees, it's just gorgeous." Tina puts her hands over her lips and practically tears up.

Sofía just grins at me. "It's very nice," she whispers.

"Yup." I nod. "When I saw it online, I knew it would complete my look, but I never imagined it would be so . . . fiery."

Sofía's eyes speak for her. "I know. It's like looking into a blue flame."

"It's exquisite," Tina whispers as I lift it up and hold it against my neck.

"Here, let me help you." Sofía puts the necklace on me, and I caress the huge azure teardrop as it sits cradled within the open neckline of my button-down shirt.

29

"Lovely." Tina's eyes glimmer as she makes eye contact with me in the mirror. "But is it really what you need—for the occasion?"

"It's not what I need," I tell her, distracted, as I fuss with my white shirt to make room for the Royal Teardrop as it rests against my skin. "It's what I want."

"Yeah, but Don Rafael picked the other one." Tina's voice is low, a mere whisper, as she tries to caution me. I know what she's doing and why she's doing it. She doesn't like to see me stressed, but she also knows my padrino will not be happy if I don't take what he's picked out for me.

"Yes, I know," I say, unclipping the necklace, putting it in its case, and pushing it toward the register.

"Oh. Will you be taking that too?" Bernice asks, looking sideways at the navy velvet box.

"Too?" I ask the store owner. "You mean instead."

"Well, this one's already paid for," she says, pushing the diamond necklace she has placed in its velvet box over to me.

I shove the Royal Teardrop closer to her. "But I want this one," I insist.

Tina picks up the diamond necklace and offers it to me. "But you didn't even try this one. Can you put it on? I just want to see how something like this looks on a real person."

I let her put it on me. To humor her. She's my best friend, and I know she wants the best for me. That's why she doesn't get along with Jackson. She doesn't think he's good enough for me. She can't explain why; it's just the way she feels when she sees us together.

"It's gorgeous," Tina says, as she reaches up and adjusts the diamond necklace so it sits perfectly between my breasts. "Take it. So I can borrow it for my big gig next month," she whispers, giggling. "We can return it later."

"Stop that," I tell her, and I shove her away playfully.

"Would you like me to wrap this for you?" Bernice asks, her eyebrows high over her eyes, her lips pursed, because I suspect she overheard us.

"What?" I ask. "No, I'm not taking that one."

Bernice's perfectly shaped eyebrows furrow, and a deep, crinkled line forms between her eyes. "Oh, well, then . . . I'm going to have to call Don Rafael because, you know . . . ," she stammers again. "It's his credit card. You understand."

"I do," I say, putting the diamond necklace on the counter and stepping back. "Why don't you just keep them both and do a full return. Email him the receipt. I'm sure he'll appreciate it."

Sofía and Tina glance at each other before they turn away, to peer at things under the lighted glass. I can tell they're uneasy, but they know there's no need to step in. I don't need saving.

"You don't want either of them?" Bernice looks stunned. "If you want them both, I can ring them up and call your father later. I'm sure he'll be quite happy when he sees how much you love the Royal Teardrop."

"I'm sorry I wasted your time," I say, and I start walking away from the counter. Tina and Sofía drop everything and quickly catch up to me, flanking me on either side as we head toward the door.

Shocked, Sofía asks, "I thought you needed something for the gala? What are you going to wear if you don't get either of them?"

"Nothing," I tell her.

Tina frowns. "Nothing? Like no jewelry at all? That makes no sense. You need something sparkly, something flashy, something to help you turn heads."

"Nope." I toss my hair and take a right at the door. "I don't need another noose around my neck."

CHAPTER

5

In the dream, I am Gregorio Chan, but not in the present.

From the cars, architecture, and clothing, it's the late 1940s.

I glance at my reflection in a shop window. I look twenty years older, wearing a double-breasted tweed suit and fedora.

I'm hurrying along Juárez Avenue to the building that houses Telefónica Mexicana. My investigative team has tracked down the next candidate, a young operator.

As the head of Grupo Tolchan, I gain access to every floor in the building. I'm ushered into an empty office. The woman is brought before me.

Could it be her?

I take her hands in mine.

She smiles shyly at their warmth, confused but not unhappy.

Then the warmth becomes heat, becomes a blaze.

She begins to scream.

I sit up, shuddering, sheets damp. For a moment, I don't know where I am. My bedroom juts out over the lake, three walls of solid glass that give the illusion that I'm floating above the water. Beautiful, but unnerving.

"Just a dream," I whisper to the dawn sparkling all around. "Nothing more."

Then the glittering grows into a glaring light that bores into my skull . . .

And I remember!

A lifetime of memories rushes into my mind, in painful flashes like highlights. My body starts twitching, and I grit my teeth as a hiss of effort becomes a groan and then a howl.

Teresa and Stilson burst into my bedroom.

"Goyo!" the woman says, grabbing my hands. "What's happening?"

"How . . . is . . . this . . . possible?" I pant. "I died! Fifty-two years ago. I climbed that volcano, old as I was, and entered a chamber. You . . . you were there! All four of you. How can there be four of you? And you laid me down on a slab, reminding me that the life I had lived would fade away, leaving just . . . just . . ."

Her fingers tighten around mine. "Just what you require. Yes. Do you have them? Those necessary memories?"

I shrug. "How am I supposed to know? I remember being Greg Chan *Quechol*. Waking up in 1920, looking . . . pretty much the way I do now. Coming down the slopes to take over Grupo Tolchan from other fake parents. Then searching. I remember every dead end, every frightened girl who turned out not to be . . . *her*."

I look up at Stilson. Tears are running down his wrinkled face.

"And I remember you. As a child. Playing with the boy who would become my next father. How . . . ? It's too much. I don't understand."

Putting her palms on the sides of my aching head, Teresa closes her eyes and begins mumbling in a language so alien it gives me goose bumps, as if I were listening to an angel whisper to heaven.

Without opening her eyes, she switches to English. "It's safe to say that you did not die. For fifty-two years, your soul wandered the slopes, keeping watch."

Stilson adds, "You don't remember that time because your brain was not involved. Besides, the Four were cleansing your mind, a memory at a time. We humans aren't made to retain so much experience. It damages us."

Teresa has opened her eyes. "How do you feel now, Goyo?"

"Physically? Better, thanks. Mentally? Clueless, with jumbled memories of another life. They don't quite feel *mine*."

"It will take time to assimilate them," she says, standing. "And I must warn you, without going into much detail—prepare for more."

I want to ask if that means this cycle has happened before, but nausea stops me, as does a glance at the clock, which tells me it is 6:45 a.m.

"Oh, great. My first class starts at eight a.m. School does not care about my identity crisis."

"Indeed it doesn't," Stilson agrees.

———————————

After showering, I style my hair in a pompadour. Next, I step into my closet to select from among the tailored clothes.

Stilson is setting out breakfast as I make my way downstairs to the dining room.

"Teresa has prepared a delicious meal."

I sit down and dig in. As I take my last bite, Teresa pops in, smiling.

"Thank you. I was starving," I tell her.

"Ah, your appetites are such fun," she replies with delight.

I raise an eyebrow. "Well, I'm off. I'll let you know if I find any leads."

In my former life, I loved expensive cars. Of the dozen vehicles in the garage, the Lotus Evija is the most over-the-top. Its ignition has been keyed to my biometrics, so it roars to life at a single touch. Soon I'm heading north along Highway 580, way over the speed limit.

Fifteen minutes later, I pull into the parking lot of Galena High School.

There are clusters of friends scattered all around. Most eyes turn toward me as I activate my car's alarm with a *click*.

The vehicle cost nearly three million dollars. It is a pretentious display, absolute overkill. And that's why I chose it. The same reason my father had Stilson acquire what locals call the Glass Castle.

I now remember that I was a good CEO. Benevolent. But deep down, I know without a doubt I *lead*. I never follow.

There's no point blending in.

A trio of girls catches my eye. As I casually turn my gaze toward them, I recognize a teenage version of Teresa and Daniela.

Are we clones? I mouth at her.

Wrong genre, she replies, exaggerating her lip movements and rolling her eyes.

After a moment, I get it. We're not in a science fiction story.

So the question remains: What sort of tale *is* my life?

Last night I studied a map of the school, so I head straight for the registrar's desk, ignoring the stares and whispers.

Mrs. Paola Alaniz looks up.

"Good morning, ma'am. My name is Gregorio Chan. I think my parents sent over my transcripts? I'm starting my senior year."

She blinks at me. "Where are you transferring from?"

"Le Rosey School. In Switzerland."

Students search for information on their smartphones as Mrs. Alaniz fumbles through files.

"Oh, I think I flagged that packet. Hang on a sec. Switzerland, eh? You don't look Swiss to me."

"No. It's an international school. My family's from Mexico. But I have dual citizenship in the US."

"Ah!" she exclaims. "Found it. Gregorio Chan . . . *Ihpotok*? That how you pronounce it?"

"Yes, ma'am. But I only use my paternal surname. Chan."

"Just turned eighteen, local address in St. James Village . . ." She trails off, looking up at me. "The Glass Castle?"

I simply nod.

"Wow. Not sure why your parents decided to transfer you to Galena High School, Mr. Chan."

Before she can continue, the door to the principal's office swings open, and out walks a prim woman in her mid-sixties. I recognize her at once—identical to Teresa, but fifteen years older.

"Welcome, Greg," she says in clipped tones. "I can call you Greg, yes? I'm María Primo, instructional leader of this campus. Mrs. Alaniz, if you can print Greg's schedule, that would be lovely. I've already plugged him into the appropriate courses."

The registrar's expression shows that the principal doesn't usually get involved. Ms. Primo gestures at the knot of excited students behind me.

"You, there. Tony Alsobrook. Be a dear and give Greg a tour of the campus before class begins. Think of yourself as our ambassador for this newest international student."

36

Mrs. Alaniz hands me a sheet of paper, and I turn to my guide. The kid is about my height, with long black hair and skin nearly as dark as my own. A smile cracks across his strong, handsome features.

"Come on, Greg. Let me show you around."

Several girls whisper and giggle as we exit the office. Tony shakes his head. "Looks like you're gonna be a big hit, and not just because you're fresh blood. Fashionable, hot, insanely rich."

"You don't have many inhibitions, do you, Tony?"

"And just listen! That accent! That gravelly voice. Dang, boy. Plus, I heard Mrs. Alaniz mention the Glass Castle. Is that where you and your folks are living?"

"Well, I'm living there alone with my butler and housekeeper. My parents are running the business in Mexico."

Tony's eyes widen. "Holy crap! That massive house, all to yourself? Let me start over."

He points to a bear painted on the wall. "Galena's mascot. We're the Grizzlies, which is why there's that *G* on the hill outside. I'm on the football team. The quarterback. I'll be leading the way to the state championship this year. First of us to make that happen."

He gestures back and forth.

"Us?" I ask.

"Yeah, you know, Natives." His dark eyes narrow. "Unless you're mestizo or whatever they call it."

Until this moment, I haven't thought about my race or ethnicity. But I know the answer without hesitation.

"No. My blood's one hundred percent Nahua. Not a drop of Spanish."

"Good for you, brother! Nice to have another one of us up in this place. My moms and pops are from the Reno-Sparks Indian Colony. We're Washoe. Let me see your schedule?"

I hand him the paper. He nods, excited.

"We've got a couple of classes together, starting with first period. And we need to head over there now if we don't want to be late. If you're cool with it, I can guide you as we go throughout the day."

A little too eager, but he's got good intentions. And I need allies.

"Okay," I agree. "I'm cool with that. Lead the way."

First period is AP US Government, with Mr. Townsend. As the teacher calls roll, I check the names Teresa gave me, which I stored last night on my phone: Valentina Zochi Gorena and Blanca Rosa Montes.

"The gods arranged those names," Teresa explained. "Among the signs of a candidate is a connection to roses and mountains."

Valentina Zochi. *Valentine flower* or *rose*. And Gorena is Basque for *mountaintop*. Blanca Rosa Montes is almost insultingly obvious.

But neither of the girls is in this period. Hiding my disappointment, I act polite and engage.

Our next class is AP Chemistry, taught by a woman in her thirties, Amanda Bashir. After reviewing the syllabus with us, she asks us to introduce ourselves.

Tony goes first, mostly recapping what he has already told me, with different jokes. Bobby Benavides shyly reminds his peers of his love for chess and shoegaze rock.

Yawning, the next student speaks.

"You almost put me to sleep, Bobby. All right, most everyone here knows me. Jackson Caldera. Star wide receiver for the Grizzlies. Fastest player on the team. Hottest guy on campus. Heir to Caldera Resorts. Future governor of the great state of Nevada."

I feel his eyes fall on me for a second. This guy is the sort of narcissist my displays of wealth are meant to push aside. But I can't get a read on how much further I've got to go so that he gets out of my way.

Ms. Bashir glances at me. "I believe we have a new student on campus this year. Greg?"

"Yes, ma'am. Thank you. Good morning, all. I'm Gregorio Chan, but just call me Greg. I'm from Mexico City, but I've been studying abroad for nearly a decade, until a skiing accident brought me home. Now my parents want me to spend my last year at a public high school in the US, so once they found a decent home here in St. James Village, down by Joy Lake . . ."

Someone whispers, "The freaking *Glass Castle*."

". . . it was clear I'm destined to be a Grizzly. Like Jackson, I'm also a corporate heir. Grupo Tolchan. You may not recognize the name, but we own a few industries in the US you probably know."

The tension is palpable. I've drawn a line in the sand.

Luckily, the next few introductions are less confrontational.

Then Ms. Bashir says a name I have been waiting to hear.

"Blanca Montes? Can you catch us up on your life, dear?"

The girl who begins to talk is beautiful. Long black hair. Dark brown eyes surrounded by long lashes. Pale skin, flawless, like freshly fallen snow upon a distant peak.

"Hey, everyone. Blanca Montes. As student council president, I got my fellow officers to volunteer with me this summer as part of the Sustainable Communities Program at Lake Tahoe. We even got a chance, with help from Tony Alsobrook, to assist the Washoe Tribe with the Restoration Project at Meeks Meadow. So that's what I've been up to. Montes Realty is about the land. Not just selling McMansions"—she looks at me pointedly, cold disdain flowing from her eyes—"but stewarding our natural resources."

"Sofía Cisneros. You're an exchange student, aren't you?"

"Yes, ma'am. My parents are professors in Puebla. When the volcano started to erupt in the spring, they decided to send me to live with a colleague of theirs, here in Reno. And, yes, I know my English is very good. I attended private schools in Puebla where most instruction was in that language. My interests? More than anything… counseling. You know, relationship advice, matchmaking, blind-date planning."

I can't resist making a comment. "Are you any good at it?"

Sofía cocks her head. "Oh, yes. The best."

The class giggles and groans. Other people introduce themselves. A few students later, I hear the second important name.

"Tina Gorena. Tell us about yourself."

This girl has auburn hair, but her eyes and skin are dark brown, and her full facial features suggest a mostly Indigenous heritage. Her warm and cheerful demeanor stirs something inside me.

"So, yeah, speaking of the volcano that erupted—y'all know my girl Blanca took me with her to Mexico City in May, which was dope until old Popo blew his top, hahahaha. Then I helped her with her thing this summer. Got to spend a weekend at Lake Tahoe with the parents. Even if it's just in snatches here and there, time with family is the best. Plus, I had lots of time to practice with my band, so I can't complain. And, y'all—we're seniors! Let's enjoy our last friggin' year together."

"Tina," warns the teacher half-heartedly, grinning.

The girl rolls her eyes and waves her sun-kissed arms.

I feel drawn to her. Could she be the one?

Time will tell.

"Hey, where you going, girl?" Tina hollers as I come out of the girls' restroom. I stop and stare back at her and Sofía, standing across the hall from me.

"Oh my God, I didn't see you there," I say. "Thanks for waiting for me."

"Take the blinders off," Tina teases, pulling my Gucci sunglasses off my face and trying them on. "Dang, girl. No wonder you didn't see us. This thing's got some tint! Who you hiding from? Paparazzi got you running or something?"

"I was going to cut through the courtyard, to catch up with you, but we can take the long way if you want," I say, taking my Guccis back and putting them in their case before tossing them in my matching bag.

"We have to; I still need to find my locker," Sofía says, shifting a stack of books from one arm to the other. "Why can't teachers just give us e-books?"

"They like to torture us," Tina says, grinning at Sofía.

"Some do, some don't. It's a matter of preference," I say. "So, where's your locker?"

"I'm not sure," Sofía says, pulling her phone out of her jeans' pocket and losing herself in it, scrolling through her picture gallery. "I took a screenshot of my schedule. It was on there, right? Somewhere at the top of the page."

Tina and I wait, standing around while Sofía sorts herself out.

"Do we have to do this right now?" Tina asks. "I'm getting older the longer we stand here. I can feel my little skin cells dying." Tina pulls at her cheek with her fingertips to mimic aging. She's always on high gear, and humor is how she deals with life's little setbacks.

Ignoring her, Sofía turns back to me. "I found it. It's 4002."

"Mine's 4034. We're right in front of the nurse's office," I tell her. "Let's go. I don't want to carry this book bag around all day."

"Mine's 4904. If anybody wants to know," Tina says as we start heading to the 400 hall.

After unloading our stuff, I walk into our Dual Enrollment Pre-calculus class with Tina and Sofía at my side. Jackson saved us seats, so we sit clustered together, opposite the new guy, who is way too formal and a bit arrogant when he talks about himself, if you ask me.

Tina and Sofía do very well introducing themselves to the class and, consequently, the new guy. As for me, I don't know what kind of impression I made. The fifty minutes just sped by in an instant, I can't remember anything I said. It all happened so fast. And I couldn't think. Couldn't concentrate. That new guy was staring at me, like, the whole time. Just burning through me with those fiery amber eyes. It was so—*unnerving*.

Because I can't help but take notice of him, I scrutinize my rotating schedule, wondering how many more classes we'll have together. Assuming he's taking all AP courses, I'm sure I'll see him multiple times each day.

"Excuse me," Greg Chan's voice, smooth as honey, whispers beside me. I jump back because I didn't feel him get this close to me. His scent, earthy and fresh as a gentle rain, lingers between us as he leans down to talk to me. He's taller than I expected, and something about looking up at him warms my cheeks. "Do you know where the gymnasium is? I want to check out the facilities."

"The gymnasium." I repeat the words, but they make no sense to me. His warm breath on my exposed shoulder is so—*intimate*.

"Yes," he says. "Where students exercise or prepare for athletic competitions."

"Oh, the gym. Yes," I say, as I look around, orienting myself before giving him directions. "That way. Down the hall. Take a left, go down the stairs, then a right and another right . . ."

Greg Chan's eyebrows wiggle quizzically, and I get it. I'm not very good at giving directions. "That sounds complicated."

"Would you like me to walk you there?" I ask. "I can take you halfway and point you in the right direction. My class is on the way."

Greg's full lips extend themselves into the most gorgeous smile I've ever seen in my life. *It should be illegal to be that handsome and easygoing*, I think, as I turn away and start heading down the hall, walking slowly so that Greg can catch up.

"This is pretty . . . advantageous, since we're both going the same way," Greg says as he sidles up to me.

Advantageous? The word can't really be used to describe what has happened, because Jackson catches sight of us and joins us as we make the first left.

"Hey, gorgeous? Where are you going?" he asks, sidling up to me and reaching over to drape his arm around me.

I stop walking and wiggle out from under Jackson's arm, because the way he's looking at Greg feels like he's trying to lay claim to me or something.

"Blanca's escorting me to the gym," Greg says. His smile is easy, secure, like he sees Jackson's showboating too but is not flustered by it. "Are you headed that way?"

Jackson's eyes shift from me to Greg before he answers, smiling as he says, "As a matter of fact, I am. My next class is nearby; then I've got Athletics. Planning to try out?"

"I'm considering it," Greg says. "But first I thought I would size up the facilities."

Jackson's lips twist sideways. "Do you know how to play football—American football?"

"I excel in many sports, Jackson. Rugby. Hockey. Polo. Kumite. Fencing. Boxing. And, yes, football. All three varieties—soccer, American, and Aussie Rules."

"Ah. Sounds like you might have a chance, make the team. It's not a given, you know," Jackson says, placing his hand on the small of my back and putting the slightest of pressure there, as if to motion that it's time to move away from Greg.

Just as I am about to take Jackson's hand off my back, to show him I don't appreciate what he's doing to me or to Greg, his best friend, Spencer Bodine, comes bouncing up the hallway.

"Hey, what you all doing?" Spencer asks.

Jackson takes his eyes off Greg and says, "Just escorting the foreigner. Down to the gym. Wondering if he's got what it takes to be a Grizzly. Greg Chan, meet Spencer Bodine, our best running back."

"Chan? Where you from, dude?" Spencer asks Greg, lifting his chin with a slight jerk of his head. "Cambodia or something? You don't look Chinese."

Greg's eyes crinkle at the corners as he smiles, a relaxed, quiet smile that says he's not intimidated by the two friends flanking him. "I speak Mandarin pretty well, but, no, I'm not from China. *Chan* is also a word in my native language. I'm Nahua, if you must know."

44

"That's a Native group in Mexico, Settler Boy," Tony says, as he joins our little congregation standing in front of a gleaming glass trophy case.

"What did you call me?" Spencer asks, and I roll my eyes.

How is he graduating this year?

I take a deep breath and let it out quietly, slowing my heart rate down before I speak, lacing my voice with the coldness I feel building up around me. "If you all are done measuring each other up, I'm going to class. The bell's about to ring."

I hurry off, not wanting any part of their shenanigans. Jackson groans in irritation and follows me. "Babe, slow down. Let me walk you."

I can still make out Tony's voice behind us.

"Come on, Greg. You can hang out in the gym during last period, when we work out and practice. You're scheduled for study hall, but they'll let you wander wherever. Right now, though, let's follow Galena's most gorgeous couple. Time to get our literature on."

Another class with him?

My heart flutters against my will.

What's wrong with me?

CHAPTER

7

"Galena's most gorgeous couple" is having trouble. I can sense coldness when Blanca flinches at his touch. Jackson may find himself suffering from frostbite. He escorts Blanca to the door of one classroom before entering the next. Tony guides me inside on her heels. The front is dominated by a small stage, with desks and a wooden lectern filling the rest.

Blanca has joined Tina and Sofía close to the lectern and the instructor's desk. I head that way, hoping to engage them in conversation.

"You sure about this, Greg?" Tony mutters behind me.

"Yes," I reply as I take a seat behind Tina.

"Good morning!" the teacher—a tall woman in her mid-twenties with blond hair and blue eyes—takes her place behind the lectern. "I'm Ms. Dresch. In addition to AP English Literature, I also teach drama, hence the stage, which we will have some opportunities to use as well."

She turns to walk toward it, and Tony draws in air.

"Beautiful," he whispers.

I shake my head. "She's like seven years older than you."

"Nah," he breathes. "She's an angel, bro. Eternal."

Ms. Dresch pivots to address us again.

"This class is meant to get you ready for the AP exam. But more broadly, you're meant to experience literature, to interpretate its themes and evaluate its artistry through timed writing that will help you develop a mature style. If you'll pull up the syllabus, you'll see that our first unit is titled 'Love, Family, or Kingdom.' Our principal texts will be two plays: Shakespeare's *Hamlet* and *Electra* by Sophocles. But, inspired by the recent experiences of some students, I've decided to add a Mesoamerican legend with many of the same themes."

I glance at Sofía. She smiles and winks.

"Now, you won't be thrilled, but you were assigned summer reading, so I want you to write a paper in which you compare the themes of *The Color Purple* and *No Country for Old Men*."

There are groans, but not from me. I finished both books the very day I came out of the coma, reading off and on during the rides to and from the airport, on the plane, and before falling asleep. Given how much I read in my previous life, it wasn't all that taxing.

Without hesitation, I begin composing what strikes me as a straightforward discussion of the books' lessons about tradition and progress. When I look up, Blanca has set her pencil down. Tina is drumming her fingers against her desktop.

"Want me to turn your papers in with mine?" I ask.

"Sure!" Tina answers, her pretty face lighting up. For a moment, it's like a flame has sparked in my heart.

Standing, I take her essay. Our fingers brush lightly, and Tina shudders.

"Here," whispers Blanca, shoving her paper between us and shaking it. "Why offer if you're going to move like molasses?"

"Dude," Tony mutters when I return to my seat. "Tina didn't take her eyes off you the entire time you were up there."

I steal glances at the girl, trying to detect any hints of her real identity. She catches me looking and blushes. She leans over to whisper something to Sofía, who nods and whispers back, eyes flitting to me.

I raise an eyebrow like a silent question.

Sofía shrugs.

"Okay," announces Ms. Dresch, "that was the last paper. There's about a minute before the bell, so feel free to talk or use your phones."

I don't hesitate.

"Excuse me . . . *Tina*?"

She turns back to me, a grin crinkling the skin around her lovely eyes. "Yes, Greg?"

"What class do you have next?"

Sofía interrupts. "We're in choir. Rumor has it you've got study hall, which is close by. Walk with us, no? We'll show you where."

Blanca raises an eyebrow. "Best behavior, Mr. Exchange Student. I've got drama next, so I won't be able to keep my eye on you."

I nod. "Yes, ma'am. I wouldn't dream of being anything less than a perfect gentleman."

The bell rings.

"Hey," I say to Tony. "I'll head to the practice field after a bit."

He winks. "Gotcha. Take your time."

Tina, Sofía, and I head out the door. As they tell me about the mariachi group they're helping to organize, we come across Jackson and Spencer, who are tormenting a frazzled freshman.

"ESL class," Spencer is saying, "ain't in this direction, hermano."

As he aspirates the silent *H*, he slaps the skinny boy on the back.

"Ey, ¿qué tal, amigo?" I interrupt. "¿Andas perdido?"

"Sí, pero estos gachos no me dejan ir."

Jackson rolls his eyes. "This 'gacho' speaks Spanish, pendejo."

"Jackson!" Tina warns. "Leave the kid alone."

I pull the boy away from them casually, my arm around his shoulder.

"What's your name? I'm Gregorio."

"Carlos Sáenz," he says.

"Okay, Carlos. This is Sofía. She's going to explain how to get to your next class. Give her your schedule."

He does, his hand trembling a little. I notice that his left sneaker is untied, so I bend down and take up the laces.

"You need to do a double knot," I tell him as I retie his shoe. "That way you won't trip and bump into random bullies."

Tina has raised a hand to her mouth in surprise.

"Thanks, Gregorio," Carlos says as Sofía returns his schedule, having highlighted a route on the campus map on its back.

"Look for me if you need anything. Estoy a tus órdenes, Carlos."

Once he is gone, Jackson and Spencer glare at me as the girls lead me away to study hall, a few doors down from the choir room.

"Until tomorrow, then," I tell them. "It was nice meeting you, Tina."

Her eyes go wide as I enter my class.

After checking in with the instructor, I get permission to head to the practice field and watch the football team train. The coach is putting the players through their paces as I take a seat in the stands. Tony notices me and waves before going back to tossing the football to teammates.

Many of the boys are agile and strong. An unexpected part of me wonders what they would be like on the battlefield. Would they fight well? Could they follow commands while also responding to

49

unexpected situations? In the midst of this weird reverie, I sense an object flying toward me. Instinctively, I raise my left hand and snatch the football out of the air before it hits me in the face.

Below on the field, Jackson gives a slow clap of appreciation.

"Not bad, foreigner!" he shouts at me. "Now throw it back."

Flipping the ball to my right hand, I get to my feet and balance myself *just* so. Then I hurl the pigskin back at him. He cups his hands to receive it and pull it to his gut, not anticipating the force of the impact.

His wince surprises me. I don't know my own strength. The thought makes me smile a little.

After the team heads for the showers, I make my way toward the parking lot. School has been out for a while, but students are still getting into their cars, having stayed after the final bell for clubs or extracurricular activities.

No one has dared touch my car, though the film of dust on the hood annoys me. I pull out a chamois and begin wiping it down. As I finish, I hear someone calling my name.

It's Tony Alsobrook, hurrying toward me.

"Holy crap, Greg!" he exclaims as he nears. "A Lotus Evija? Dude. You're richer than all these posers."

Walking around the car, he whistles.

"Two thousand horsepower, but totally electric. Never thought I'd even glimpse one up close and personal."

"You know a lot about cars. What do you drive?"

Tony sighs. "Right now, just my dad's Bentley. If he lets me. I don't get a car till I graduate. Normally Jackson drops me off, but today . . ."

His face tightens even as he waves away the unspoken problem. "Did that fool do something?"

Tony forces a smile. "Nah. He's just a jerk and wants me to be like him. No worries. I'm used to ignoring his stupidity. But now it means I have no ride."

I decide to take advantage of the conflict and get more information.

"Where do you live?" I ask.

"In Montreux, with a bunch of the stuck-up morons you just took down a notch by enrolling here. It's on the way to St. James Village if you take Mount Rose Highway."

The name makes me turn around and face him in surprise. "Mount Rose Highway? Mount Rose?"

"Yup. Named for the extinct volcano." He points over my shoulder. "About fourteen miles that way. Great skiing."

I lean against the car for a moment as thoughts tumble in my mind.

Mont Rose Massif, where my cover story says I fell into a coma. Le Rosey School, where my double attended classes in my name. Now Mount Rose.

Rosa. It's what people living in Santiago Xalitzintla in Puebla call the dormant volcano Iztaccihuatl. And a version of that name is prophesied for the girl who was lost.

It's like a neon sign from the gods.

"Want a ride?" I finally say.

"Uh, obviously!"

The drive to Montreux is quick, but so is Tony. As he lovingly examines every bit of the interior, he manages to tell me all about his family. Washoe, though he clarifies, "We don't live on the colony anymore." His father's an actor, one of a few Native Americans

51

getting constant work in Hollywood. Now starring in some *streaming series*, whatever that means. His mother's a professor at the nearby satellite campus of the University of Nevada, Reno. He's got a younger sister named Katie, who attends Herz Middle School.

I turn off on Bordeaux Drive and drop Tony off at his house, a stone and timber affair overlooking a golf course. Then I head back toward the pines that surround St. James Village, so like the mountainside forests of my previous life in Mexico.

I pull up to the guard house, taking the resident lane, but the guard steps out to stop me from entering the community.

I roll down my window. The portly white man keeps his hand on his pistol as he approaches.

"Yes?" I ask. "Didn't my butler put this car's license plate on the list?"

"Forget the car, son. Who are *you*, and what business do you have in St. James? The homeowners association has its own team of gardeners and its own maintenance crew."

I blink at him. This country is riddled with fools. A fire crackles to life in my heart.

It takes every ounce of my will not to grab his collar and shake him.

"I'm Gregorio Chan. My father owns the four-acre lot at the end of Timberlake Court, beside Joy Lake."

His breath catches for a moment, but he's too invested in messing with me to stop now.

"Can I see some ID?"

My blazing eyes focus on his name tag as I pull my wallet from my back pocket and start yanking items from it.

"No problem, Bryan Cummins. Here's my driver's license. And my passport, in case you need it. Would you like to see the premium credit card"—I wave the gold-plated rectangle about—"issued to me by my father's international corporation? Not too long from now, he's going to replace you with something less ignorant and racist. Maybe a baboon."

Realizing that he has made a terrible mistake, Cummins takes a step back. Without waiting for him to wave me through, I peel out and head for my castle, my veins roiling.

Bursting through the front door, I find Teresa and Stilson watching the news on the screen that covers one wall of the living room.

"I'm here live at Steamboat Springs," a reporter is saying, "where an unprecedented amount of steam and smoke has been pouring from fissures in the ancient lava domes for the past fifteen minutes. Dr. Irene Alsobrook, professor at the University of Nevada, Reno's Redfield campus, is on the scene as well. Dr. Alsobrook, what can you tell us about this activity? Should the public be worried?"

Tony's mother shakes her head. "No. Though Steamboat Springs used to be a volcano, it's essentially extinct. For the past ten thousand years, the only activity has been hydrothermal. In other words, magma deep underground heats water above it to create the hot springs and fumaroles that we all know and love."

To her cautious smile, the reporter counters, "We had earthquakes back in 2008, didn't we? Could we see a repeat of that?"

"I don't think so," Dr. Alsobrook replies, "but the university, the city, and the state will be monitoring this activity. We'll let residents know if there's any further risk. But I suspect this is just a small hiccup. It'll calm down soon."

Teresa spins to look at me. "You need to stop."

I scoff. "Stop *what*?"

She waves at the flatscreen. "*That*. It's you. Why are you so angry?"

"The security guard," I spit. "Stilson, I need you to do something."

He bows his head and waits. "Yes, Master Gregorio."

"Call Silver Star Security. Get them to fire Bryan Cummins. Use whatever pressure you have to."

"Yes, sir."

"Today. Now." My voice creaks with barely contained rage.

Stilson exhales raggedly. He has been holding his breath.

"At once," he rasps, hurrying away.

"This side of you," Teresa says, "is partly responsible for the situation we're in, Goyo."

"I can't let cretins like him step all over me."

"I get it. But you're not a normal person. Your wrath has uncommon consequences." She motions at the TV with her head. "Now that you're in Reno, your special connection with Popocatepetl passes through local volcanic phenomena."

I shake my head. "Why? My new memories are too fuzzy about this bizarre link."

"If I explain, you might snap. I can't risk putting the people of this city in more danger. When the time is right, you'll remember what you need to know. Until then . . . calm down."

It takes a few hours and finally a phone call from my father. But the fissures at Steamboat Springs keep steaming until I see Bryan Cummins's dismissal notice and watch video of the scumbag being escorted away from St. James Village.

Then, bit by bit, as my pulse slows, the volcanic field falls quiet.

Monday afternoon, the girls come over to the house to help me redo the seating arrangement for the casino's grand opening because Denise Hernández, the most incompetent event coordinator in the world, messed it all up. She put everyone associated with Caldera Resorts lumped up in the back of the room and everyone from Montes Realty sitting front and center.

"It's like she doesn't know how to do her job," I tell Tina and Sofía as I start removing some of the blue sticky notes associated with Montes to make room for the yellow ones for the Caldera associates. "Doesn't she understand the press will be there, filming, taking pictures? We can't just segregate people like that."

"Yeah." Tina watches me ponder the whiteboard I put up in the family room. "It's just not cool to hog the limelight."

I stop mid-move and take stock of the emotions driving Tina's comment, but the impish grin on her face tells me she's not sore about how this grand opening is affecting her.

"I'm sorry I can't go to your show," I tell her. "I would if it weren't on the same night."

"No te preocupes." Tina shrugs, and her hoop earrings catch the light, drawing attention to her gorgeous eyes. "It's not your fault."

"I tried," I remind her. "But my padrino insisted the date couldn't be changed."

"I blame Denise," Tina says.

"Me too," Sofía says, chiming into the conversation. "She's the worst!"

"But if I can't be at the benefit concert, we can make sure important people come to our events."

"Double our efforts!" Tina grins at me. "I like that."

As the girls and I shuffle sticky notes, I sense a bit of unexpected tension between Sofía and Tina.

"So . . . are you interested in the new guy?" Sofía asks Tina.

"Greg Chan?" Tina takes a deep breath and frowns. Only her half smile tells me she's not immune to Greg's charms. "I don't know. He's so . . ."

"Charismatic?" Sofía asks, grinning as she teases Tina. "Rich? Handsome?"

"Smart!" Tina says. "He's a walking search engine, and he talks like he's older than everyone else. Even the teachers look a little intimidated when he gets going in class. Did you hear him talking at lunch about global warming and what that means for the world's economy? I mean, I couldn't understand half of what he was saying."

I could. It felt like he was speaking directly to me.

Sofía nods, her bright eyes gleaming with something like pride, which makes no sense because, like the rest of us, she just met Greg today. "He's sophisticated."

"Yeah, that's it!" Tina snaps her fingers. "He's uber sophisticated."

I switch two more sticky notes on the whiteboard.

"So, you like him," Sofía says, prodding, like she wants to find out what's going on inside Tina's head.

But why? What does she care if Tina and Greg get together?

Tina shakes her head. "I'm just not sure he's my type, you know. All that brain power. I'm exhausted just thinking about talking to him."

"What about you?" I ask Sofía, trying to sound nonchalant, even though her attention to Greg has me intrigued. "Are you into him? Is that why you're asking?"

Sofía looks shocked, but only for a moment. "Who? Me? No. I told you, he's not for me." Only, I can see it in her eyes; she's hiding something.

"Come on," I say, turning to look at Sofía. "What's the deal? Why are you so fascinated with Greg Chan?"

"I'm not fascinated," Sofía says, turning and walking away to plop down on the sofa across the room. "I just thought one of you should snatch him up. He's a real catch. And you two are definitely on his radar."

Tina turns to me, and I shake my head before I sit opposite them on the love seat. I want to deny what Sofía is saying, but the truth is, there is something there. I caught him looking over at me a couple of times in chem.

A notification dings. Tina glances at her phone.

"It's Tony," she tells us. "He says his mom's on TV."

With a flick of the remote, I turn on the local news. Dr. Alsobrook is in the middle of Steamboat Springs, gesturing at fading vapor behind her. "We'll be keeping our eye on the lava fields, just in case," she says. "Further volcanic activity is unlikely, but still possible."

Unexpectedly, I raise my hand toward the flatscreen.

"Love is a smoke made with the fume of sighs . . ."

As the strange words escape my lips, the world around me dissolves.

Suddenly, I am not in Reno anymore but in some strange land, in a foggy, mystical forest, atop a great mountain, enveloped in Greg's arms. Only it's not the Greg I met today who holds me, but another Greg, with longer hair and softer eyes. And I don't feel like myself either. I am some other me, in another time, resting against Greg's chest, arching my neck as he leans down to kiss me. The earthy scent of him in my nostrils, his soft breath on my skin, and his lips touching mine—it's all too much, and I feel faint.

"Blanca? Are you okay?"

I blink, open my eyes, and glance across the family room. Tina and Sofía are staring at me. "What?" I ask them.

"What's going on?" Tina's brows knit themselves together over her eyes.

"Nothing," I say, and I shake myself awake, push the memory of that other Greg as far away from me as I can, because I don't know what to make of it.

"Really?" Tina asks. "Because that didn't look like nothing."

Sofía cocks her head. "Who were you talking about? Who makes you sigh? OMG! Are you . . . into Gregorio Chan?"

"No," I huff. "I have a boyfriend."

"Poor Greg." Tina presses her lips together and shakes her head. "He has no idea what's coming if he sets his sights on you."

"He's not into me!" I exclaim, more forcefully than I intended because I'm not sure what's happening to me. I think I was quoting Shakespeare. But why?

"Well, he *was* making ojitos at you in the hallway," Tina says, raising an eyebrow.

Sofía sighs. "Why do I get the feeling Greg's about to hit an iceberg?"

"Because he is." Tina grins. "With his face!" Then she lifts her feet off the floor and throws herself back on the sofa, laughing hysterically.

"Oh, no, I can't watch him go down in flames like that," Sofía says. "Please don't be rude to him. He's a really nice guy."

"Tell me again why you're not into him?" I ask Sofía, because I can see the disappointment plastered all over her face. "I mean, you said so yourself; he's a nice, good-looking guy."

Tina stops laughing and tucks her feet under her legs on the sofa. "Yeah, why are you interested but *not interested* in him?" she asks Sofía.

"I'm just looking out for him. He's new," Sofía mumbles. "He doesn't know anyone in town."

"I can see that," I say, because she makes a good point. "We shouldn't leave him out in the cold. We should be kind. Generous."

"Listen to you. The so-called Ice Princess, asking us to be nice to the guy she's about to freeze out," Sofía pipes up.

Sofía's snarkiness catches me by surprise, but I take a deep breath and measure my words.

"I'm not heartless," I finally say. "I'm just . . . cautious. And besides, it's senior year and I'll be leaving town before long."

As I finish my thought, I see something moving to the right of me. I turn sideways to catch my padrino Rafael entering the sala. His presence chills the living room as he stands there, tall and domineering, his suit jacket laid over his left forearm.

"Good afternoon, ladies," he says, glancing at the whiteboard. "Who are you talking about?"

"No one you know. A new kid at school, a foreign exchange student," I tell him, wondering how long he's been standing there, eavesdropping on our conversation. Then, because the seating arrangement on the whiteboard reminds me of something important, I jump up.

"Oh! I've been meaning to talk to you! Do you know Lorraine Fillmore, from the Washoe Tribe of Nevada and California?"

My padrino furrows his brows. "No. Why?"

"You're kidding, right?" Tina sits up. "Lorraine Fillmore is huge! She's like a major ecological warrior! I would have given her passes to my gig, but it's my debut performance, so I have no pull."

"Well, despite our company's *ecological consciousness*, I've never heard of her," my padrino says, turning to leave the family room.

"She's heading up the Native water conservation efforts at Lake Tahoe. I'd like to invite her to the grand opening. We still have some seats." My words make my padrino stop and look at the board. I point to a table on the left side of the chart. "We could give her two seats. Four even."

Padrino Rafael examines the layout more closely. "Four, huh?"

I can feel it building up around him, the cold disdain my padrino has for anything that doesn't benefit him, and I just know he's about to turn this down. But I can't let him do that.

"Yes," I tell him, inching closer to the board so that he has to make eye contact with me. "It would make you look good, don't you think?"

Padrino Rafael twists his pressed mouth sideways. "I'll consider it," he finally says, and he heads back the way he came.

"I can tell Denise to send Ms. Fillmore an invitation," I holler after him. "If that's okay with you."

As the girls sit quietly listening to my padrino's retreating footsteps, I reach for my phone and send Denise a text message, giving her the information she needs to reach out to Lorraine Fillmore. Then I write out the name *Washoe Tribe of Nevada and California* on four sticky notes, place them on the whiteboard, snap a picture, and send it to Denise.

CHAPTER

9

I'm at the prow of a ship, one of three bearing riches acquired during my travels. We are entering the Caribbean, returning to Mexico.

Though I've roamed widely, my search has been in vain.

As I've done every morning for weeks, I stand staring at the water.

Today, however, another vessel comes rising up over the horizon— a clipper with a fluttering black banner.

Pirates.

The captain rushes over. "She's faster than us, Don Gregorio, but if we turn now and release a broadside . . ."

"No," I reply. "Escort the men below. Signal the other ships to do the same. The sea will take them."

"But, sir . . ."

"Trust me, Captain."

He obeys. The clipper is closing fast. I raise a hand, palm pointing outward.

"Ma chinolo," I whisper, and the sea beneath the attacking ship begins to boil. Dead fish rise to the surface, belly-up. In seconds, the hull of the clipper is steaming, smoking.

Then I make a fist, and the ship erupts in flames.

The memories hurt less this morning. A second previous life spills into me without overflowing, just enough discomfort to make me kick my feet. When the flow stops, I remember being Gregorio Quechol Chimal in the nineteenth century.

Not a clone. The same body, growing old each time, then spending the next fifty-two years de-aging. Every passing day stripping a day's wear and tear from my flesh. Teresa tells me my soul performed the work of a guardian during those decades. And I've already seen evidence that my emotions are connected to nearby volcanoes. But I only remember curated moments from my mortal existence.

In every one, I'm searching for her.

The girl I lost, not in the two lives I remember. Before.

The idea boggles my mind. Just how long have I lived?

How long have I been searching?

Tuesday morning, I have AP Environmental Science with Blanca Montes. Her friends are in other classes, and I'm surprised to find that I miss them a little. I guess I'm starting to think of them as my friends, too. Being me is weird. I have memories from two lifetimes, records of my actions and thoughts from multiple decades of adulthood. But mostly? I feel exactly like what these kids think I am—a smart, rich teenager who behaves weird and aloof mostly because he's a fish out of water.

After reviewing the syllabus, the teacher has us grab a laptop to set up our online Environmental Issues Portfolio, where we're going to upload articles and our critical responses. As I struggle with the school district's strange interface, Blanca leans over to peer at the screen.

"Ah, you must've clicked on the wrong icon. Want some help?"

I sigh in relief. "Please."

She scoots closer and pulls the laptop toward her at an angle.

"I didn't expect technology to be your weakness," she says, getting me to the right subfolder.

"That's the drawback of a classical private education," I explain. "Lots of Latin and Greek, but not much computer science. Keep mum, though. Don't want the other students finding out the new guy struggles with email."

Blanca laughs, a pleasant and soft sound. She feigns a British accent: "Your secret is safe with me."

"Okay," announces the teacher, "I'm going to pair you up to do an icebreaker. You will talk with your partner about what matters most to you about the environment. Then you will each make up a story about your partner in which they are an environmentally enlightened character, making an effort on behalf of an ecosystem."

Blanca and I are paired up.

"Water is vital to human life. Before colonization, the people of this land were excellent stewards of it," she explains. "Now corporations control it. So we need to be using our wealth to do good things for this community. It behooves us to take care of our world, and what better place to start than with local water conservation efforts . . . ?"

She grinds to a halt, looking sheepish and self-conscious, as if just realizing she's been monologuing earnestly.

"Sorry," she mutters. "I get a little carried away."

I see that there's more to Blanca than just her beauty. I'm disarmed by her basic nobility, her goodness, her desire to protect the world and its inhabitants with her power and wealth. Such traits are absent in modern corporate heirs. They belong to an older time, when the aristocrats of the Americas sealed their duties to gods and common folk with sacred, unbreakable oaths.

Then I share my love of mountains, my desire to see their slopes kept pristine, without the gouged scars left by mines or logging companies. As we craft our fictional stories about each other, we're each inspired by the other's earnestness, the truth of our desire to see the world better stewarded. And that common goal is a wonderful place to start a friendship, one that might grow into something more.

In all the curated memories spilled into my mind, there's no moment like this, when I have allowed myself to be inspired by the mind and heart of another human. I always led, always was the one to inspire . . . or, more often, to command obedience. And my search for the girl I lost in some forgotten time has kept me from opening my heart to any other deep connection.

What if Blanca isn't her? Why should I care? Who says I must keep searching?

Which god bid me never love another? How can I obey such a cruel command?

"Okay," the teacher says. "Let's start with Greg and Blanca."

I stand, looking down at my new friend.

"Among the students at Galena High School," I begin, "one of them wasn't human. Blanca Montes was secretly a mermaid. Not just any siren, mind you: she was Cihuamichin herself, a sea goddess whose songs command the very waves, a lovely voice no human can hear and forget. And in Reno, the most unlikely city in the world for such a being, she came to live among us mortals to rally us to her sacred cause: the protection of the coral reefs where her beloved mer-folk have lived for millennia."

The other students laugh and clap. Blanca stands as I take my seat.

"Gregorio Chan," she says, giving me a wink, "was also pretending to be human. He was actually a duende."

The Mexican American kids chuckle.

"But not one of those mischievous goblins that steal keys and knock over lamps. He was one of the most ancient, a gnarled old nature gnome who used a magical glamor to look . . ."

"Hot," a nearby girl suggests.

"Let's say *normal*. Why had he traveled from Mexico to Nevada? Because of the ski resorts and forest fires. You see, this duende had been placed by the gods on earth to keep mountains safe, but humanity had encroached on those sacred places. Greg needed to protect them . . . and thereby, ironically, protect the very people who would destroy them."

I give her a high five as she sits, and the students tell their increasingly bizarre fictional stories.

When the bell rings, Blanca and I walk out together.

"Cafeteria?" she asks.

"Yes! I'm starving. Fun assignment. Thanks for being cool about my silly story."

"Oh, no problem. You inspired me to be more creative than usual!"

"I think that's going to be my favorite class," I say, looking over at her. "I know your friends aren't with you, but at least we'll have each other."

"Yes," she replies, cheeks rosy.

I wonder if I've embarrassed her or if she feels a little of the excitement that flutters in my gut.

During lunch, though, Sofía reads my mind—one of the abilities of the Four not-clones—and she urges me not to waver in my task.

"It could be either of them," she mutters to me as Tony tries to convince Tina to sing some popular tune. "Don't get hung up on one before you're certain."

"That's really unfair," I whisper back. "What about my present-day feelings?"

"Trust me, you don't want to wind up falling for the wrong girl after all this time. You'll screw up our plans and burn your brains out. You may end up condemning us all."

"You don't make any sense," I say.

Blanca looks across the table at us. "What do you mean?"

Sofía laughs. "Can you believe this dude roots for el América? ¡Puro Cruz Azul, güey!"

Playing along, I roll my eyes. "A soccer club named for a cement company? Por el amor de Dios, Sofía . . ."

Our pretend argument is interrupted as Tina gives in and starts belting out what I later learn is Tony's favorite song: "You Gotta Be," by Des'ree. He joins in, a little flat but full of joyful energy. Nothing he does can take away from the power of Tina Gorena's powerful contralto, which can shrink to a husky whisper and then swell like a choir of angels, filling the cafeteria and bringing kids to their feet to dance and sing along as she almost raps the famous chorus.

Sofía looks at me pointedly. And there's no denying it. Tina is amazing. Talented, tough, funny. And grounded in ways that perhaps Blanca isn't. Though her mom has power as a leader in the Washoe Education Association, her family isn't wealthy. She's had to struggle in ways that make the suffering of others immediate and important to her.

Another truly decent human being.

After lunch, I find myself in AP Spanish Literature with just Tina. None of the others are as advanced in the language, except Sofía, who already took the exams for the previous course, AP Spanish Language and Literature, last May, right after enrolling.

La profesora Otheguy asks me to read a passage from *Quixote* aloud, so I stand and clear my throat, letting the Early Modern Spanish roll off my tongue as if I've been speaking it for centuries. Which I have.

"I have been pursued by enchanters, enchanters yet pursue me, and enchanters will continue their pursuit until they find me and my exalted knighthood in the deep abyss of oblivion, and they harm and wound me where they see that I feel it the most; because to take away from a knight-errant his lady is to take away the eyes with which he sees and the sun with which he warms himself and the sustenance with which he endures. I have said it many times, and now I shall say it again: the knight-errant without a lady is like a tree without leaves, a building without a foundation, and a shadow without a body to cast it."

I feel Tina's eyes on me the entire time. When I take my seat, she points at the textbook.

"You didn't even look at it. Did you really memorize it that fast?"

"To be fair, I have . . . read the book several times."

She twists her lips to one side, a goofy but endearing gesture. "It's easier with poetry. Like lyrics."

When she's called upon, Tina recites Sonnet 173 by Sor Juana Inés de la Cruz. We lock eyes, as if I'm the Alcino the speaker of the poem addresses, making the last lines hit differently:

> *"Do you see my blood spilled on the path*
> *as I follow your trail of illusory charm?*
> *Are you quite surprised, Alcino? In truth:*
> *worse should befall the one who did me harm."*

The energy between us is real, no doubt. But she's telling me not to toy with her emotions. Could this spark be the sign that there's a spiritual tie between us, the kind that can bind two souls across time? Because that's what I've been waiting for. As much as I admire Tina as a friend, a singer, a lovely girl with a big heart, I just don't know if it's enough. A part of me wishes it could be, the confused and lonely amnesiac teen who just wants a normal life. But the rising tide of past that I feel looming over my soul?

It won't settle for anything less than eternity.

That night, another dream. I am Gregorio Chinolo Popocatzin, looking to all the world like a twenty-six-year-old wealthy Indigenous merchant. It's the year 1720, and I am raging.

One of my properties has been seized by a distant relative of the viceroy. The village that sits on that vast tract of land is being dismantled, its women forced to work as servants in other regions, its men conscripted. Families shattered.

What if she is among them?

My heart crackles with blazing anger.

I can't contain that flame. It will consume me.

So I thrust my silent scream deep into the roots of the earth.

And seven leagues from my estate in Amecameca, the volcano Popocatepetl erupts.

Out of thin air, the Four step into my drawing room. In the dream, I know their true names. Not María, Teresa, Daniela, and Sofía. Tiyacapantzin, Teicuihtzin, Tlahcotzin, and Xocotzin.

Eldest Sister, Younger Sister, Middle Sister, and Little Sister.

Collectively, they are Ixcuinan, goddess of vice and forgiveness, weaver of fate.

Four faces of the divinity that has protected me when Chaos would see me broken.

"Dearest Popoca," they whisper in calming unison. "Do not despair. We have sensed a strange stirring in the north, where the Christianized heirs of Tlaxcallan have settled along the Great River. Seek her there among the distant cousins of your people."

As it turns out, there is magic among those folk, though not of the sort we had hoped. Instead of returning to Amecameca, I spend forty years roaming North America, searching for her among other Native peoples.

Finally, I feel the volcano drawing me back. I am old, nearing the end of this life.

The year is now 1760. Flanked by mounted Comanche guards, I cross the Río Bravo and pull my wagon up to the settlement at the heart of the triangle formed by the missions of San Francisco Solano, San Juan Bautista, and San Bernardo.

As if she can sense my arrival, Ruth Mixtle comes to greet me, her face impassive.

"Ruth," I say. "I hear you married."

"Yes," she replies. "Pedro de la Cruz. He did not care that you rejected me."

"I'm sorry. I believed that you were her, that the gods had sent her back to be one of the Luminous. But I was wrong."

She bares her arm to show the scarred skin my burning hand left decades ago.

"Yes. But my people have a saying, Tlatla ijkon teochiualos. It's a blessing to burn. Why have you come back?"

"My time has come. I must return to the volcano. I wanted to leave you the wealth I've accumulated during my search. Your people may need it as they try to hide what they are."

"Very well. Leave the wagon, Popoca. Walk back. Suffer a little. It will lighten my heart."

I don't argue. I just start walking.

When my guards offer me their horses, I refuse.

Penance can't be avoided.

After this third life has flooded my mind, I find Teresa, preparing breakfast. "The eighteenth century," she remarks. "A tough time."

I wonder whether I should get on my knees. She doesn't seem all that divine—just a sweet surrogate mother who I'd rather hug.

Smiling despite the tears that sparkle in her eyes, Teresa sets down her spatula and wraps loving arms around me.

"Yes, my child," she whispers. "This is the worship I always prefer."

After she pulls away and serves me, I keep thinking about the pain in the dream.

"Why the burns?" I ask. "What happens when I think I've found her?"

"It will be her time to remember, too. None of us can move on until she does. And if she doesn't, you may have to . . . prompt her."

It's a horrifying idea. But there's no hurry, I tell myself. I'm still just a high school senior.

A glance from Teresa suggests that I'm fooling myself.

Wednesday, I think as I pull into the parking lot. *Hopefully I'll get some clarity today.*

In AP Chemistry, the instructor has us organize ourselves in triads to review safety rules and the equipment at each of the stations throughout the class.

"Tony," calls Jackson, "come over here."

"Nah, man," Tony responds. "Find somebody else."

Jackson's eyes narrow. "Sure you want to play that way?"

"Let's team up with Tom," Tony tells me, gesturing at Thomas Willet, a drum major with red hair and freckles.

Behind us, Blanca, Sofía, and Tina have put on their safety glasses and are following the steps to light the Bunsen burner.

I stand sideways so I can observe them better.

As Tina turns the valve, Blanca ignites the gas.

But there's a malfunction.

The burner shoots a jet of flame that nearly reaches the ceiling and begins tilting toward the girls. Without thinking, I extend my hand and jump toward the flame.

Before I can put my flesh between them and danger, however, a blast of cold shoves me aside. The fire goes out, and Sofía shuts off the valve.

Ms. Bashir hurries over. "Blanca Rosa Montes! What were you thinking? Are you okay?"

I look up from where I'm lying on the floor. The pale beauty is clutching her hand to her chest, but the flame never touched her skin. What's causing her pain?

"Frostbite," Sofía mutters as she bends to help me up.

Blanca stammers at the teacher. "I . . . I don't know."

Jackson shakes his head. "This school is *asking* to be sued. Want me to call your godfather, babe?"

"No. I'm fine."

"Tina," Ms. Bashir says, "can you take her to the nurse's office? The rest of you, carefully store your equipment." She twists a master valve shut at the back of the room. "We'll have to postpone any labs until a technician checks all the gas connections. This is *not* supposed to happen. My apologies."

As Tina and Blanca leave the room, I brush something stiff from my shirt and jacket.

Ice.

Pulling Sofía aside, I demand softly but sternly, "What the hell is this?"

She smiles, excited. "Good news, that's what it is. Blanca. She's the girl who was lost."

"You're not explaining anything," I point out in frustration.

"Your soul is tied to a volcano. One that is living, active, dangerous. She has a similar link."

She stops, looking at me expectantly. I consider the implications.

"I tried to block fire with my hand just now. In my dreams, my memories, I wielded a sort of volcanic power."

"Yes."

"So . . . the wave of cold . . . came from Blanca . . . Rosa . . . Montes. And like Mount Rose here in Nevada or in Switzerland or back home . . . her volcano is dead, dormant, covered with ice and snow!"

Tony looks up as I almost shout these last words.

"Everything okay?" he calls. "You took a nasty fall, bro."

"I'm fine, Tony. Thanks."

Ignoring him, Sofía stares into my eyes intently. "What are you feeling right now?"

I take stock, shake my head. "I'm not sure. Numb."

She nods. "You're still in shock. Emotionally and physically. I wonder if this was the first time she's ever tapped into that power."

I raise an eyebrow. "From the look on her face, yeah."

Then Tony and Ms. Bashir come to check on me, and Sofía quietly sweeps ice chips out of view with her foot.

At lunch, Blanca shows her bandaged hand to the small crowd gathered around. "It's nothing. The nurse said it seemed more like light frostbite than a burn. Some ointment for the next couple of days, and I should be fine."

"You look kind of shook, though," Tina says. "Maybe you should go home for the rest of the day."

Jackson gives an exaggerated sigh. "Quit babying her, Tina. She says she's fine. Besides, a little extra heat could help melt the Ice Princess a little. Her boyfriend's in danger of frostbite himself."

In an instant, my numbness melts away. The bridled blaze of my heart threatens to burn its way through my chest.

"Instead of being a jerk," I interrupt, "maybe you could show some sympathy. Maybe even some respect."

He pushes his tray aside and glares at me.

"Do you really want to do this now, boarding school baby?"

"What did you just call me?" I demand. "You pampered fool."

Jackson surges to his feet. "Right here, right now. Just say the word."

All eyes have fixed on us. More students have gathered around our table.

I step close to Jackson, so close I can feel his nervous breath on my face.

"Guys!" Blanca warns. "Knock it off. No testosterone battles in the cafeteria."

I give her a thumbs-up without taking my eyes off Jackson.

Then I laugh, low and mean.

"You want to fight me, eh? Don't you understand? I'm not the sort of person that you can touch."

Jackson's eye twitches. He's afraid, but he isn't used to backing down.

"Let me guess—if I lay a finger on you, your father's lawyers will make my life hell."

"No, Jackson. If you don't come to heel, I'll beat you like a rabid dog. In front of the entire school. You won't ever recover from the encounter. Physically or socially."

Something nasty writhes across his face before he scoffs and walks away.

"Hey, Greg," Blanca says coldly. I turn. Her eyes are narrowed in fury. "I didn't ask for your help. I can handle Jackson on my own. Why don't you focus on Tina or whatever?"

"Hey, wait a minute!" Tina objects.

The words come blurting out faster than I can think. "I'm not interested in Tina, Blanca. It's you I want to get to know."

The crowd lets loose a collective sound of surprise and admiration.

"Then the first thing to remember is that this is the twenty-first century," she quips. "Acting like a tough guy is *not* attractive. Come on, girls. Let's get to English class."

The three of them saunter off. Sofía gives me a parting glance and a shrug.

Tony grabs me by the elbow and pulls me away from the crowd.

"Dude, that was kind of cool, sure. But also really stupid. If you like her, you've got to be more subtle, bro. You can't announce it to the whole school."

I almost jerk my arm out of his grasp, but instead I remove his hand calmly.

"This is going to sound weird," I explain, "but it feels like . . . I've been waiting forever for that girl, Tony."

"What?" He shakes his head, dumbfounded. "You've known her for like three days, Romeo. Give it a few weeks at least. Jesus."

Then the bell rings, and we run to class.

CHAPTER
10

With the teacher's permission, I leave English class early, wandering toward the front entrance, lost in thought. But as I step outside, I'm greeted by an impossible sight.

Snow—dear, delicate, divine snow—is falling everywhere. The air is full of soft flakes, drifting gently, swirling in my path. I stop and stand there, mesmerized.

Then I begin shivering, not just with cold—but also from the inside out—because there are all kinds of unexpected, complicated, unbridled emotions stirring within me, and I don't know what to do with them.

Hurried steps come rushing from behind, and someone drapes a jacket over my shoulders. I turn my head, startled, but then breathe easier when I realize it's just Greg, making sure I'm warm. I relax and give him a weak smile.

"Are you okay?" he asks gently. "This snow's pretty unexpected."

Pulling his jacket tighter around my shoulders, I smile and nod. Then, feeling a bit remorseful, I take a deep, shuddering breath. "I'm sorry I snapped at you in the cafeteria."

"Not to worry. You'd just had quite a scare. Who can blame you for getting upset when a guy you hardly know decides to defend you against your own boyfriend?" He sighs. "Saying it aloud makes me realize just how ridiculous I was. Please forgive me."

I blink feathery snowflakes off my eyelashes. "Forgiven and forgotten."

Just then, a black Escalade pulls into the parking lot.

"That's me," I say, handing the jacket back. "Thanks for keeping me warm."

He looks at me intently, and something passes between us, something strong and strange and surprising, but oh so sweet. I feel it in the air around us, bits of it revealing themselves in the snow that swirls and soars between us.

"Anytime, Blanca Rosa Montes," he whispers, his warm words creating a soft little cloud that floats toward me as they leave his lips. "Anytime."

Then my padrino's driver opens the door for me. I turn from the magic and the snow, jump into the vehicle, and we drive away from Greg. Looking back, I catch a glimpse of him standing in the snow, staring after us.

Back home I switch on the TV. Our local meteorologist is surprised.

"Scientists are still struggling to understand these climate changes—what's brought these intermittent cold snaps to Reno over the past decade and a half."

My padrino walks into the living room. Taking the remote control, he lowers the volume.

"You look pale." He puts the back of his hand against my forehead. For a moment, I almost expect warmth, tenderness. Paternal affection. But his fingers are as icy as his heart. "Your chemistry teacher left a message with my secretary. Are you all right? Should we go to the hospital?"

I shake my head. "No, I'm fine. I'll change into something warm and take a nap. That's what I really need. Rest."

He stares at me for a moment, then nods. "I'll have some hot chocolate taken to your room."

September 28. 6 p.m.

Something strange happened in Chemistry class today. Something I've never experienced before. There was an accident. A burner exploded and, before its flames reached me and Tina, I stopped it.

With my mind—my will—I stopped it.

I don't know exactly how I did it, but when I felt the heat, I was suddenly not myself anymore. I was in that foggy place again, seeing a whole other kind of explosion. In my mind, I stood on a white, stone balcony, high above a pine forest. In the distance, an angry volcano erupted, sending seething snakes of molten lava slithering down toward a village. But I didn't panic. Didn't jump back or scream. I just put my hand up and pushed the volcano's flames away.

As the lava slowed, cooled, blackened, the world began to slip away, and I realized my balcony was not part of some earthly building at all. I was standing amid the stars, in paradise, watching over someone I could no longer see.

Then I was back in class, where my station had frosted over and everyone was staring at me. Greg Chan was there—his amber eyes glistening with concern. But it wasn't his eyes that held my attention. His head and torso were covered in tiny icicles. It was weird; I couldn't make sense of anything. I guess it could all be explained by that storm that swept into Reno late in the afternoon, just before the bell rang.

It's strange, how that storm echoed my state of mind—how the coldness I felt inside was suddenly everywhere I looked as I went outside. But that's not all. There is Gregorio Chan—his eyes haunt me. And I feel, when I am with him, like we're connected. I don't know why, but I feel a familiar warmth coming from him. It was in his jacket, when he put it over my shoulders—seeping into my bones, melting something cold and bitter inside me. Making things better, somehow.

What does it all mean?

I don't know. I don't understand what is happening to me.

If my parents were alive, if the brakes on their car hadn't failed that night . . . maybe if I were still seeing a therapist, I would tell them all about it, but neither one is an option. I am alone, always. As much in wakefulness as in that other realm, that wishful, fearful world we inhabit when we go to sleep, I am utterly and desperately alone.

My phone pings, and I put my pen down. It's Tina. She's at the door. I use the app on my phone to let her in. Then I close my diary and shove it into the secret compartment behind my bed before I rush halfway down the stairs, stop at the landing, and wave for Tina to come up to my room.

"How are you?" she asks.

"I told you," I say, turning back to look at her as she follows me up. "I'm fine. Why's everyone making such a big deal?"

"Because Greg just told the whole world he's into you . . . that's a big deal," Tina says as she jumps onto my bed. "A huge deal."

I lock my door and sit beside her on my bed, clutching my favorite throw pillow against my stomach, because this complicates things so much.

"Do you think it's time to . . . you know?" I ask her.

Tina sits up and looks at me closely. "Break up with Jackson?" she asks. "That depends. Is it definitely over with him?"

"It's been over for a while," I tell her, plucking a tiny piece of lint off the plush purple pillow on my lap.

"Okay, so . . . why did you wait so long?"

I take a deep breath and let it out slowly, because the answer is *not so simple.*

Everyone I know, Jackson's parents, my padrino, their friends, our friends, they all think he's the perfect match for me. *How will they take it,* I wonder, *when I tell them we're not together anymore? What will his mother say? She's always been so sweet, so supportive of me—a real caring, maternal presence in my life. I don't want to break her heart. Will she hate me then? Because I just don't think I could bear it if she never spoke to me again.*

More important, what will my padrino do? Will he threaten to take my inheritance away? Can he do that? As executor of my parents' estate, how much control does he have once I turn eighteen? What kind of power can he enforce over me, legally?

It occurs to me then that I don't really know much about my own inheritance. Padrino Rafael has always said we'll talk with the lawyers, once I turn eighteen, *to see where things stand,* but he's never really laid it out for me. What I need to know, what I need to find out is, *what does the paperwork say? What's in my parents will?* I wonder.

"Hello?" Tina snaps her fingers in front of my face. "Are we still talking here?"

"Yes." I shake the distressing thoughts out of my head and pay attention to her.

"Well?" Tina prods.

"I'm not sure if this is the right time," I tell her. "I mean, we have the grand opening coming up, and I invited Lorraine Fillmore. So, I can't have any drama. Not when we're sitting at the same table with her. She's like my idol."

"Sure. I get it." Tina nods. "You want to make a good impression."

"Exactly," I tell her. "I want to partner up with her someday, help her bring her project to fruition, make sure our Native communities have access to clean, sustainable water."

"And your padrino's on board?" Tina asks, taking the purple pillow out of my hands and tossing it aside before I can pluck it to death. "I mean, with you funding the project . . . spending his money."

"*His money?*" I blurt out. "You mean my parents' money, don't you?"

Tina makes caras at me. "Well . . ."

"What?" I ask her, my voice a bit harsh, because I'm annoyed with the notion that breaking up with Jackson has financial repercussions for me.

"His, theirs, that's a bit of a gray area," Tina says. "He has worked hard to expand your parents' business, hasn't he? I mean, he's kinda built up Reno. Brought it up to standard. Before he came along—"

"Stop. Don't say it." I push myself off the bed and go stand at my window. The courtyard below is gleaming in the sunlight, and I play with the frilly curtains as I talk. "Before he graduated and came to work with us, my parents' business was more than established. This house, every luxury in this room was their doing. They worked hard for it, and they left it to me. Not him."

Tina leaves my bed and comes over to wrap her arms around me. "I know," she whispers. "I'm sorry. I didn't mean to upset you."

Tears are pricking at my eyes, and I fight to hold them back. "I don't owe anybody anything," I tell her.

"Of course you don't, preciosa!" Tina says, and she squeezes me tight.

I look up at the bright late afternoon sky. The usually blue heavens outside my window are white, resplendent, and I close my eyes. Then it happens again. *I am no longer in my room, warm in my best friend's arms, but rather in a strange place, some kind of dark and musty cavern, I think. The dimness of the hollow, empty space is nothing compared to the coldness that surrounds me, a frigidity that fixes me, holds me down, traps me, like a thick layer of snow.*

Chilled to the bone, I shudder, but there's nothing I can do to warm myself.

I am numb.

"Are you okay?" Tina asks, and I open my eyes and gaze at her. "Look at your fingers. They're like little icicles."

I can't talk, because I am busy conserving my strength. I need every ounce of energy I have to keep from freezing. Tina pushes me away from the window, and I let her cover me up as I lie curled up on my bed.

"I'm so cold," I whisper, as Tina rubs my hands and blows warm air over my bluish fingertips.

"You shouldn't have gone outside," Tina says, pushing my hair out of my face and touching my forehead. "I knew standing out there in the snow wasn't good for you. But then I saw Greg, and you two seemed to be having a moment, so I hung back. Now look at you."

"He makes me warm," I whisper, recalling Greg's jacket, his eyes, his lips. "So warm."

Tina smiles, and her brown eyes shimmer. "Good. You need

82

warmth," she tells me. "And Greg Chan brings the heat in spades. God knows Jackson doesn't have it in him."

I nod. "Never has. Never will."

Tina nods and sighs, and I smile at her.

"So, you're, like, *into* him too?" she asks, tucking my blanket tightly around me. "For sure. For sure."

"I don't know why," I admit, grinning as I snuggle inside the layers of my blue quilt. "But I am. I really am."

"So, is it finally happening?" Tina asks, in a teasing tone of voice. "Is Gregorio Chan *the one* Galena High has been waiting for? Is he about to prove once and for all that this is no fairy tale? That our Ice Princess is actually human?"

"Stop it," I warn. "I'm not in the mood."

"No, seriously?" Tina asks, laying her head down on the pillow beside me. "Is Greg the boy hot enough to melt the Ice Princess's infamous frosty façade?"

Instead of rolling my eyes at her, I give Tina a steady, cold glare—something I learned to do well from my padrino.

"What?" she asks. "What's that look for?"

So I remind her.

"It's not a façade."

CHAPTER
11

The fourth life before this one. I've spent the eight years since my reawakening traveling throughout the Hispanic Empire, looking for signs of the lost girl's reincarnation.

Teicuihtzin, using the alias Teresa Segundo, accompanies me as I visit the viceroyalty of Peru, seeking an individual with special insight: thirty-year-old recluse Isabel Flores de Oliva, known to everyone as Rosa.

Though Rosa cares for the needy and sick of Lima from a room in her parents' house, it's tough to get an audience with her. But Teresa works her divine magic, and soon we are sitting on the floor while the woman who will one day be canonized as a saint emerges from a grotto built into one wall of the room. She lifts a heavy silver crown from her head, and I see that spikes inside it have cut wounds into her scalp, which bleed for a moment before closing miraculously.

As her eyes focus on us, Rosa understands who we are.

"He told me a pair of the minor Native apu would visit soon. Welcome and blessings."

After some pleasantries, I get to the point. "We are looking for another . . . apu. A former princess. Iztac."

"Ah," Rosa says, smoothing her habit before running the beads of her rosary through her thin fingers. "She whose heart is chained to the icy slopes of a dead volcano. Yes. I caught sight of her, looking down from a mansion in the highest tier of heaven. Watching over you, Don Gregorio. Full of compassion for you and those your rage might harm. Surely you have felt her calming touch down the centuries."

I am overwhelmed. The soft assurances that I have heard in my darkest hours?

They came from her lips, whispered from on high.

She has not forgotten me.

I wake up sobbing. Just as I have searched for her, she has kept her own vigil. Before this moment, my love for this long-forgotten lost girl was an idea. But for the first time, I feel her absence in my gut, a raw and seething hole in the center of my being.

Stilson rushes in and takes a seat beside me on the bed. I need relief from the sudden flood of anguish, so I bury my face in the starched white of his shirt, and he pulls me close, patting my head.

"Ca cualli, notahtzin. Nican nimopil," he whispers, and his words wrench even more tears from me: *It's okay, beloved Father. Your son is here.*

No wonder I fell into a coma. No human being could hold all this sorrow at once and remain sane or whole. "How many?" I groan, pulling away. "How many more lives, Stilson?"

His rheumy eyes flit toward the door, but then he sighs. "Eight more, Master Gregorio. This life you now live is the thirteenth."

I feel for a moment as if I've been punched in the stomach. "And the last, yes?"

"We pray it is. For your sake. For hers. For Ixcuinan, who has risked her standing among the Divine to help you and the others do penance. And for those of us whose families have spent centuries hiding your identity, aiding in your search."

Though my memories are like a highlight reel of films someone else made, I can picture the dozen or so people like Stilson or my parents in Mexico City, raised to serve me when I returned from my cavern. Hundreds of others from a small Nahua village near my volcano. All trapped in the cycle of my regeneration, in the web of my search.

"Finding her is just the first step, isn't it?" I ask.

"Indeed," Stilson says. "Until she remembers, she cannot help free you from your punishment. But we must avoid overwhelming her. A coma would be a terrible outcome."

Sighing, I lean back. "I wish I could sweep her up and fly her away to one of the islands we own. It would just be the two of us. I could help her remember."

Stilson shakes his head.

"Ms. Montes cannot be forced. She was lost because men tried to take her agency away."

My eyes go wide. None of my curated memories have held a clue as to how she was lost, though now I can calculate how long ago it happened.

Twelve hundred years ago.

"Apologies. That was way too flippant. Of *course* I wouldn't put her through such an ordeal."

Stilson puts his hand on mine. "Ahmo zan inon," he begins.

"Precisely. It's not just that." Teresa is standing in the doorway to my room. "She has a life here. Family and friends. Dreams for her future. You will never sway her unless they matter as much to you as

86

they do to her. For she must be swayed. She must come to love you as Gregorio Chan. Otherwise, she won't remember. None of them will. That is the bargain we made with Chaos, my child. And her soul accepted it, in paradise."

Confused, I squint at him. "None of them?"

Stilson looks around, nervous. "Does it not seem strange to you that all Four aspects are here in Reno?"

"Yeah, actually. Principal. Agent in the DA's office. Student. It's like they're trying to keep an eye on . . . more than one person!"

My head swims a little at this recognition. Stilson squeezes my hand. "Try not to think too hard about it, young master. But there are others whose souls are emmeshed with hers. And their destinies—*all* our fates—depend as much on your actions as hers does. So hear me well. *Blanca Rosa Montes* must be swayed. Even when you fully remember who you are, you will have to face one crucial question, Master Gregorio: Whom are you trying to reach, truly? The person she is now or the person she once was?"

At school, I can hardly focus on calculus, so anxious am I to see Blanca again. When I walk into our AP Environmental Science class, she's watching the door, as if eager to see me as well.

We're paired together again for today's activity, which is to find two similar biomes separated by at least two thousand miles and create a comparative chart.

"I've been thinking about this recently," I tell Blanca. "The Great Basin we find ourselves in is similar to the Mezquital Valley of Mexico."

"Oh!" Blanca says, her fingers flying over the keyboard of her laptop. "That's perfect. I've spent years studying up on the local biome, thinking of ways to improve preservation and access to water. What state?"

"Hidalgo."

We spend five minutes comparing the two regions, filling out the planning grid we've been given. Then Blanca pulls out a blue container filled with markers and other craft tools as I spread a sheet of butcher paper across our table.

"It's so weird," she mutters as she starts to trace a line down the yardstick I hold in place. "Maybe because of how similar it is to the Great Basin, but I feel a real connection to this valley. It seems so familiar to me."

I'm still pressing the yardstick down. As her hand passes mine, her fingers graze my skin. There's a sort of crackle of energy, as when two masses of air meet, one warm and one cold. It's not just a physical sensation, though. We're in a sort of vibe, the two of us, working in tandem on something that's important to us both. The closeness is intellectual as well. Perhaps even spiritual.

Blanca almost drops the marker, but quickly recovers. She can't help blushing, though she gives a little laugh. "It's this crazy low humidity. All kinds of static shocks and bad hair days, let me tell you."

I cock my head and make a surprised smirk. "Yikes. Yeah, no— Mexico City's like at ninety-nine percent all month long, so it's definitely a change for me."

But I can see in her eyes that she also felt something more. We stare at each other for a few seconds. Then the instructor walks by, checking on our progress, and we get back to work, clearing our throats, caught between nervousness and embarrassment.

———————

During lunch, I sit with Tony, Carlos, Tom, and a few other boys that I've become friends with. Some used to hang with Jackson, who now sulks in a corner of the cafeteria with his band of muscle-bound lackies, staring at Blanca as she eats with her friends.

The girl is facing a dilemma. She steals glances at Jackson and at me, whispering with Tina and Sofía. I hope Little Sister is doing her part to tip the scales in my favor.

"Just give her time," Tony reiterates to me. "Trust me. Her life is complicated. She's going to weigh all the pros and cons. And a big one is her father. I mean, her godfather. You've kind of wedged yourself into a situation you don't totally understand."

He's right. I need to know so much more. And the perfect informant is sitting in front of me.

"What are you doing after practice, Tony?"

"Besides homework? Not much, really."

"Would you like to . . . hang out at my house?"

His expression seems an indictment of my sanity.

"At the Glass Castle? Dude. Absolutely!"

I have to give Tony the tour, of course. It takes what seems an eternity because he has to fiddle with every cool gadget he encounters. When he realizes that there are multiple video game consoles set up in the movie theater (Stilson's doing, not mine), he insists I turn on the digital projector and play some post-apocalyptic game with him. While the visual effects dazzle me at first, I get tired after a half hour.

Tony obsesses over the gym, but he is too exhausted to use any of the equipment. Instead, we end up in my Olympic-size pool, one end of which extends beyond the wall. We swim under it to the glass-bottomed end of the pool, which juts into Joy Lake itself.

Beneath us, trout dart back and forth.

"Dude, there are no words for how awesome this is," Tony mutters, clinging to the lip of the pool and looking out across the lake.

"It's nice to have someone to share it with."

"Oh, I can come hang out anytime you want, Greg."

I approach the subject of Blanca from an unexpected angle.

"The day I moved in, the district attorney came by. She was very interested in Montes Realty. It sounds like she's investigating the company."

Tony slicks back his long hair. "Probably investigating Rafael Montes. When he built this place, rumor was that he was laundering money for some mob or cartel."

I narrow my eyes. "Ah. So my dad buying this house at the asking price may have made that successful. Didn't you call Don Rafael the *godfather* of Blanca Montes? Where are her parents?"

Tony blows mucus from his nose into the lake. "Dead. Car accident when Blanca was a little kid. Rafael is her dad's . . . cousin? Second cousin? Rafael agreed to raise her if anything ever happened. It was in the will. But so was a wrinkle that I don't think Rafael liked."

"She inherited the business, not him," I guess.

"Bingo. He's her legal guardian, and he manages her trust. Ton of money."

"That really sucks," I reply, sighing. "Not a recipe for a loving relationship."

"Why do you think she became the Ice Princess?" Tony flips to float on his back. "There's no love in that house. Not since Blanca lost her parents twelve years ago."

That night, I dig deeper. Oscar and Belinda Montes died when the brakes on their vehicle failed, and they plowed into a semitruck that suddenly veered in front of them on an icy highway. Oscar had been an only child, CEO of the family business. But Oscar had ensured jobs for many of his cousins within the company, including an executive slot for his favorite, Rafael.

These facts and hints connect to my curated memory, and a loose picture forms. Blanca inherited a big chunk of shares in Montes Realty. Rafael Montes may be the president of the company, but when she turns eighteen later this fall, Blanca will be the biggest shareholder.

In my dreams, I've seen rivalries, family members grasping at power when their patriarch falls. It's easy to reach conclusions, though I have no evidence. I send a message to my father, asking him to look into Montes Realty.

More than the complications of corporate civil war, however, my mind echoes with Tony's chilling observation.

There's no love in that house.

I think of such loneliness, such solitude, the way it chills one's very soul.

I imagine Blanca sitting in her godfather's frigid house, a robe drawn tight about her shuddering flesh, going blue with cold like the robe itself, like her lipstick, like so many of her clothes and accessories.

Tears spill from my eyes. And, with a flash that brings with it a splitting migraine, I see an image of a blue flower, blooming from snow at the summit of the world . . . and my hand reaching for it.

After the ache in my head has subsided, I go to my computer, where I've been creating a table of the cycles of my lives and some pertinent information, trying to get a better handle on what I am and who Blanca might be.

I feel someone standing behind me.

"That looks about right, yup." It's Teresa.

I turn to look at her. "Santa Rosa called me an *apu*. Looked it up. Means *mountain god* in Quechua. So I'm guessing I'm a tepictli."

Narrowing her eyes as she takes a deep breath, the goddess nods. "Yeah. Which means you were a human first, of course. That's the part I can't get into just yet. You'd blow a gasket."

"Sure, I get it. But the mountain . . . It's Popocatepetl, right? There's a whole lot on the internet about that legend. Just sayin'."

She puts her hand on my shoulder. "Don't push, Goyo. Let the true story come to you. The details are *super* important. Like, *vital*. Because Blanca and you were *not* the only players in the actual historical events, and if you go down a rabbit hole of nonsense that's accrued over more than a thousand years . . ."

"I hear you. Still, I'm a little worried. Right now, I feel something special starting to happen between Blanca and me. When Stilson asked me this morning whether I was trying to reach Blanca or the girl who was lost, I wasn't sure what to say. Right now? I *know* Blanca. Or I'm getting to know her, anyway. I don't remember . . . who she was."

"But you're going to."

I swallow heavily. "Exactly. And that's what worries me. Because in every life I remember, you have said the same thing to me."

Teresa closes her eyes as she repeats it. "She has to love you. Or the cycle never ends."

I don't want the tears to come, but they do. "In order for her to love me, Teresa, I have to love them both. The person she is now *and* the person she once was. But what if I can't? What if the girl who was lost overwhelms Blanca Rosa Montes?"

Her eyes open, and I catch a glimpse of her terrifying divine nature.

"Then *all of us* will be lost, Goyo."

CHAPTER

12

I feel Jackson's presence before he lays his hand on the small of my back, moves my hair away from my neck, and whispers, "So, you gonna miss me?"

"What?" I push him back with my elbow, because spooning at the lockers is just not cool.

"Why do you always do that?" Jackson leans beside my locker and stares at me.

I put my books in my locker. "Do what?"

"Push me away," he says. "When I'm trying to get close to you."

Because I want to break up with you, I want to tell him, but I don't. "You were saying something about missing you. Are you going somewhere?"

Jackson's eyes almost pop out of their sockets. "Really?" he asks. "The game? On Friday night?"

"Oh, yeah," I say.

When I close my locker and turn around, I catch sight of my friends. Tina, Sofía, and Tony are clustered together around Greg's locker. Whatever Tony is saying is interesting to everyone but Greg, whose beautiful amber eyes zero in on me. I smile at him, and he smiles back.

"That's why I'm not going to the grand opening, remember?" Jackson rambles on. "Super important game."

"Sure, sure," I tell him. "But you'll be at the reception. Right? Your parents are expecting you to get there as soon as the game's over."

Jackson wraps his free arm around my waist and pulls me in close. He leans down so that his nose is touching the tip of my ear, and I freeze. "And you? What are you expecting?"

"Stop it," I tell him, slapping his hand off my hips. "People are looking."

"People?" Jackson lifts his head and glances around. He stops when his eyes focus on Greg, who is still watching us. "You mean *him*? What's going on? Are you—you're not thinking of trading me in for that clown, are you?"

"I don't know what you're talking about," I tell him.

"Well, it's pretty obvious you're not into me anymore," he says.

I roll my eyes.

Rather than firing me up, Jackson's neediness leaves me feeling completely cold. But breaking up with him, like this, in front of my locker between classes, would make him flip, and then God only knows what he'd do. I can't let this escalate.

"I have to get to class, but I'll see you at the reception. Okay?"

Jackson glances over at Greg again.

"Yeah, sure, okay," he says absentmindedly, because once he gets an idea in his head, he won't let it go, even if he's wrong. He's just that focused when he spots an opponent. It's what makes him a good football player, but it's also his downfall.

I turn away from him. He walks beside me, and when we pass Greg, Tina, Tony, and Sofía, he puts his hand on the small of my back. I skip ahead and turn the corner.

"See you!" I yell, as I rush down the hall, away from all the potential drama.

––––––––––––––––

The rest of the day breezes by, and I am glad to be home again, getting ready for dinner. However, thoughts of what to do about Jackson keep my mind busy, and I can't shake the feeling that this has to be dealt with soon.

We always sit at the big table for dinner. Padrino Rafael insists on it. He likes using this space. This tall, hollow formal dining room with its massive, glittering chandelier, sparsely decorated walls, and cold marble floors suits him. He's as silent and dignified as the statues of ancient Maya warrior gods, artifacts he's collected during his travels, relics he values more than living, breathing things, like plants, or pets, or people. That's why there have been no pets in this house since my poodle, Chacha, passed away when I was in sixth grade.

One mutt in this lifetime is enough to contend with, don't you think? You've learned how to take care of things, how to be responsible. No need to repeat the experience, he'd said, six months later, when I was ready to give my affection to another living creature.

I didn't beg him for another puppy. I didn't need to because he made it very clear that dogs were no longer welcome here.

Who's going to pay for everything he destroys while you're housetraining him? Are you going to buy every piece of furniture he chews up? Will you replace the stained carpets with your allowance? No. It's final. We don't need the headache of keeping something that stupid and incorrigible around.

Rosario brings out the soup course, and I take my time eating, savoring the delicate soup, because flor de calabaza was my mother's favorite. Every single sip is a fragrant memory, her beautiful smile, her warm brown skin, her laughter tinkling in the air as we chased each other inside the formal garden where my parents held charity events.

The thought reminds me that I haven't heard anything official from Denise on my request for four seats at the grand opening, and I am glad to have something to take my mind off Jackson.

"Oh, I've been meaning to ask." I lay my spoon down gently. "Have you talked to Denise about Ms. Fillmore?"

My padrino takes his time eating his soup before he looks up at me. "No," he says. "She didn't mention it, and I didn't think about it."

"She didn't mention it?" I can't help it. My mouth drops open as I stare at him. "But I asked and you said you'd look into it!"

"And I will," my padrino says. "It just slipped my mind. I had other, more pressing things to do. Things your parents would have prioritized. To secure your future. You understand."

"Ah, yes, my future," I mumble the words, and they remind me of the one thing I was trying to forget—Jackson—and how pissed my padrino is going to be when he finds out I'm breaking up with him.

"How is school going? Is it everything you hoped it would be, this final stretch?"

Rosario picks up my padrino's empty soup bowl and walks over to collect mine.

"It's okay," I tell him. "I can't complain. We have a new student from Mexico. He seems to know a lot about environmental sustainability, which, as you know, is very important to me. So, I've worked with him a couple of times. Other than that, everything's the same."

My padrino's favorite dish, roasted rack of lamb, sits untouched a moment too long after Rosario serves it, because he is sitting with his hands steepled in front of him over his plate, watching me.

"And Jackson?" he finally asks, picking up his silverware and cutting into his lamb. "How is he doing?"

I take my time chewing a small bite of my lamb, deciding what to say. As I force down the morsel of food, delicate and perfectly prepared, I realize I don't like costillas de cordero. I've been eating food I can't stand all this time without saying anything about it because I didn't want to offend my padrino. That's been my life. All these years. Living with things I despise to keep the peace. But this thing with Jackson has to end. There's no way around it. And there's no use dragging it out any longer.

"I've decided to let him go," I tell my padrino, after I take a sip of water.

"Let him go?" Padrino Rafael puts down his fork and knife. He wipes his lips carefully and puts the napkin back on his lap. "What do you mean, let him go?"

"You know, cut ties with him," I say. "Take my losses and just walk away."

Padrino Rafael scowls, a deep, disapproving frown followed by a quizzical look. "Well, that's a disappointment. You two are so well matched."

"Well, we're not trying out for the Olympics here," I remind him. "Dating someone just because you're *well matched* doesn't mean it's going to work."

"I'm just saying, this is going to affect a lot of people," my padrino says, because he can't mask the fact that he finds the prospect of me and Jackson ending up together very appealing. Come to think of it, I wouldn't be surprised if he feels the same way Jackson feels—that this would be a great financial move for us.

"Oh God, you're not thinking about money, are you?" I ask, horrified. "Because *mergers* and *acquisitions* have absolutely nothing to do with love."

"No. Of course not." My padrino flushes. His dark olive skin burns bright red as he looks up at me. "I just know his parents, especially his mother, are very fond of you. They will be devastated to hear you're giving him the boot," he reminds me. "Our families have long been—"

"Our families don't have a say in this," I tell him. "I decide what I want. And neither you nor anyone else has any say in this."

Padrino Rafael's hands are tight fists. "I am your legal guardian," he blusters. "I have every right to express my opinion. Advise you, even, if I think you're being foolish."

"And I've taken your advice, many times," I say, cutting into my lamb again.

"But this time—" he starts, only I don't let him finish.

I put my fork and knife down. "This time I'm choosing to do what I want," I tell him.

"And can I ask why you are choosing to *let him go*?" My padrino pushes his plate away from him.

"He's too much," I say. It sounds a bit ridiculous, because it's true.

Padrino Rafael raises a brow at me. "Too much?" he asks. "I'm not sure I understand what you mean."

"He's infantile! An immature bully, always pushing people around, making everything about him. I can't take it. Can't—won't—deal with it anymore." The reproachful mouthful comes tumbling out of me like a long, convoluted series of complaints, and I shut my lips, cringing.

"So, call this to his attention," my padrino says. "Why make a mess of things? Why not communicate with him, show him how to behave around you?"

More than indignant, I am hurt by my padrino's suggestion. His words remind me of that puppy I wasn't allowed to have. Anger overwhelms me, and I feel myself getting colder and colder, as I lean back on my chair and stare back at the man who's denied me everything I've ever wanted, ever needed, from a parent. If my parents were here, if my padrino hadn't gotten them tickets to the Eureka Opera House on a rainy, miserable night . . . but I can't think about that right now.

"I don't have the time or the desire to train Jackson Caldera." My voice trembles because I can't find the right words to tell him how much I resent this conversation.

Before I can say anything more, Rosario steps into the room, quietly, like she doesn't want to disturb us. My padrino waves his meal away, and Rosario picks up his almost untouched dish.

"So that's it, then?" my padrino asks, when Rosario has left the room and is clearly out of earshot. "You won't even try?"

I play with my napkin, folding and unfolding it on my lap while I try to find exactly how to express my feelings. "Let's just say I *don't need the headache of keeping something that stupid and incorrigible around.*"

My padrino is silent for a long moment before he finally speaks. "I don't need to remind you of how much our families care about you two," he says. "How much it would mean to us all if you could find a way to salvage things between you."

"Are you telling me who to date?" I ask. "And will you also tell me who to marry? How far does it reach, this power you think you have over me?"

My padrino's eyes are cold, dead, as he stares me down. "I'm just asking you to be careful. Don't break anything you can't mend. Once something is broken, it can be discarded, disposed of, so make sure you know what you're getting yourself into. Don't expect this to go well."

"What do you mean?" I ask, my whole body shaking, shivering as I try to hold myself together. "Are you going to send me away? Throw me out? Disinherit me? You can't do that. You don't have that kind of power."

"Do I have to remind you—" my padrino starts, but I don't let him finish.

"I'll be eighteen next month," I remind him. "And when that happens, I'll do things for myself, make my own decisions. I'll get an MBA here, at Nevada, and start working on things that matter to me."

"You spoiled, ignorant child. You have no idea what I've had to do, what I've sacrificed, to take care of you!" My padrino's voice rumbles through the halls as he lays down the law.

"You call living here, like this, a sacrifice?" Tears start pricking my eyes as I look around me, at what he's done to make my parents' house his own. "Oh, I'm sure it was a hardship, moving in here, living in luxury, waiting for my parents to die so you could take over!"

I stop myself, because I can't believe I just said that. I have no idea where that awful thought came from, but it came out, unexpectedly. So it must have been living in my heart for a while for it to slip out of me like that.

I look up at my padrino. His face is flushed again, only I see something different, moisture, the semblance of tears, glistening in his narrowed eyes.

"Your life is so simple." My padrino's voice is low, restrained. And by the way he pulls his shoulders back before he continues, I can tell he's completely recovered from my assault. "You think your little social ventures, your justice-warrior nonsense, will survive if you take over this empire without an advanced degree? You're delusional if you think a measly MBA from this little community college is going to prepare you for that."

"It's a university," I say, interrupting his rant.

"It's a cesspool!" my padrino hollers. "It won't prepare you for the intricate job of CEO. You'd lose everything without a proper education, and then how would you help the little people you love so much? Your precious lake will dry up if you don't know what you're doing. No. Nevada is out of the question. You're going to Harvard, just like Jackson. You need a doctorate in international business to run our corporation."

I shake my head and press my fists against my stomach. "No," I tell him. "I need to start working on my passion projects now. I don't want to wait ten years to start living my own life!"

"You'll do as I say," my padrino says, his voice calm, collected. "You'll follow the plan, and you'll let me help you."

Let me help you. The words swirl around in my mind, repeating themselves over and over again, and I close my eyes, because I am remembering something I put out of my mind long ago.

A dark door opens, and he's there, my padrino, standing in the winter storm with the lightning flashing behind him, outlining his form. My parents are dead, he tells me. They're gone. Gone. He goes down on one knee, reaches for me, but I step away.

Then I'm out the door, running. Running down the street as fast as I can. Running against the wind and the rain and the sleet. Running from the coldness in my padrino's eyes. Running from the shadow of a snow-capped mountain. Running from the bitterness that is now home. Running from his words—"Let me help you."

CHAPTER

13

A fifth life. I descend from Popocatepetl in 1504. I use resources from my former life to become king of a city within the Triple Alliance of Anahuac—the Aztec Empire, as it will be called. By 1520, Ixcuinan and I find a possible reincarnation of my lost love, but the Spanish arrive, and the smallpox they bring sweeps through Anahuac, killing millions—including the girl.

In a rage, I climb my mountain to wield its power against the invaders, to wipe them from this continent so that nobody else from their distant land will ever attempt to come near us. But my anger is so great that it slips from my control, and the blast I would hurl at Cortés and his Tlaxcaltecah allies collapses upon me.

In my dreams, there's what Tony calls a *glitch*, as when a video game reaches the limits of its program . . .

And I find myself in my *sixth* life. I come to a small community at the edge of Moon Lake, part of Acolhuacan, a confederacy of kingdoms united under an honorable overlord. As I use my resources to search for the girl who is lost, I get wrapped up in the war between Acolhuacan and the Tepaneca Empire. With the help of the Isle of Mexico and rebel Tepanecas, we triumph, establishing the Triple Alliance.

But in all my travels and battles, even with a four-in-one goddess on my side, I find no trace of her. As famine and flood threaten to destroy everything I've helped create during my fifty-two years of life in this century, I drag my aching, old bones up the slope and lay myself down in the alcove that's becoming way too familiar.

As my mind slips away, I feel relief.

"Teresa!" I call as I wake up. She shimmers into existence before me.

"What? Are you okay?"

"Couldn't you just . . . walk over here? That's really unnerving."

"You shouted my name, Goyo."

I bob my head from side to side. "Fair. Okay, I was remembering my life during the Spanish invasion, but the memories cut off . . ."

"Oh." Her face goes expressionless. "Well, you didn't make it very long in that lifetime. But we learned a lesson! The volcano sustains you. It's not a weapon. And you are not actually immortal, just hard to kill . . . and hard to bring back to life, ugh."

"So I caused my own death. Yikes."

Stilson walks in, carrying breakfast on a tray. "Summoning such power out of unbridled rage invariably recoils upon the user. So say the archives."

As he sets food on the bed, I reach for a piece of toast. "The archives?"

"Yes. Your memories are curated, but your watcher records everything. I read all previous volumes while writing my own. And I've had them digitized for easier searching."

Teresa raises her hand. "Before you ask, no. Not until you've remembered all we prepared for you."

With my mouth full, I grumpily mutter something about being the heir to Tolchan.

"You may be a rich kid from Mexico," Teresa quips, smiling her

103

enigmatic smile, "but we're a goddess, the Four of us. No archives until your mind is whole."

Before I can make some snarky response, her head jerks to one side the way it does when another aspect is communicating with her.

"Little Sister says that Blanca is *so* close to severing her relationship with Jackson. Excuse me. We're going to strategize."

After she leaves, I put my fork down and regard Stilson. "You're married, right?"

"Indeed. He is patiently waiting for my work to be finished. I have promised him quite the retirement paradise, you see."

The thought brings a grin to my face. "How did you win him over, Stilson? You were such a serious, weird little kid. Even as a teen. I figured you'd end up a monk."

"Ah, young master, the grand gesture is key. I swept my beloved off his feet with unparalleled displays of affection, gifts that chipped away at his fears and insecurities. In the end, he could not help but fall in love, even with a weird little kid like me."

The joy that glistens in his eyes makes me want to shove breakfast aside and hug him. I've spent centuries experiencing that happiness vicariously. When the people around me find love, I could be jealous, but instead I rejoice and celebrate them.

"Grand gesture, huh? What about . . . a blue *Eryngium monocephalum*?"

Stilson lifts an eyebrow. "Inspired choice, Master Gregorio. Let me make some calls."

Sofía gives me a heads-up at school: I should be nice and normal around Blanca, without pushing anything. And that's fine. I spend the day being a good friend to her and the others, not worrying too much about the unusual gift I plan to give her tomorrow.

At the lockers between class, it looks like she's about to break up with Jackson, but no—she confirms that they're on for a reception this weekend, after the football game wraps up.

Jealousy tries to force its way into my brain, but I ignore it. I really like Blanca. I need her to like me. But Stilson and Teresa are right—it's got to be her free will. It's got to happen naturally.

All I can do is be me. Honest, respectful, and caring. A true friend.

And, yeah. I can also start with the grand gestures, as long as they come from my heart. That's a fair move.

That night, my seventh life before the present. Calling myself Tenoch, I descend from Popocatepetl and arrive among the Mexihtin, nomads in captivity on the plains of Colhuacan. They've been here for a while, intermarrying with their Colhua overlords.

I rise through their ranks, becoming their chieftain. When the Four tell me that the daughter of the Colhua king might be the incarnation of my lost love, we work to arrange a marriage alliance. All goes well until I attempt the fire trial.

It isn't her. She is burned, and her father goes into a rage. I flee, and my adopted people come with me. We are pushed to the marshes at the edge of Moon Lake, and the goddess whispers that we should swim to the barren island at its heart.

Floating children on shields, we make our way to our new home.

Mexico, we name the isle. Land of the Mexihtin.

And near the only freshwater spring, we establish our first

town—Tenochtitlan, named for the leader who came down from a volcano to lead the Mexihtin to their promised land at last.

Most of my morning is spent reflecting on the role I've played in historical events. Then a notification dings my phone. It's Stilson.

I ask permission to go outside to retrieve the precious object my keeper has brought from the airport. It was expensive to have it plucked from such heights and flown here overnight.

We'll see what effect the grand gesture has.

Holding the insulated black box carefully in my hands, I hurry inside. The principal is waiting for me, an eyebrow raised. She gestures me into her office.

"Aren't those containers used to ship chilled pharmaceuticals, Goyo?"

"I've brought her something special. Do you mind paging her before the bell rings, Firstborn?"

Without hesitation, she picks up her phone. "Mrs. Rosales, please have Blanca Montes come to the conference room."

Moments later, I am standing in the conference room as Blanca opens the door, flustered and out of breath. She does a startled double take when she sees me.

"What's going on?" she asks.

"I've noticed you've been a little down lately," I explain, "so wanted to give you something. A gift as rare and beautiful as you. My ancestors discovered it millennia ago on the slopes of the three legendary volcanoes."

I unseal the container. Nestled among thick, curling, spiny leaves sits a unique indigo-blue flower, shaped like a bright pinecone thrusting its way through a maguey plant.

Blanca gasps.

"La rosa de las nieves," I tell her. "The snow rose. Plucked thirteen hours ago from the drifts atop Iztaccihuatl."

Her pale hand, which was reaching out to touch the flower, stops at the sound of that name.

"Iztaccihuatl? I was there back in May, with Tina. Such a beautiful place. It felt . . ."

I hold my breath expectantly.

". . . like home, if that makes sense. I guess it's because of the snowy peaks around Reno."

"Maybe. You know, the snow rose has special meaning for the nearby Nahuas. It appears dead through late spring and early summer, when the air is warm. But once the dormant volcano is covered by snow again, it blossoms like an echo of the promise."

"The promise?" Blanca asks, her fingers brushing against the flower. For a fleeting moment, recognition flashes in her eyes.

"That Iztaccihuatl will awaken."

My voice hitches.

Blanca sees the tears in my eyes and responds with tenderness.

"It's beautiful, Greg. Thank you. I'm . . ."

We stand there, mere inches apart. There's a tingling between us, like when the barometric pressure drops before a massive storm.

Then the bell rings, breaking the reverie.

"I can't carry this around with me, though. Do you think Mrs. Primo will let me leave it here until after school?"

"Yeah, totally, I already asked her permission."

I lead her from the conference room into the busy hallway. Jackson sees us walking to AP Chemistry class together. He looks *furious*.

"Where were you, babe? I went to Calc to pick you up."

Blanca shrugs. "I got called into the office. My padrino."

Jackson seethes as she walks past him into the classroom. I don't even bother to look his way as I follow.

Something has shifted between us. I catch her stealing glances at me during the lecture. When we break for lab work, she suggests that our two groups share our findings in a sort of debriefing.

When we pull our chairs together, she sits next to me.

Little Sister winks.

Tony sends me a text: *ur really into her huh? Careful bro.*

But the time for careful is over. I'm going full-on grand gestures from now on.

Toward the end of lunch, I walk over to the girls' table.

"Blanca, do you have a sec?"

She looks up with a smile that almost makes me stagger. "Sure. What's up?"

"Can we talk outside?"

Sofía nudges her.

Tina giggles. "Go on. We'll throw your trash away for you."

The sun is scorching, so I guide Blanca to the meager shade of one of the trees lining the parking lot.

"I figured you had more to say after that gift. Spill. What do you want, Greg?"

I steel myself. "A date with you. I know you're seeing Jackson. But all I ask is one evening. If you decide there's nothing between us by the end of the night, I'll back off."

Blanca laughs, but I see joy glint in her eyes. Her face flushes, and not just from the heat. "All right, Greg. Here's a compromise. The Grizzlies' first game of the season is next Friday. That means

Jackson can't attend the grand opening of Imperial Silver Casino, though he'll show up for the reception. You could escort me to the event itself, but when he arrives, everyone will expect me to be with him. It's not a date, exactly, but you would accompany me for most of the evening. We'll see how you do mingling with the crème de la crème of Reno."

I nod. "I'd be honored to escort you. I'll also meet your godfather, no?"

Blanca looks at me strangely. "I'm sure you've heard all sorts of things about us. But, yes, my padrino will be there. And Rafael Montes is your biggest hurdle, Gregorio Chan. Let's see how you do against him."

I clear my throat. "Against him? You make it sound like a duel."

She gives a wry smile. "For Rafael, life is a series of battles. Every interaction is a scrimmage, at minimum. Here, give me your phone."

I unlock the screen, and she taps on the glass with fast fingertips.

"All set. Details forthcoming. Don't leave me on read."

I give a soft laugh. "Never."

Tina, Sofía, and I spend the weekend shopping, because we decide that even though we can't be together on Friday, we're still going to act like we are and wear complementary outfits. Finding them, however, proves to be easier said than done. It is actually hard work.

We go to twenty different stores, starting out in Reno and heading south to Carson City before rounding back up to Incline Village, exhausting every single shop owner within a thirty-mile radius. On Sunday, we even cross the state line into Cali and browse little boutiques and antique stores in Truckee. It is worth it, though, because in the end, we have them, three perfect outfits that make us look like moon-bathed goddesses.

"Ay, pero, you look bien chulas, like muñecas," Tina's mother, who insists I call her Tía Mague, says Sunday afternoon when she and her comadre come over to my house for a group fitting. We stand before her, all gussied up, while her comadre, Gloria Amescua, marks and pins the alterations she needs to make before she brings them back Thursday evening.

"Muñecas?" Tina says. "I wouldn't go that far."

Tía Mague lifts her hand up in the air. "I mean it, you all look so beautiful, parecen de mentiras, como La Barbie."

"Thank you, I get it from you." Tina touches her mother's shoulder.

"I'll take that." Tía Mague's eyes soften, and I wonder what my mother would say if she were here, right now, in this small, supportive circle of strong women. I shake the sadness that threatens to overwhelm me, because Tía Mague is admiring my gown.

"I don't think I've ever seen you look so radiant," Tía Mague tells me. "I mean you always look real nice, but this brings out your light."

I lean over and give her a hug. She kisses my temple and smooths my hair, the same way she does to Tina. "Gracias," I say.

Sofía caresses the shiny fabric of her royal blue A-line dress and swings her hips back and forth, making the skirt sparkle as it dusts her toes. Then, grinning, she reaches up and traces the edges of the wide, scalloped neckline that shows off her soft, round shoulders. "I think what she means is that trying to look like Barbie is just out of style," she tells Tina's mother.

"That's 'cause we got all the style now," Tina says, and she strikes a pose and raises her hand, palm up, waiting for someone to give it a gentle slap.

"That's right! And we ain't giving it back!" Sofía says, affording Tina the much-anticipated high five.

We're all giggling so much we don't see a dark figure approach. Not until he raps his knuckles against the wall and clears his throat, do we all turn to look at my padrino, standing halfway inside the archway that connects the loft to the upstairs family room.

"Ahem." Padrino Rafael steps into the loft. "I see you've been busy, getting ready for the grand opening."

"I know this is going to break your heart, but I won't be there," Tina sasses, tossing her hair back and grinning at my padrino, daring him to deny it.

"Yes," I say. Looking around at the large, upturned boxes, the scattered bags, and crumpled tissue sheets strewn about the room, I cringe. Then I walk around trying to match the tops to their boxes and gathering the tissue paper, because my padrino hates disarray. "I'm sorry about all this. I'll make sure it's all put away when we're done with the fitting."

Uncharacteristically, Padrino Rafael shrugs a shoulder and starts walking toward us. "Don't worry about it. I'm sure Rosario can take care of it for you."

"Good evening, Rafael," Tía Mague says. "Gloria and I are almost done here. We'll be out of your hair before you know it."

"There's no hurry," Padrino Rafael says, waving a hand in her direction before turning to look at me. "I just wanted to give you this. You look wonderful by the way. Like an angel. Azul celeste has always been your color."

I stare at the familiar emblem on the jewelry box he is holding up to me. "What?" I ask, not moving to take it because, to be honest, I am frozen in place, chilled to the bone. "I told the woman at the store I don't want the necklace. It doesn't go with my dress."

"Open it," my padrino says, smiling in a way I haven't quite seen before. The softness in his eyes is something between gentle and sensitive. It's almost . . . *paternal*. "Please. I think you'll find that it goes perfectly with your gown."

I look away from the box and turn to Sofía, Tina, and her mother, who are all waiting for me to either take it or flat-out reject it. My best friend raises her eyebrows, and Sofía lowers her gaze. Tía Mague, however, lets out an exasperated breath. Before anyone can stop her, she takes the gift box, places it in my hands, and opens it.

"Oh my santitos!" Comadre Gloria gasps, and she leans over my shoulder to get a closer look. "Is that . . . the *Titanic* thing . . . what's it called?"

"The Heart of the Ocean. And, no, it's not. It doesn't look anything like it," Tina says, rolling her eyes. "This one's called something else, Noble Teardrops, Regal Tears . . . something like that."

"The Royal Teardrop," I whisper, sneaking a sideways glance at my padrino. "How did you know?"

Padrino Rafael puts his hands in his pants pockets and shrugs again. I don't think I've ever seen him shrug so much. Or ever, actually. "Bernice told me."

"She called you? To talk about me?" I ask, snapping the lid on the velvet box closed a bit too harshly.

My padrino looks taken aback.

"What? No. Bernice is more discreet than that. But she was at the club this afternoon. I asked her how things were going, and she went on a long-winded discussion about the younger generation's preference for gems and their disdain for diamonds."

"That is concerning, for many of us, but, honestly . . . I just . . . Well, I just like what I like," I start blubbering like a fool because I am shocked that Bernice would be so wily as to construct such an elaborate scenario just to sell a piece of jewelry. I see right through her.

"She mentioned that she ordered this for you, said this is what you really wanted to wear Friday, but that you wouldn't let her call me to make the exchange." Padrino Rafael sighs. Because I'm not expecting it and have no recourse other than to let it happen, he takes his hands out of his pockets and puts them on my shoulders. "I'm sorry I didn't go to the jeweler with you that day. This business, taking care of it for your estate, well, it keeps me from being better at this. There is no training, no guidelines, no rule book for good guardianship. Trust me. I've looked."

"It's okay," I whisper, chilled to the core, unable to think, to define what exactly has shifted in our dynamic or why.

"I hope you know I wasn't trying to dictate what you should wear to the gala. How you dress, what you look like, who you take as your plus-one, that is all your prerogative. Your choice. Always."

"Awww!" Comadre Gloria puts a hand to her heart and looks swooningly at my padrino. I flush, because I don't know where this is coming from. Is this his way of apologizing to me for the other day? Why? This is so not like him that I can't help but wonder . . . *What does he really want?*

"That's so sweet." Tía Mague fans her flushed face with the top of a small box.

Sofía and Tina exchange inconspicuous glances with each other. I suspect that, like me, they're seeing right through my padrino's *transformation.*

Emboldened by the older women, Padrino Rafael reaches down and picks up the jewelry box. He taps the lid gently, thinking for a few seconds, before offering it to me.

"Will you accept this, please?" he asks, his eyes full of that strange emotion again—his attempt at displaying kindness, I think. "As a token of my devotion to you. I can never replace your parents, but I can make sure you are well taken care of."

"Yes, she will, and she'll let me borrow it. To wear on the red carpet. When I win my first Grammy," Tina says, snatching the box out of my padrino's hands and opening it up to show it to her mother, who's reaching out to touch it, eyes shining brightly.

I shake my head, ignoring her, before I turn back to my padrino.

"Thank you," I say.

Then, because I don't know what else to say, what else to do, I reach out and offer him a hug. My padrino's eyebrows lift, then settle over his sparkling eyes, before he leans over, puts his arms around me, and we stand there, holding each other in the most unnatural way.

It's awkward. Very awkward. And I breathe a sigh of relief when it's over. It's like both of us know better than to try to give it more time, more effort, because there's no use forcing it. There's no real love here.

My padrino gives the older women a winning smile, before he steps back and bows slightly toward them. "Ladies," he says, "I leave you to your important business."

15

By Saturday morning, my eighth life before this one swirls in my head. Those fifty-two years happen in the middle of the dark ages that came after the fall of the Toltec Empire. I spend most of five decades fighting against the fierce Chichimecas who pour into Ana-huac, snatching up princesses and kingdoms. I'm not going to let them take the lands near the volcanoes, so I give military aid to other Toltec kings. Our empire may have fallen, but we still have our pride and our people.

My main rival is Chief Xolotl, leader of the invaders. Not only does he try to gather power and establish an empire—he's also after a Toltec princess named Camaxochitzin, who the Four believe is a candidate. Our conflict over her leads us to a duel on the battlefield. I manage to slay him, but his heir, Nopaltzin, makes the rest of my life miserable, especially after I discover that Camaxochitzin isn't the reincarnation of my lost love.

After I wake up, I decide to shake off the negative vibes with some intense shopping. He isn't a Chichimeca chieftain, but if I'm going to meet Rafael Montes on his own turf, I need to be ready. So I fly to

London for a fitting of a bespoke tuxedo at my favorite shop on Savile Row (which I haven't visited since my last life). It's run by a family that has tailored clothing for three hundred years.

On the flight back, I have a videoconference with the man everyone knows as my father, Roberto Chan Texis. It's easier to talk with him now that I remember preparing him for this role when he was young. I feel some guilt. A family in my sacred town of Santiago Xalitzintla put him in my care. His name was changed. His connection to his relatives had to be hidden. It's a tough way to live. But I was good to him, and he's managed Grupo Tolchan for fifty-two of his seventy-five years.

On the screen now, he bows his gray head and gives me a knavish grin.

"You look happy. I hear you've found her at last."

I nod. "Though I'm kind of hazy on the particulars, the Four tell me that all the ceremonies that are required will be done within a year. Are you and Dolores ready for some freedom?"

He laughs, wrinkles crinkling in a way that makes my heart hurt. "More than ready. She's looking forward to 'ending this charade,' she insists."

"Ha! Sounds just like her. I'll keep you in the loop. Be well."

"You too, Gregorio."

———————

Sunday brings memories of still another life. I emerge from my cavern to find a prince named Huemac has ascended the throne. But Huemac is a weak leader, and the Priests of Chaos do all they can to ruin his reign. I become one of his generals, but I'm pulled away from that civil war when Princess Xiuhcozal, Huemac's only child and possibly the reincarnation of my former betrothed, is kidnapped by a Huastec warlord named Tsok Tsan.

117

My pursuit of Tsok Tsan leads me into a trap. The warlord is in league with the Priests of Chaos and their leader, the dark wizard Tezcatlipoca, the incarnation of Chaos itself. As he stands laughing over my broken body, I die a decade before my time.

"So I've died twice?" I ask Teresa when she brings me breakfast.

"Well, three times, if you count the first. At this rate, you'll remember that death soon enough. Eat up. Get plenty of rest. Wednesday is going to be rough on you, Goyo. But it's important you reawaken to the lessons of the past. Reuniting with the girl who was lost means dealing with *how* she was lost and *how* you responded to that knowledge. Chaos is hoping you'll lose control again. If you die before we're done . . . well, even our spindle whorls and spinning bowls can't predict what would happen. So don't."

I swallow heavily. "Whoa. Death. Are things really going to get that intense?"

"I'm afraid so."

I take her advice and eat as much as I can all day, taking multiple naps to fight off jetlag and reincarnation overload. When I check my computer in the evening, an initial report about Montes Realty is waiting, detailing its corporate structure, assets, shareholders, and so on. Blanca's going to inherit a 40 percent stake in the company when she turns eighteen. Right now, her godfather manages her shares plus his own 12 percent, making him the decisive vote on any issue.

Rafael Montes is both CEO and president of the board of directors. I'm sure he wants to retain those roles. But to remain in power, he'll have to continue managing Blanca's wealth or make sure she votes with him at shareholder meetings.

It's weird that he's treated her so coldly. What was he thinking?

There are too many possible variables. My father says he'll keep researching Raphael Montes and Montes Realty, giving me regular updates on his findings. I ask him to be discreet. Blanca wouldn't appreciate me snooping around her family business.

Monday's memories are different. Every other life, upon awakening in the cavern, there would be a human protector waiting with one of the Four to ease my transition into the mortal world again, like Stilson and Teresa in the present. But when I opened my eyes in the year 984 CE, there was just a teenaged boy named Tlecoyo. He took me by the hand and led me down the eastern slope to the town of Xalitzintla, whose inhabitants worshiped me as a god. One of their priests had met my spirit on the slopes, they claimed, before entering the cavern to find my body growing younger.

I lived a pampered, gentle life among them. My memories returned slowly, over many years, and it wasn't until middle age that I remembered my vital task.

The people of Xalitzintla mobilized a search. They spread throughout Anahuac, keeping in mind the three markers—*a girl born into a powerful family, somehow connected to the cold, with a symbol like the snow rose appearing upon her person, on her clothing, or in her name.*

As they scoured the cities near the highland lakes, I began to fast and pray, crying out to Ixcuinan, to the Four-in-One, the goddess who had sworn to be always by my side.

At the very end of my fifty-second year, bitter and heartbroken, I received a visit at last.

"Oh, dearest boy," they said, weeping. "Chaos has kept us from you, playing an awful trick. But we know better now. When you awaken as a young man once more, we shall be waiting by your side."

And I know. Because I've remembered every life that is to come. They keep their promise.

CHAPTER

16

Monday, I hang out with Greg when I'm not with the girls because I plan to avoid Jackson as much as possible. My plans, however, come to a screeching halt when Jackson comes sauntering into AP English Lit, waving a schedule change right in the middle of our discussion on *Hamlet*. The question that has everyone popping right now is whether Hamlet's madness is real or feigned, and I wonder how Jackson is going to be able to keep up with us.

Frankly, watching him pull up a chair between me and Greg, making us all shift our fishbowl seating arrangements, is disrupting more than my rhythm. He's making me want to jump up and go get a schedule change too.

"Of course it's real," Greg says, filling an especially tense moment of silence. "To return to your palace, your *home*, and find betrayal shattering your family—how could you *not* go crazy?"

"And Ophelia?" I ask him, ignoring Jackson. "If Hamlet isn't acting, he can't be blamed for her suicide. Pretty convenient, no?"

Greg answers me with complete confidence, speaking respectfully.

"Well, her father pushes her to break up with him, to return his letters and things," he says. "The toxic scheming of Polonius harms her psyche, sure. But she also despairs to see the mind of the man she loves broken, to know that her prince is lost to her, his family twisted by envy and deceit."

Sofía looks at him pointedly. "Deceit. That's at the heart of the tragedy, no? Not madness. Deceit and betrayal, which lead to vengeance instead of forgiveness and atonement."

"It's all a matter of perspective," Jackson cuts in. "The play doesn't let Claudius explain himself. Maybe there's a good reason to get rid of his brother. Like keeping Norway from invading Denmark and getting revenge for the death of their ruler at the hands of King Hamlet. If the prince had just stayed at school and not stirred stuff up, everyone would have survived."

"You've read the book?" Ms. Dresch asks, surprised. Though I doubt she's as surprised as I am.

"Googled it," he admits, winking at me. "Had to. No time to read at practice. But I got the gist of it, the politics, the rivalries . . ."

He turns sideways, and I see his eyes boring into Greg before he continues. "It's Hamlet's arrogance, not his insanity or his uncle's betrayal, that brings all the tragedy down upon their heads."

Tina laughs. "Y'all are way too smart for your own good."

Tony gives her a high five. "Agreed. Which is the best movie version to watch this weekend, Ms. Dresch? Like Jackson, training is keeping me from reading as, uh, closely as other folks in this room."

We leave class clustered tightly together, Sofía and Tina flanking me so close Jackson has to fall back and follow us. After school, however, I have no choice but to deal with him, because he accosts me in the parking lot.

"So, where's Loverboy?" he asks, following me to my SUV.

"I don't know. I'm not his mother," I tell him, unlocking my Jeep, jumping in, and waving for Tina, who's talking to our precalculus teacher, asking him for more time to turn in her late assignment, when the poor guy is just trying to go home. I wish I could just speed off without her, but I can't. I'm her ride.

Jackson puts his hands on the roof of my Jeep and leans down to look at me. When I ignore him, he taps on the glass impatiently.

"What is up with you?" he asks when I roll the window halfway down.

"Nothing," I tell him. "I just have to get to Dreamy Affairs and make sure Denise Hernández doesn't ruin things for the gala. I know you don't get it, but I have to be on top of everything with her."

"What is it? What's going on?" Jackson asks.

"It's a lot of little things. I just saw her latest post online, and I almost threw up. So gaudy. Don't worry about it," I tell him. "I can handle it."

"Hey, you ready?" Tina asks, jumping in the Jeep beside me.

"See you tomorrow," I say. Then I roll up the window. Jackson looks confused, but he presses his lips together and nods as he steps back onto the curve and watches us take off.

"See you tomorrow? Really?" Tina asks. "I don't know why you're dragging this out. If I were you, I'd have cut him loose a long time ago."

"Hmm." I speed up to beat a red light and keep going, because I really want to avoid rush hour.

"Come on," Tina says, reaching over and giving my shoulder a sturdy shake. "You're giving me nothing here. What is it? You look worried. Is it Denise? I can't believe she hasn't gotten back to you yet."

"Yeah, but she's used to having her way," I tell her. "If you ask me, my padrino's given her too much cuerda. But I have to make sure everything turns out just right. I don't want Lorraine Fillmore to think we're a bunch of classless casino cats."

"What about Greg?" Tina asks, as we hit the strip, heading toward the Imperial Silver Casino. "And Jackson! What was up with those two today? Were you uncomfortable sitting between them?"

"Nah." I shrug. "I was all right."

"Why do I have the feeling you're holding out on me?" Tina looks at me closely. "Come on. What's going on?"

The long red light gives me a moment to think. "He asked me on a date."

"Ah!!!" Tina screams, an ear-piercing howl that makes me cringe and smile at the same time. "So? Come on . . . spill the frijoles."

"So," I say, keeping my eyes on the road, "he's going to escort me to the gala."

"The gala?!" Tina's shock and excitement can't be contained. "Oh, my freakin' fudge! Now you've gone and done it. You're flying in the face of everything your padrino wants. I'm like totally impressed with you right now!"

"Okay. Calm down. Time to switch gears," I say, grinning, as I pull into the parking space. "Come on. I'm gonna need backup."

Denise Hernández is toying with me. I'm sure of it. Because no matter what concessions she makes one-on-one, she turns right around and tells her crew to do otherwise.

"Wait," I tell her. "Why are they adding more glitter to the centerpieces? I thought we agreed, no glitter. It looks like fairies barfed all over them."

"I don't understand," she says. "Why don't you like glitter?"

"Because this isn't a party for five-year-olds!" I hiss.

"Well, it's too late now," she says.

"Oh, no it's not," Tina says. "If you don't toss the glitter, I'll take every one of those sparkly barf bags and use them as target practice."

"Excuse me, but . . . who are you?" Denise asks. "Because I don't remember getting the memo about your coronation."

"This isn't about me," Tina starts, and I put my hand on her shoulder, holding her back before she gets more riled up.

"Stop, please, let's just take a breather, give them time to get those centerpieces out of here. Come on, let's go check out the balcony," I tell my champion, pulling my phone out of my pocket as we retreat, because I just got a notification.

Tina walks with me to the sliding doors and follows me silently as I step outside to read my text messages.

GREG: Hey, I forgot to ask, what time do I pick you up Friday?

"What's going on?" Tina asks, when I turn away from her and start typing something. "Oh my God . . . Is it Greg?"

"Yes," I say, trying not to smile.

"And?"

"And what?" I ask dismissively because, frankly, I'm having too much fun teasing Greg about getting forgetful in his old age.

GREG: Then you better hurry up and answer my question, before I forget what we're talking about.

ME: The Opening is at seven, so six? I need to get there early.

Just as I send that last message, another message comes in—*from Jackson!* I look up at Tina, who's busy eyeing Denise through the wall of windows.

"Hey, you wanna check on Denise?" I ask. "Tell her I mean it about the glitter. And tell her absolutely no balloons. I saw a helium pump in the corner, by the bar. God. What's wrong with that woman?"

Tina grins.

"It would be pure pleasure to deal with Ms. Party Pooper," she says. Then she takes off, opening the door dramatically, letting the air blow her hair back, before making an entrance and heading straight for Denise.

JACKSON: hey babe just taking a quick water break how are things at ground zero?

I struggle, because I'm not sure if I should text Jackson back or not. But after the stunt he pulled today, forcing his way into our lit class, I don't want to instigate any more *surprises* from him.

ME: Catastrophe. But I'm dealing with it.

I keep it short, because I also don't want him to think he has to come to my rescue. Jackson and Denise at the same time? The combination might be my demise. As soon as I answer him, I check back on my conversation with Greg.

GREG: I will be there, with a very special flower for your wrist.

ME: Don't you need to ask what color my dress is first?

GREG: No. I'm pretty sure I've got this.

ME: Okay, Einstein, we'll see how observant you are.

There's a moment of silence, wherein no text messages come through, but then my phone pings again, twice, and I see that both Jackson and Greg have texted me back.

JACKSON: So, what exactly was the problem?

It would take too long to explain the problems, because there are more than a few things wrong with the setup for the gala, so I switch back to see what Greg had to say.

GREG: Didn't I do enough to prove my sophistication the last time I did this? Did not my simple gift, my tender blossom, la rosa de las nieves, bring forth from you some faith, some hope, or in the very least some tender thoughts?

Faith? Hope? Tender thoughts? His directness is unnerving, but also exciting. Most guys his age are a bit uncertain, even downright clueless. But not Gregorio Chan; he's full of confidence and charm. Even his texts are perfectly put together, not a comma out of place.

I turn off my phone, close my eyes, and consider what to say, how to express what I'm beginning to feel when I think of him. How even though we are so different, we are like two totally different elements, fire and ice, drawn to each other in ways I cannot explain.

Why, yes. Yes. It did, I want to say. Though I know I shouldn't—not until I figure it all out. Opening my eyes, I look at the scenery before me, Carson Range and Mount Rose. Is this why I thought of this analogy, because this view reminds me of the two volcanoes I visited last spring? Just thinking about the connection I felt when I hiked the trails on Itzaccihuatl fills me with emotion. So, I open my phone and text Greg back.

ME: I know I thanked you already, but I wanted to say, I really did appreciate all the work you put into getting that perfect flower for me, having it brought all the way up here from Mexico. It was the sweetest, most beautiful, most thoughtful gift anyone's ever given me.

There is another moment of silence. I grip my phone tightly in my hand, wondering . . . *Did I gush too much? Sound disingenuous? He doesn't know me that well, and maybe he wasn't expecting me to be so . . .* But just as I am beginning to doubt myself, my phone pings again.

It's Jackson again. I roll my eyes and open it.

JACKSON: flowers? from who? not that mestizo guy? he wouldn't dare! did he? tell me the truth did he send you flowers?

I'm reading the message with my heart in my throat, half panicked and shivering, because it's obvious I used the wrong thread. But I don't have time to smooth this out because, in that very moment, the door flies open and Tina yells, "Blanca. Get in here. You're not gonna believe this!"

CHAPTER
17

Tuesday night. It's 880 CE. The beginning of my second chance at life. But I'm not in the cavern. I'm standing in full battle gear at the edge of a massive slag of volcanic rock. Red veins betray the heat beneath the blackened crust.

Behind me awaits a squadron of soldiers. Hearing of the tragedy that has occurred, we have marched for two days to this place. Tetempan, Place at the Edge of the Rocks. A town of two thousand souls.

It is utterly gone. It appears that I buried it in the blindness of my rage.

But I can't remember doing so.

We return to Tollan. I'm installed as King Ce Tecpatl, hailed as the return of the demigod Mixcoatl. I dedicate myself to ruling, making alliances throughout Anahuac, forging a peaceful empire to make up for whatever horrible deeds my mind has blocked.

I pray to the gods again and again. They've brought me back to life, but what about her? Has she returned? Where can I find her?

I don't marry or have children. When my hair begins to gray, I learn of a brilliant scholar and warrior who lives in a nearby hermitage. Ce Acatl is his name, a supposed miracle worker.

I call him to the palace. There is a woman with him. His sister, he says.

But I soon learn the truth. They are both gods.

Quetzalcoatl, made flesh. And Ixcuinan, the goddess of fate, she who tempts us to sin and then devours that sin once we truly repent.

"Chaos would use you," they tell me, "but cannot fathom our plan. The path will be long, dear child, and arduous. Yet at the end, Order and Creation and Love will reassert themselves."

I crown Ce Acatl Quetzalcoatl my heir. Then, seeming to all the world like a very healthy seventy-year-old man, I disappear from my empire, following Ixcuinan up the slopes of the volcano, which my people have renamed Popocatepetl in my honor.

———————

I get through these increasingly tough nights by reminding myself I'll see Blanca in the morning. Hanging out with her, Tina, and Sofía is a welcome relief. Tony has been busy preparing for the first game, so today I only see him in class. Honestly? He seems more distracted than he should be. I've gotten used to his foolish jokes and friendly company. I hope everything's okay.

Jackson's also around less. When he shows his face, he's usually scowling at our knot of friends. Not happy to see Blanca and me spending time together.

I can't stop looking at her. The way she treats others shows her goodness, wisdom, and leadership. Any coldness of hers is never cruel. She is quick to follow up abrupt responses with a smile and an apology.

I'm moved. It's not her fault that her warmth and humanity are cloaked by an icy mantle. She makes her way through life as best she can, the jabbing of those icicles perceived as arrogance. Does she want to shatter the barrier, to fan the embers of her spirit into a bonfire?

If she asked, I'd lay down my soul as tinder for that flame.

But I'm also content to accept her heart of snow.

Sofía leans close as I think this. "Start with text messages, drama queen. Act your age."

And I do. Blanca and I spend most of Wednesday evening exchanging texts and memes. Being silly and slightly flirtatious feels good. We just *get* each other in every way.

I can't wait till Friday.

As I finally plug in my phone and switch off the light, Teresa pokes her head in.

"Tonight's the night, Goyo. If it gets to be too much . . . just dissociate yourself."

I narrow my eyes at her silhouetted form. "What do you mean?"

"You've been a king many times. Imagine the royal bard, singing the tale. Put some distance between yourself first. Then ease in."

And she closes the door, whispering, "Good night, dearest child."

———

At last comes my original life as Popoca. My birth in 832 CE. A noble family, related to the emperor himself. A happy childhood with loving but stern parents who teach me the Toltec Way: centering life on the arts. Music. Engineering. Painting. Poetry. Architecture. And, in my father's case, the martial arts, a love of which he passes on to me. At the school for noble boys, I train body and mind. When the time comes to defend Tollan and its allies against those who would destroy our livelihoods and hopes, I plunge into battle. I rise quickly through the ranks. My men adore me, and I care for them as I would my own children.

But I have another love. The youngest daughter of the emperor. Lady Iztac.

Who pledges her heart to me in the gardens. Whom I swear to wed. But then . . .

Pain beyond words. Beyond screams. Sadness and regret that make me want to obliterate myself from the cosmos. I do not deserve her. I do not deserve life. I do not deserve love. Or power. Or wealth. Let me die. Let me die.

A hand touches my shoulder in the darkness of the nightmare. It is Tlecoyo, my first protector, his smile as bright as dawning skies.

"Peace, my lord. Do not despair. There is a deeper truth. None of us deserves life. Nonetheless, Creation gives it to us freely. Out of boundless love, Order looks at the wreckage lying in the wake of Chaos, and smiles, whispering, 'All must be broken to be made whole.'"

There is a flicker of light, a warm and gentle fire. All the people I have loved are gathered in a circle, smiling at me with care and forgiveness.

"Rest your heart, Popocatzin. Let us recount those times. Listen and remember. We are with you, always. Lean on us. Take our hands in the darkness."

Tlecoyo begins, taking a brand from the fire and lifting it before his face. "In the mists of the early ninth century, we Toltecs came under the rule of Emperor Tecpancaltzin."

A tall, wiry man steps forward to accept the torch next. It's the emperor, or my memory of him, regal except for nervous eyes.

"Empress Maxio bore me a daughter whom we named Huixachin. We were happy until tragedy arrived a few years later when Maxio, heavily laden with a second child, succumbed to the pains of child-birth, leaving me bereft with two daughters. I called the newborn Iztac, for she was born on the day of the year's first snow."

A beautiful woman takes his place, black hair plaited severely to reveal smoldering eyes capable of love or fury. Xochitzin, who raised Iztac, smiles at me.

"In his heart," she continues the tale, "the emperor knew that his daughters should not face life without maternal warmth. Fate led him to me, the clever daughter of a farmer. I had learned the secret of pulque. Enthralled by my beauty and wisdom, the emperor made me his queen. Time, as you know best, passes swiftly. Within a year, I blessed the emperor with a son, Meconetzin."

Now my father takes the burning brand, and I begin to shudder with sadness. He reaches out and pulls me warmly against his imposing bulk for a moment before releasing me.

"Weep not, my son. Listen as I speak of your bravery. The tranquility of the palace was shattered when Meconetzin turned ten. Assassins, silent and deadly, slithered in, aiming for the young crown prince. But salvation would soon arrive, brandishing an obsidian blade. You, dear Popoca, a gallant soldier and my only son. Your courage and loyalty earned you the mantle of captain of the palace guard, and young Meconetzin came to view you as an elder brother. Lady Iztac, now in the bloom of her youth, fell in love with you. You returned that love. You began meeting under the veil of night within the imperial gardens. But your romance was not destined to last."

My former protector Tlecoyo once more accepts the torch. He kneels before me, taking my fingers with his free hand.

"This part is difficult. For a shadow of envy and ambition lurked in the empire: Captain Tzinacan. The officer harbored hate because his noble family had been repeatedly passed over for positions of power. His rage grew when he discovered your secret romance with Iztac, and he went to the emperor. But Tecpancaltzin saw an opportunity for you to prove your worth. He tasked you with a dangerous mission: conquer the Totonac territory. And you, bound by honor and love, accepted. Wanting to ease the tensions among factions, you made Tzinacan your second-in-command. But he betrayed you to the enemy. After your capture, Tzinacan assumed command and returned to the palace, spreading the lie that you had died. His family seized the chance and pressured the emperor into arranging a marriage between Lady Iztac and Tzinacan. Tecpancaltzin, to prevent civil war, agreed, ignoring his wife's pleas."

My body goes from trembling to spasms of agony. I don't want to remember this part. I could go the rest of my life without seeing these images again.

In the flickering firelight, a young woman approaches: Huixachin, looking just as she did the day I returned, wearing undyed mourning clothes woven from maguey fibers.

"Ah, Popoca. It falls to me to help you remember that most horrifying of discoveries. Heartbroken and horrified at the prospect of marrying Tzinacan, my sister Iztac sought solace in the Queen of Death's cold embrace. She had no way of knowing that you had freed yourself from captivity and were making your way back to her. You arrived to find her lifeless, and in your fury and sorrow, you slew Tzinacan. Then you took Iztac's body and ascended the mountains, collapsing in the heart of a blizzard. You begged the gods to revive your beloved, whose lips went the blue of the snow rose as you screamed . . . Your pleas echoed unanswered until the harsh wilderness claimed you, too."

In my dream, I begin to wail, and those dear avatars of my loved ones gather round, holding me as I shake and weep. Then one by one they pull away, leaving a teen boy. Meconetzin as he was before I first died, dimpled and big-eared, with a smile to warm the soul.

"Ah, Popoca. It brings me shame to tell my part. While grief and chaos consumed the royal family, I blamed Father and was driven to madness by the loss of you and my sister. A seer sought to calm me, revealing that your hearts had been bound to nearby volcanoes, but I closed my ears. Chaos tempted me, and I sought revenge, conspiring with Huixachin, also broken by the tragedy. We claimed the southern kingdom of Colhuacan by murdering her husband, an ally of Tzinacan's clan. Then I waged war against Father, dealing the fatal blow myself. Mother, however, would not yield without a fight. She rallied Father's surviving soldiers, training them for the battle against her children. Yet in the end, she too fell beneath my sword."

Shame on their faces, the four stand before me, unable to look one another in the eye.

Emperor and empress, sister and brother. Their hearts shattered like mine.

I open my mouth to address them. "As you did these unspeakable things, I lay dead upon the mountains beside Iztac. Two years after you killed your father, I was awakened by the goddess of fate, Ixcuinan. She explained that I was now a tepictli, a mountain god linked to a volcano's heart, and recounted what had occurred in my absence. Enraged, I returned to the palace of Tollan and avenged the deaths of my sovereigns, the parents of my beloved, by killing you, Meconetzin, and you, Huixachin, when you attempted to stop me. But the fury I let loose that day took more casualties. It triggered a massive eruption of my volcano, erasing the village of Tetempan from existence . . . along with all my memories."

One by one, the revenants of the past step into the fire, immolating themselves. The flames leap higher and higher, blazing brighter and brighter . . .

CHAPTER

18

"He's ghosting you," Tina says, disgust edging her voice as she falls back against my headboard and sighs, disappointed.

"What? No," I say, speaking quietly, even though we're alone in my room. "He's a good guy. He wouldn't do that. Something's happened. I can feel it."

"You're right. He wouldn't be ghosting all of us," Tina surmises. "Tony said he hasn't heard from him either. And Sofía . . ."

"Wait!" I practically yell at her when I feel my phone vibrate against my thigh. My eyes feel moist when I see who it's from. *What's happening to me? Why am I so emotional?* "It's him."

"Oh, wow. Really?" Tina asks. "What's he got to say for himself?"

"I don't know. I haven't read it," I say, turning the screen off and putting the phone down. I'm trying to sound nonchalant, or at least somewhat like myself, but inside I am trembling. All kinds of emotions are fighting within me. Joy, anger, relief, disdain, pride, every single one of them is vying for my attention.

"You haven't looked at it?" Tina hollers. "What the heck are you waiting for?"

"Shush, will you?" I say. "I'll look at it when I'm good and ready. Just like he did."

"Okay," she says. "I just hope he wasn't in an accident or something."

Horrified at the thought, I pick up my phone and read the text. "No way," I say. Then I flip my phone to face her. "How did you . . . eres bruja?"

Tina's eyes widen and she shakes her head. "Honest. I had no idea. Call him! Now! Life is short. Love the one you're with. Don't put off till tomorrow . . . Didn't anybody ever tell you that?"

"Hush," I say, because I'm already dialing.

"Hey!" Greg's voice sounds different, softer . . . weaker.

"Are you okay?" I ask, shame warming my cheeks. "I'm sorry about all my texts. I didn't know . . . you were . . . in the hospital."

"No problem," he says. "It was a short stay. They had to keep me there for observation . . . I just got home, but I'm taking it easy tomorrow, so I won't see you until I pick you up for the gala. We're still on, I hope."

Tina, who's leaning in to listen, nods vehemently and gives me a big, enthusiastic thumbs-up.

"I mean, sure, yes," I say, stammering on my words because my heart is still pounding a mile a minute. "If you think you're all right to come. I mean, I understand if you need to cancel."

"No," Greg says, sounding firm, despite his situation. "I want to escort you to the gala. I've been preparing for this night . . . all my life."

Tina puts both hands against her heart and mouths, *Awww!*

I swear, she looks like she's about to burst into tears.

"Okay then," I say, my voice unusually soft, because I am having all the feels right now. "I'll see you Friday night. And please," I add, because I can't help but tease him, "get some rest. You're going to need it."

Greg's low, timbering chuckle sends chills up my spine, and I grip the phone and grin as if he could see me enjoying his laughter.

"Okay," he says. "Will do."

At the appointed hour, Greg's Phantom pulls up to our driveway. I watch him get out of the car, carrying a precious orchid in his hands.

Wearing an azure gown that glitters like a twilight sky already filling with stars, the string of sea blue pearls with the single sapphire, the Royal Teardrop that sparkles upon my skin like a drop of sacred water hanging around my neck, I feel like the best version of me is stepping out tonight. I piled my black hair high, held in place by a netting of the same rare pearls. Only this piece used to belong to my mother. So, it's special.

"You look quite dashing," I tell Greg as I reach the last step and take his proffered arm.

"And you look like a goddess freshly emerged from the waves." Greg's eyes are glimmering with something akin to pride. Or is that love I see reflected in their depths?

"Is that flower for me?" I ask, looking down at the corsage in his hands. "I'm going to guess there's a story behind it, too."

He takes my hand and secures the deep azure bloom over my wrist with the attached silky blue ribbon.

"Dendrobium azureum," he says, his voice soft, quiet. "A true blue orchid, one of the rarest in the world. It only grows at high elevations on Waigeo Island in Indonesia. Some of the locals call it the Lady of the Mountain."

"Another unusual beauty that thrives in the cold," I murmur, wondering how he finds such delicate things. "What are you trying to say, Gregorio Chan?"

He lifts his head and looks deeply into my eyes. "Only that I see you, Blanca Montes," he whispers, his voice a caress on my heart. "I see you."

Clearing his throat, Greg's chauffeur opens the door for me, and, I'm suddenly aware that we are not alone out here, I giggle nervously.

"Madam," he prompts. "I should rather not make you late."

In the back seat of the Phantom, Greg tells me more about the flower on my wrist and I talk about my love of blue flowering trees and shrubs.

Before we know it, Stilson is pulling up to the front of the looming glass towers of the Imperial Silver Casino. The paparazzi of both Reno and Las Vegas are out in full force, thronging near the entrance with cameras and portable lighting. Greg gets out first, ignoring the flashes as he walks around and helps me exit the Phantom.

"Miss Montes! Where's Jackson Caldera?" is the one question that gets repeated as we make our way along the blue carpet toward the arch of the entrance. I stay calm, even though I'm nervous because this is a big night for me. Not only am I bringing Greg into my social circle, but I'm also meeting my idol, Lorraine Fillmore.

"Who's the handsome young man on your arm, Blanca?"

"This is Gregorio Chan," I say, with a bit of pride, because, honestly, he looks uber handsome tonight. "Heir to Grupo Tolchan in Mexico. Go on, Ms. Romero. Google him. Now, if you'll excuse us."

An impeccably dressed hostess escorts us to the most luxurious of the ballrooms. More media are arrayed around the theater-style seating. Greg and I take a seat in the front row, and soon the manager of the casino welcomes the crowd before introducing Rafael Montes and Ted Caldera.

The whole time they are up there, I'm not listening or paying attention to anything that's going on because, in my head, I am practicing the series of questions I came up with for when I meet Ms. Fillmore at dinner.

"The joining in a business partnership of the two most prominent Hispanic families in Reno marks a new era for our community," my padrino starts reading his prepared speech.

Then, because I realize I haven't been necessarily present all this time, I look over at Greg. He meets my gaze and smiles.

"Thank you for being here," I say, leaning over to speak quietly to him.

"It's an honor to sit here." Greg looks a little uncomfortable. Like he's trying to listen to what my padrino is saying, but also doesn't know what to do while I'm talking through it.

"So, what Ted and I have done is to tap into the Mexican American values shared by our families, that lift up *communal* fun above all other types of entertainment," my padrino drones on, and I shift back to face the front.

"I'm sorry," I say. "I'm sure you're trying to listen."

Greg shifts, takes my hand, and looks at me lovingly. "No, I'm sorry. I want this night to be about us, not them."

I grin. I can't help it. His words fill me with something that I've never experienced before. Joy. Love. Warmth. "It's just that I've been to a bunch of these, and, after a while, it all sounds the same. Even though I know I should still pay attention, because someday that's going to be me up there, I can't . . . It's just all so . . . *irrelevant.*"

"Well, it's a lot to have hanging over your head," Greg whispers.

"It is," I say. "But let's not talk about that. Tell me how I look. Do you like the dress? Are you impressed by my sense of fashion?"

With a soft laugh, Greg picks up on my silly vibe and runs with it, asking about his own attire, smoothing back his hair and schooling me on the history and sophistication of the pompadour.

Afterward, the media shuffles off to another room. Greg and I mingle for a bit as the guests stand and begin making their slow, social way out. I look for Ms. Fillmore among them, but I don't see her anywhere.

"Blanca, my dear," my padrino calls from somewhere behind me. "You failed to mention that you'd have a different young man with you this evening."

Greg offers his hand. "Gregorio Chan, a su servicio."

They shake briefly.

"Chan? Oh, your family bought the lakeside estate from us!" My padrino turns to me with a look that says he approves. "Your father is the CEO of Grupo Tolchan, correct?"

Greg nods, and, because my padrino's looking so pleased with me, I turn to him. "Oh, have you met Lorraine Fillmore? I haven't seen her yet."

My padrino's eyebrows crinkle together, but before he can reply, DA Flowers arrives out of seemingly nowhere.

"Mr. Montes," she drawls, arching an eyebrow. "What an impressive place you and Mr. Caldera have built. I feel drawn to it, frankly. I think I'll be spending lots of time here."

My padrino smirks. "District Attorney. What a surprise to see you here, especially as I gave strict instructions to neither invite you nor let you in."

"Oh, but I have my ways, Mr. Montes, as well you know," the DA says, eyes sparkling mischievously. "I had to be here. To make sure everything's on the up-and-up."

Horrified by her implications, I pull on Greg's sleeve and lead him out of the ballroom and into the photographer's area, because I haven't checked for Ms. Fillmore there.

"Where are we going?" he asks.

"I want to get a pic with you," I tell him. "Before Jackson shows up."

The crooked, sexy smile on his face tells me just how okay it is, so I motion for him to follow me. He rushes after me as I run off, heading to another ballroom. The official casino photographers, Monica and Ben López, a husband-and-wife team, get excited when they see us coming their way.

We're waiting our turn, standing face-to-face and looking into each other's eyes, when I catch wind of a commotion. The media is snapping pictures of Jackson as he walks right up to us. Grinning from ear to ear, he taps Greg on the shoulder and wedges himself between us.

"Thanks for stepping in for me, man. I owe you one," he says as he tugs at his lapels and smooths back his blond hair.

With the flash of the paparazzi around us, I put my hand on Jackson's chest and push him gently away from us. "We're not done yet."

Jackson grits his teeth and glares at me.

I lift my chin and match his unblinking stare, daring him to make a scene at what is perhaps the most important evening of his father's life.

"Seriously?" he whispers between clenched teeth.

"Seriously," I say, stepping back so that I'm standing next to Greg again.

Jackson turns away to leave, but not before grazing Greg's wide shoulders with his and growling, "I'll deal with you later."

———————————

Because we have so many requests for pics, Greg and I pose facing each other, flanked one in front of the other, left, right, this way, that way, but not once does Greg touch me. I'm relieved because I don't want the paparazzi to splatter those kinds of pictures all over social media with some sordid rumor attached to them.

"Glad that's over," Greg says, and I laugh as we head upstairs for the reception.

"This is me," I say, standing behind the seat to the right of Jackson and his parents, who all smile and nod at us. "You're there. Not too far, right?" I ask, looking around the ballroom for Lorraine Fillmore.

The place is getting full; many of our guests are already here, milling about, chatting with one another. I look from smiling face to smiling face, craning my neck, straining my eyes, but it's no use. I can't find my special guest.

"Looking for someone?" Denise Hernández asks.

"Yes," I say, looking past her. "Lorraine Fillmore, from the Washoe Tribe. I don't see her. I hope nothing's wrong."

Denise takes the seat Greg has pulled out for her.

"The water conservation people?" she asks, as she plops her gaudy, navy-blue purse next to my Chanel metal minaudière. "Oh, they weren't invited."

I feel my face reddening as I think of the gall of this woman, to just blurt this out, like she's discussing the weather. "But I asked you to invite her."

Denise's smile is so self-satisfying it disarms me, and I don't know what to do when she says, "It wasn't me. Rafa just wasn't interested."

Refusing to give into the rage that is threatening to overwhelm me, I give Denise a cold once-over before I turn to Greg. "Wanna get out of here?"

"Now?" Greg asks, his eyes curious, as Denise babbles on about me needing to stay.

"Yes," I tell him, grabbing my handbag and getting up.

Jackson looks up at me, shocked. "Where are you going?"

"Nothing that concerns you," I tell him, pushing my chair in. "Oh, in case you haven't noticed, we're through."

"What?" he calls after me, but I ignore him and start walking away, weaving quickly between the clustered tables in the ballroom.

Greg follows me as I wind around people and tables. The media outside the ballroom doors catch sight of us and give chase, snapping pictures and asking inane questions.

"Blanca, Blanca, where are you going?" they want to know. But Greg and I slip away from them, running down the street as fast as my high heels allow. We stop a few blocks down from the casino and hide behind a huge bougainvillea, bright fuchsia petals fluttering all around us.

"What now?" Greg asks, his beautiful smile resplendent.

I glance around, orienting myself.

"This way," I tell him.

We walk down two more blocks and make a quick left. After entering a dark alley, we scoot to the right and hug the dark wall when a car passes by, a vuelta de rueda. I'm sure my padrino's sent someone out here to look for us by now. But there's no way they'll find us where we're going.

"Blanca Montes. Where in the world are you taking me?" Greg teases, when the roaring sounds of casinos bursting at the seams spill into the alleyway.

"We're almost there," I say, and we cross the street and enter another alley. This one is more familiar to me, and I walk up to a heavy metal door and knock on it.

A few seconds later, the door swings open and the owner, Miss Janet, grins at me. "Well, look at you. All dolled up. Come to help raise some moolah?"

"Of course," I tell her, hugging her before stepping inside. "Sorry I'm late. We had to make a quick pit stop. This is Greg, by the way."

"Welcome to Little Bits." Janet looks him up and down approvingly.

"Has she gone up yet?" I ask Janet as we walk through a small kitchen where Moses Woo, Janet's significant other, is flipping a patty for one of his famous Mo'burgers.

"She's between songs," Janet says.

The lights dim, and I hear Con Cariño, Tina's band from Carrizo, start up again. As we step into the dining area, Tina begins to tell a story with her soulful voice.

"Oh, I love this one. She wrote it," I tell Greg as we stand in the back, watching Tina grab the mike and wail.

"Wow," Greg says, when there's a break in the lyrics.

"Yeah, not bad, huh," I say, because there are no empty seats in the room.

"I mean, I knew she could sing, but this is amazing."

"They all are," I tell him, pointing to another group of people standing to the right of the stage. "That's Moonstruck Madmen over there. They're from Las Vegas. And that's Grupo Toki, from Texas. They're all here to help Tina raise money for her community. Carrizo has major water problems. Their streams have been diverted, and those that haven't been rerouted are polluted. Old lead pipes."

Greg nods. "So, this is a fundraiser?"

I nod. "I was sad, because I thought I wouldn't be able to make it," I tell him. "But then my padrino didn't invite the water conservation people. So, here we are."

"Looks like you're not the only one willing to help," Greg says, looking around at the packed room.

"It's okay," I tell him. "But it's not enough. That's why I invited Ms. Fillmore to the reception tonight. This is what I wanted to talk to her about."

Greg's eyes shimmer as he looks at me in the dim lights of the dining area.

"What?" I ask, cocking my head to look over at him.

"Nothing. It's just . . . admirable, what you're trying to do," Greg says.

"Thanks, I do what I can," I say and look back at Tina who's finishing her song.

The music stops. Tina hands the mike over to the guitarist. The long sequence of gems on her jumpsuit catch the stage lights, sending rays out to us as she jumps offstage and heads toward us.

"Hey, what happened to the grand opening?" she asks, hugging me tight and rocking me side to side before releasing me.

I wave the idea away. "I stayed long enough. But things got muddled, so we ditched!"

"Jackson muddled or casino muddled?" Tina asks, raising an eyebrow.

"Padrino muddled," I say, wincing. "He didn't invite Ms. Fillmore!"

"What?" Tina's eyes widen. "It was the perfect opportunity to get some good press for Montes Realty. I mean, it doesn't make sense to keep them away."

"I know, but I'm glad we came over. You're really killing it tonight!"

"Ah, you're so sweet!" Tina pulls her shoulders up and grins. Then she reaches over and squeezes my hand. "And thanks for bringing the big guns, hermana!"

Her candidness warms my cheeks, but Greg just laughs it off.

"I'm always happy to help," he says, bowing his head slightly as he grins at me.

"Great. The drop box is over there," Tina says. "But you can always give my girl here a fat check. She'll make sure it gets to the right place."

Tina goes back to the stage, but not before she procures a table for us, asking her friends to give us some room. There isn't much space, so we have to sit close. My cheeks flame again, and I'm glad Greg can't see me too well in the darkened room, but before too long the next act is taking the stage.

The rest of the evening goes by fast. Greg is attentive, charming, and funny, finding humor in the nooks and crannies of our conversation, laughing at my jokes and making a few of his own. All of which I was not expecting. We have so much fun that by the time his chauffeur brings his car around, I am sure we've made a connection.

Gregorio Chan is into me.

When we both step off the curb and reach for the car door, our hands accidentally touch, sending an electric shock wave that travels up my arm and makes me shiver. We stay like that forever, our hands fused together, before Greg finally says, "Please. Let me get this for you."

I move away, and he opens the door carefully. We ride in silence, heading north to St. James Village in the early hours of the morning, awakened to something new and strangely familiar between us.

Can he feel it too? I wonder. *This magical connection between us. So powerful. So visceral. Is he as overwhelmed by it as I am?*

We get to my house, and he opens the car door and walks calmly with me all the way up the cobblestone path. When we get to the front door, I turn around, face him, steeling myself for what is about to happen.

Don't be solicitous, I tell myself. *Let him come to you. Let him lean in first. Then you can jump him. Not before. Never before.* But instead of stepping in for a kiss, *our first kiss*, Greg takes my hand and steps back.

"Thank you for an enchanting evening," he whispers. Then he presses a chaste kiss on the top of my hand.

His lips are gentle, warm, and I feel the heat of that lingering kiss moving over my hand, all the way up my arm, making me weak at the knees. But before I can say anything, Greg lets my hand go, turns around, and practically runs back to his car. I stand on the edge of the porch, confused, a wavering candle in the darkness of the night.

"Well, that's different," I tell myself, baffled as I watch Greg's car pull away and round the circle of our cul-de-sac, and then speed off, his headlights illuminating the dark road ahead of him.

I sigh and go in the house. Though nothing went as I'd hoped tonight, I do know one thing: someday soon, I'm going to kiss Greg Chan, and it's going to be divine.

CHAPTER

19

I can't remember ever feeling this excited. It's different than the strolls through the garden with Iztac. Now I'm dating her *as Greg Chan*, a teen at her school, not some soldier who rescued her little brother.

And she likes me for who I am, not for what I've done or what I have.

Monday morning, I wait for her on the steps of the school. My palms ache as her godfather's car pulls up, and when she gets out, radiant as the first snow of winter, my stomach tingles. I'm actually *nervous*, wondering if I've misread our relationship.

Then she looks up at me, and the world seems to fade till only she exists. My girl.

Not just Iztac, though I see traces in her. This is about Blanca.

Waving sheepishly, she gives me her slightly crooked smile as her face crinkles and her eyes narrow at me in dreamy abandon.

"Hey, there," I say. I sound foolish, but I don't care.

"Hey, right back at you." She glances around and nods, as if satisfied that no one we know is going to interrupt. "Were you . . . waiting for me?"

It's hard for me to focus on anything beyond the slight bump on the bridge of her nose that begs for a quick kiss. But I give a brief nod. "Yup. I thought we could walk to class together. If that's . . . okay?"

"Absolutely."

I'm acutely aware of all the students crowding the halls as we make our way to first period, reminiscing about our date, laughing together at inside jokes.

We've started to click. I feel it.

As we near the door of the classroom, a knot of kids hurries past, pushing her against me. Our hands brush. Before I can pull away, her long, slender fingers interlace with mine.

Cold yet electrifying.

Like snow upon cypress boughs.

She's beautiful. Noble. Generous. Caring. Haughty. Funny. Uncompromising.

Everything that made my heart flutter centuries ago, and more.

How can I help falling for her again?

I still have to keep track of the other threads of my life. Especially since I now know that it isn't just Blanca I'm supposed to find. All of those people from my tragic first life have been reborn, the Four have explained—the emperor and empress, the crown prince and his half sister, even Blanca's birth mother and the cruel monster who betrayed us all.

Any of the teens or adults in this school could be their new identities.

The idea makes my head swim.

Tony hasn't called me once since the Grizzlies won their first game. I thought for sure he'd want to discuss every pass, but he doesn't seem happy about the victory. At first, he's just distant and tired, but by Wednesday it's clear something bad has happened.

Tony stumbles into AP English Lit right before the bell rings. Jackson stares at him with anger as he slumps into his seat. Whatever's going on between them has benefited Blanca and me: Jackson hasn't even noticed us spending more time together. But now I'm starting to worry.

Ms. Dresch crouches beside Tony's desk and touches his forehead. "Are you okay? Wouldn't you rather go to the nurse's office?"

My friend only manages to give a slight shake of his head to the woman he so admires—evidence that something is truly wrong.

Concern on her face, the teacher stands and leads us in a final discussion of *Electra*.

Like my fellow students—though I've read the play before—I thrill to the revelation that Orestes is still alive. His reunion with his older sister and the revenge they take on their mother and stepfather for killing their father is more satisfying to the class than the ending of *Hamlet*.

Sofía challenges our notions of justice, however.

"Remember why Clytemnestra killed Agamemnon to begin with. Not only did he sacrifice their oldest child, Iphigenia, when he left to fight the Trojans—he also brought a young lover home once the war was over."

"Triggering a cycle of revenge," I say.

Little Sister nods at me. "Yup. The only way out is to *stop*. To forgive and ask forgiveness. To pay the price, willingly. Then comes redemption and release."

Jackson gives a bitter laugh. "Some things can't be forgiven."

At the sound of that cold declaration, Tony's fingers grip his desk so tight his knuckles go white.

Ms. Dresch doesn't notice the simmering conflicts. She dims the lights and turns on the projector, fiddling with her laptop as she speaks.

"Excellent thoughts. You'll see how perfectly they connect to our next reading. Some of you may be familiar with this image."

I try not to cry out.

On the screen, surrounded by snow on the summit of a mountain, stands a Nahua warrior, features strained with grief and rage. The artist has jumbled elements from various kingdoms and time periods, but he's recognizably one of my people from before the Spanish invasion.

In his arms is the slack form of a princess, rendered too European, her clothing and ornaments inaccurate, but beautiful and lifeless.

Jackson scoffs. "Yeah, I've seen it on lowriders and in taquerías. The height of Chicano culture."

"Dude," Tina snaps, turning to look at him. "We get it. You're a rich Hispanic kid. Big whoop. Look around, Jackson. You're not the only one. But the rest of us aren't being classist douchebags."

Ms. Dresch clears her throat. "Let's save that for outside of class, yes? Jackson, you're right that the image is so popular it pops up in unexpected places. The couple are the protagonists in a legend usually called *The Volcanoes*. It's the origin story of three striking volcanoes near modern Mexico City."

She switches to a map of the Basin of Mexico as it looked centuries ago, before the lakes were drained to sustain the sprawl of the capital. At the top left of the image, to the northwest of Lake Tzompanco, a small triangle is labeled "Tollan." At the bottom right, to the east of Lake Chalco, larger triangles are labeled "Iztaccihuatl" and "Popocatepetl."

A burning fills my chest. I tremble for a moment until I feel Little Sister's hand on my back, patting gently.

"It's considered an Aztec tale," Ms. Dresch continues, "but it was old before the Mexica tribe arrived in the area, a part of the traditions of most Nahua nations in Central Mexico. The earliest versions speak of a conflict between mountain gods."

The screen lights up with the familiar slopes of Popocatepetl.

"According to folklore in the Mexican state of Morelos, a mighty volcano—Popocatepetl, the Smoking Mountain—once had as his wife the purest and most beautiful goddess: White Woman."

Now Ms. Dresch shows the snow-draped curves of Iztaccihuatl. My hands clench into fists as my pulse quickens. To calm down, I gently correct her. "Actually her name means *Lady Iztac*. 'Cihuatl' can be a noble title, you see."

"Thanks! It's amazing to have a native speaker of Nahuatl in the room, Greg. And don't feel self-conscious about correcting me. I want to respect your people's culture. But, the legend continues, another mountain god, the Nevado de Toluca, coveted the volcano's bride. So the two began hurtling chunks of ice at each other, till the volcano sliced off the mountain's head with a massive barrage. That's why the Nevado de Toluca has a . . . flat top."

Her implied joke, together with the reveal on-screen of the summit of the volcano we once called Tzinacantepetl, calms my heart and makes me chuckle.

Sofía arches an eyebrow at me and whispers, "Beheading did indeed take place."

"Later versions folded in the culture of different Nahua peoples. We're going to be reading an English translation of a version published fifty-two years ago by poet Alejandro Mier Teopixqui. It places the tragedy at the height of the Toltec Empire. Perhaps you learned this in world history, but the Toltecs were the first Nahua nation to establish itself in Central Mexico, about twelve hundred years ago."

The instructor has us come up one by one to sign for a copy of the book from her class set. It's a simple, thin volume with the volcanoes on its cover.

As I take my seat, I turn and whisper to Little Sister. "Alejandro? He was a terrible poet."

She laughs. "He did well, Goyo. Trust us."

Blanca has just picked up her book and walks back toward us. "Trust who?"

Sofía smiles brightly. "Me and Tina, hello! We're your friends. We know all the stuff you like . . . if he ever wants to buy you something cute, etcetera."

Blanca rolls her eyes. "I think his instincts are pretty solid. Did you call him 'Goyo' just now?"

"Yup!" Sofía tosses her hair to one side. "It's a nickname for Gregorio. I have a cousin that everyone calls Goyito, so I was trying it on for size."

Blanca shakes her head. "Nope. Don't like it. He's definitely a Greg."

Before I can laugh, the instructor calls Tony's name. He's slumped over his desk, eyes shut, so I nudge him awake.

"Tony, Ms. Dresch is calling on you."

Groaning, he pulls himself to his feet.

"Are you okay, man?" I ask. "Isn't she your guardian angel or whatever?"

He grunts and shuffles away.

———————————

That evening I sit at my desk, reading. The book, translated by one Oscar Garza and printed by the University of Texas Press, helps me sort out my new memories. Alejandro pulled from the archives that my protectors kept over the centuries to compose his epic verse, and while he takes some liberties, he gets the tragic tale right enough. I spend a few hours grappling with my feelings while Steamboat Springs hisses and rumbles in the distance.

A phone call shakes me free of these emotional aftershocks. It's Blanca.

"Hello," I say. "Is everything okay?"

"Yeah, totally fine. I was reading the book and felt kind of sad. Wanted to hear your voice."

"I cheer you up, do I?"

She pauses, then laughs. "You do a little more than cheer me up, Greg. I don't know what's gotten into me. Being around you makes me happy. Warm inside. But I'm also nervous. Does that make sense?"

"Yeah. It's hard for us to accept that we deserve happiness. It's been kept from us for so long. But let's be greedy, Blanca. Let's take every joy we're owed and more."

A sniffle tells me she's been touched by my words. "That sounds wonderful."

On impulse, I plow ahead. "Why don't we have dinner this weekend? Say, Saturday?"

"Like a date, date?" she asks, somewhat hesitant.

"Yes." I switch to a mock British accent. "Will you accompany me on a real date, Ms. Montes?"

"I most certainly will, Mr. Chan."

On Friday, Ms. Dresch has us carry out what she terms a "jigsaw summary" of The Volcanoes, by which she means that each of five groups crafts a synopsis of one part of the short epic poem before a representative from each presents their part.

Tony is like a zombie, unresponsive, eyes sunken, hair unkempt, a nervous tic making him wince when Jackson glances our way with disgust. So the three girls and I let him rest as we quickly sum up the main points of our section. I watch Blanca's face carefully for any signs of recognition. Her eyes twitch, and her lips quiver several times, but I can't tell if she's remembering or reacting.

"Time," calls Ms. Dresch. "Group one?"

As each group presents, Tony puts earbuds in, pulling his hoodie up and laying his head on the desktop as if to block out the world. Ms. Dresch notices, and her brow wrinkles with concern, though she leaves him alone. When we're done, she claps her hands together.

"Excellent. You will be doing some character analyses this weekend, which I'll go into in a second, but any thoughts? Reactions?"

Jackson raises his hand. "This Mixcoatl dude is one major deus ex machina, no? What a weird final act. He just pops out of nowhere and fixes everything."

I raise an eyebrow, though I don't turn to look at him. Instead, I focus on the twitch of Tony's hands at the sound of Jackson's voice.

Sofía clears her throat. "Hey, sometimes gods just have to step in, no?"

Tina raises her hand. "I don't know. See, Latanya thinks Popocatzin dies up in the mountains, but what about the seer's words? What if his soul really did merge with the volcano? Because then . . ."

Blanca's gasp interrupts Tina's thoughts..

"Wow. That means *he causes the volcano to erupt.* Like he knows terrible stuff is happening in the empire. He wants to stop it. Guys, what if the demigod in the story is actually Popocatzin?"

Out of the corner of my eye, I see Sofía put her finger to her nose with a grin.

I spend Friday evening and Saturday morning putting the finishing touches on our first official date. I've found out from Tina and Sofía that Blanca loves a good steak, especially picanha. So I've bought out Reno's top Brazilian steakhouse.

I pick Blanca up at seven. She's wearing a stunning white skirt and blue blouse, her pretty black hair once again piled up on her head.

As we drive into town, I entertain her by trying to sing along to some of her favorite pop songs, guessing at the lyrics and failing miserably.

Pulling up to the entrance, I hand my fob to the valet, and then the maître d' escorts us inside. Though I thought about closing the restaurant for the night, Teresa pointed out how awkward that might make Blanca feel. Instead, I emptied the top floor so we have that big space to ourselves. The waiter serves us some refreshing limonada suíça, which is like citrus snow swirling in a glass.

"I've already ordered," I tell Blanca. "Picanha, medium rare. I think you'll be pleased."

A slight twist of her lovely lips tells me that might've been a miscalculation.

"I've also brought some entertainment," I add hastily. "I thought about flying in Iracema Ferreira. But I decided that was overkill. Besides, I think you'd prefer my new favorite singer."

A spotlight hits the small stage in the more shadowy recesses of the restaurant, which we look down on from our table. Sitting on a stool, guitar on her knee, is Tina. She glances our way and gives us a thumbs-up.

"Good evening, everyone," she says into the mike. "My name is Tina Gorena. I know at least one couple here is on a date, so I'll play a set of softer songs to set the mood. Enjoy!"

As Tina's raspy alto voice begins to croon against her gentle strumming, Blanca reaches out and grabs my hand. "Oh my God, Greg . . ."

There are tears in her eyes, squeezed out by a smile she can't contain.

"I care about you," I explain. "And your friends, too. I get that what makes you happy is the well-being of others. And I figured that having Tina nearby would lessen the pressure of our first real date."

After the second song, our food is brought to the table. I'm watching Blanca's expressions of delight at the perfectly cooked steak when my phone begins to buzz. A glance tells me it's Tony, so I just silence the vibration. However, he continues to call, over and over.

"Who is it?" Blanca asks.

"Tony Alsobrook. Let me text him that we're on a date, and then I'll call him later."

"Why don't you just answer? It might be important."

As if conjured, there's another incoming call from him.

"Tony? I can't talk right now," I tell him.

"Greg, I'm in trouble. Big-time. Like life-in-danger sort of trouble." His voice is shaking, full of fear.

"Where are you?"

"In the parking lot of Prospector Casino. It's one of those Caldera places downtown."

"Yeah, we drove past it a while ago. Stay put. I'll be there soon."

Blanca is staring at me with expectant eyes. "What's up?"

"I'm so sorry," I tell her, "but Tony says he's in trouble and needs help right away."

She takes her napkin from her lap and sets it on the table. "Tony? Oh my God. I'll come with."

I shake my head. "No. I don't know what *kind* of trouble. I can't put you in harm's way for my friend. Please just finish the meal. Chat with Tina when her set is done. I'll send Stilson around to take you home."

Blanca sighs and then bristles a little. "Fine. But don't bother sending Stilson. I'll call my padrino's driver."

I reach out to touch her shoulder. She pulls away, less in anger than disappointment.

"Go on. Hurry up. *Your* friend needs you."

Knowing better than to push her right now, I dip my head and go outside. The valet brings my car around, and I speed down the thirteen blocks to Prospector Casino.

Tony is leaning against a light post near the parking lot exit. He is smoking, his hands shaking. I pull up beside him and roll down the window.

"What did you do?" I demand.

Tony flicks the cigarette to the sidewalk and grinds it out.

"It's . . . not what I did. It's what I *didn't* do."

I glance around at the pedestrians and unhoused folks. "Get in. Let's talk."

After Tony slumps into the passenger seat, I find a place to park.

"Since when do you smoke? You've been weird all week."

Tony sighs and smirks. "A month ago, Jackson approached me with an offer. To help him throw our first game so that some bookies who launder money through his dad's casinos can make bank. Me and him would get a pretty good cut. I was tempted. Eventually agreed."

"Then you backed out at the last moment, right?" I ask.

He nods and clears his throat. "Out on the field, I couldn't do it, couldn't set up incomplete passes with him and tank the game. Partly because I'd be the one to look bad, not him. But also because it's *wrong*. My family raised me right. The Alsobrooks may not be as rich as the Calderas or the Monteses, but we have a clear conscience."

I unbuckle my seat belt and turn to look at him fully. "You're a good person, Tony. That's why we're friends."

Swallowing, he continues. "Two days after the game, some goons snatch me from the street when I'm jogging. They say they're going to break my arms if I don't come up with a hundred grand within the week. What they lost betting against the Grizzlies. Monday was one continuous nightmare. But by the next morning, I had a plan. I used some cash I had set aside and started playing blackjack. Tuesday night. Wednesday afternoon. Friday night. All day today."

I narrow my eyes. "But you're only seventeen."

He gives a pained laugh. "Ted Caldera is happy to put his son's 'friends' on the VIP list, as long as we're losing. Like me. I won five thousand that first day. I tripled it the next. But now I've lost it all."

I stare into his bloodshot eyes. "What's the account number? I'll wire you a hundred thousand right now."

Tony pulls away, shaking his head, a little horrified. "No, man. I can't let you do that. I don't care how much money you have. How could I call myself your friend after you give that much money? No. But—if you'd lend me ten grand, I can spend tomorrow gambling, and—"

I want to slap him. "No. Your plan won't work. Either I give you the full amount, or I tell your parents everything. Your pick."

He winces, a betrayed look clouding his face. But he has no choice.

"Okay. But I'll pay you back, somehow."

I put my hand against the back of his neck, pressing my forehead against his.

"Never lie to me again," I say. "That's payment enough."

CHAPTER

20

Sunday afternoon, after seeing no response to my email letting Lorraine Fillmore know I hope to meet her someday, I take my laptop and lie down on my bed. I have to write a paper comparing our two heroines' tragic deaths by suicide for AP English Literature class. Only, I don't believe Iztac is anything like Ophelia.

There is a certain fragility in Ophelia's mental state that doesn't quite fit Iztac's regal poise as she decides to take her own life. However, I do believe that both women had a lot in common as far as agency is concerned. It's that lack of agency that has plagued women from every culture through the ages, and I make that the focus of my essay.

As I put the finishing touches on my paper, my phone rings. It's Greg, but I'm still peeved at him for leaving me out of the Tony situation, so I ignore his first call. And when he texts, I pick up the phone and stare at the curser on my open text box. It blinks, waiting . . .

GREG: *Hey, how did it go with Tina?*

GREG: *Sorry I had to leave on such short notice. It really was an emergency.*

GREG: *I can explain everything. I'd rather do it in person. Can we hang out? Maybe grab some dinner?*

I want to text him back, but I can't. I have no choice but to agree with him. This is something we have to discuss in person. So, I turn off my phone and push it away from me on the bed.

Monday morning, I show up to school ready to have this mess with Greg sorted out by the end of the day. We're too busy writing up lab reports in AP Chemistry, but during lunch I confront him.

"What's going on with Tony?" I ask Greg as he walks over.

Greg puts his tray on the table and sits down. He glances around the cafeteria before he says, "I'm sorry, notlazohtzin, but this isn't the place to discuss the problem."

"Problem? *Has something happened to Tony?*" My voice warbles as I ask the question, because Tony is absent today and he's not answering Tina's texts.

Greg takes my hand and holds it tightly. "Tony's fine. But let's go find a quiet place and I'll explain."

I pick up my tray and stand up.

"Hey, y'all," Tina says as she steps up to our table, putting her tray down in front of her.

Sofía catches up to us all. "Where are you two going?" she asks.

"I'm sorry." Greg gives the girls a half-crooked smile. "I've got to steal Blanca away. Two days is just too long to be without the light of her."

"The light of her!" Tina's eyes glimmer, and she puts a hand over her heart. "That's . . . so beautiful."

Sofía grins at us. "You two are too cute. Go on. Get out of here. We'll cover for you."

"Oh, we'll be back before the bell rings," I tell her. "I'm not blowing twelve years of perfect attendance no matter how cute we look."

We dump out our trays and walk out the back doors, into the courtyard, where the school's couples usually hang out. But Greg leads me to the edge of the school grounds, where the tree line meets the highway.

"Tony got himself in big trouble," Greg starts when we finally stop. Then he explains how Jackson put Tony in a horrible position. "I covered the debt, so he should be fine. He's missing school so he can pay the bookies. Stilson's driving him. I know you're mad at me, but I hope you understand."

"I *was* mad," I tell him. "And not just because you left, but because you excluded me. Don't forget, before Tony was your friend, he was *my friend*. I've known him since elementary."

"I know." Greg pushes a strand of my hair away from my face. Then he takes my hands and squeezes them gently again. "I'm sorry."

"He might have called you," I tell him, "but I care about him, too."

"You're absolutely right. I'll do better next time." Greg makes tiny circles around my knuckles with his thumbs as we stand facing each other holding hands under a tall maple.

"Well, I hope there is no next time," I say, as I consider what Greg has shared with me. "I can't believe Jackson would do this."

"I made him swear off gambling." Greg's eyes narrow, and he looks more serious than I've ever seen him.

"Good."

Greg takes a deep breath. "Thanks. I just wanted to make sure *we* were okay. But we should get back. The bell's about to ring, and you don't want to be counted absent, remember?"

"Ah, yes, school," I say, letting out what feels like a long-held breath. "I'm just glad we sorted all this out. We are sorted out, right?"

Greg's eyes soften, and he reaches up and caresses my cheek.

"Yes, notlazohtzin, we are absolutely sorted out. From now on, we do everything together."

———————————

"The first date was a disaster, but Greg said he's going to make it up to me today!" I tell Tina and Sofía, who have come over to help me get ready Saturday morning.

I put the jeans back on the rack in my closet and walk my fingers over the silk hangers along the wall of tops and matching pants. "I have absolutely no idea what to wear. If only I knew where we're going!"

Tina looks through my clothes rack, flipping hangers. "Maybe you're going shopping. In which case, you don't need to wear much, do you?"

"Eww!" Sofía's reaction makes me roll my eyes and sigh.

"Oh, don't be a prude," Tina says, flipping her hair and going back to looking at the items in my closet.

"Ladies, focus. You're not helping," I tell them. "Either of you."

"Well, he said to dress comfortably, didn't he?" Tina switches gears and starts to sort through the pile of outfits stacked on my dresser.

I nod and push the hair out of my face, because what I really want to do is pull it all out. "And to wear comfortable shoes," I say.

"Uhm, no." Tina puts several long, flowy dresses back on the rack and thinks. "Gosh. That could mean anything."

"Exactly!" I say, glancing at my shoe racks. "I have like, three dozen pairs of shoes. Most of them are pretty comfortable. I mean, why would I buy them if they weren't comfortable?"

Sofía gets up and picks up my white Nanette hiking boots. "These are nice. They look like they could take you anywhere, not too tough, not too flimsy, just right."

"And super stylish," Tina says, handing me the white halter top. "You should wear them with this and some jeans."

"You don't think this is too skimpy?" I ask.

"You need to show some skin," Tina says.

"Don't be crude," I tell her, taking the halter top and jeans and heading back to my room.

The girls sit on the edge of my bed and wait for me while I slip into the outfit behind my silk dressing panels. My phone pings, and I rush out and grab it.

"It's Greg," I tell the girls, as I read his text messages. "He's sending his car over. Oh, God, this better be the right outfit. 'Cause I don't have time to change."

"Trust me, it's the right outfit," Sofía says, as she grabs my white cardigan off the coat rack next to my dresser. "But you might want to take this."

"But it's like eighty-five degrees," I say.

"In Reno, yes," Sofía says. "But what if he's taking you somewhere else? Somewhere exotic. Somewhere romantic."

Behind Sofía, in the window, the shadow of a vehicle is rounding our circular driveway.

"He's here!" I say, pushing my hands through the arms of the cardigan and rolling it over my shoulders.

I put my feet in my boots and lace them up quickly. Checking my hair and lipstick one last time in the mirror, I wave for the girls to follow me. We rush down the stairs together. At the door, Tina and Sofía fuss with my hair before they push me out.

"Go, go," Tina says. "Before you turn into a pumpkin!"

Sofía grins. "Don't worry about us," she tells me. "We'll leave as soon as you drive away."

"See you guys later!"

Stilson is his usual, reserved self. Other than the pleasantries about weather and such, he just lets me relax in the back seat while he drives. When we get to the airport, where Greg stands waiting for me at the top of the stairs of a private jet, Stilson opens the door and helps me out of the car. Though I am not surprised that Greg's family has a private jet, I am surprised to see him dressed like an anthropologist on his way to an excavation, little brown Panama hat and all.

"Good morning, Professor," I say, as I ascend the stairs. My hair is blowing everywhere, and I wish I had a piochita in my purse so I could pull it up and out of my face. But I didn't know I was flying anywhere today.

"Ma cualli tonalli, Blanca." Greg takes my hand to help me up the last few stairs.

I size him up. The white shirt showcases his dark, rich complexion, and my heart flutters when his lips turn up and form a gorgeous, wide smile that takes my breath away.

"Why do I get the feeling I'm overdressed?" I say, checking out his cool duds.

"You're perfectly dressed for the occasion." Greg walks ahead of me into the cabin of his father's luxurious jet, and we sit down on the wide bucket seats. As I buckle up, Stilson opens the curtain on a partition that leads to the back of the plane and hands Greg a big white box before he disappears behind the curtain again. "I hope you don't mind, but I got you a small gift—something fuzzy and warm."

I take the long box. "Please tell me it's not a puppy," I say, grinning and shaking the box slightly before putting my ear to it.

Greg laughs, and his perfect white teeth glint in the light from the window. Everything about him is perfect.

"I had you pegged as a cat person," he says.

I open the box and pick up the beautiful garment to look it over. It's a white Moncler Grenoble fitted jacket that goes perfectly with my outfit.

"How did you know? Are you some kind of sorcerer?"

Greg laughs.

"Not quite," he says, his eyes twinkling with pleasure. "I bought three of them, in different shades. One of them was bound to match."

"Ah," I say, nodding. "Makes sense. Thank you. It's beautiful."

I put the jacket on and check my reflection in the mirror in the far end of the cabin. Greg reaches over and pushes a strand of hair behind my ear, and my pulse quickens when his fingertips caress the curve of my earlobe before he sits back. I exhale, shuddering a little, when I realize I've been holding my breath the whole time.

"So, where are we going?" I ask. Greg's intense gaze is making me so nervous, I don't know what else to say.

"I wanted it to be a surprise," Greg says. "But I can give you the coordinates if you need to let your padrino know where you're going."

I think about it. *Coordinates.* Well, that sounds intriguing.

"No, that's okay," I tell him. "I like surprises."

Stilson comes back to remove the box and takes our drink order. Orange juice for me and mineral water for Greg. The ride is smooth, and, before I know it, we arrive in Montana.

"Glacier Park International Airport," Greg says as we unbuckle our seat belts.

"Oh, Greg, I love this!" I squeal when I step outside and catch sight of the gorgeous views of mountains and lakes from the top of the stairs. "Are we going down to the water?"

"We can," Greg says. "But I thought we'd hike one of my favorite trails."

I grin. He's thought of everything. "Lead the way!"

From the airport, we take a helicopter that drops us right at the start of a trailhead. Greg pulls the jacket's hood over my head. He zips me up all the way to my chin, and then he pulls a pair of sunglasses from his pocket and slides them onto my face. His breath on my cheeks is intoxicating. I want to slip into his arms and just stay there.

We hike up amid light flurries of snow. Greg leads the way, trekking ahead of me, and showing me where to step so that I don't slip and fall. I've been on more than my share of trails, so I can hold my own. Nevertheless, I am flattered by his attentiveness.

As we reach the summit, Greg reaches back and offers me his hand. I take it, and, as I step up, he moves aside so that I can set eyes on the spectacular sight awaiting us. There, on the wide plateau of the mountain, is a white canopy surrounded by the most gorgeous setting.

I pull my sunglasses off and just stand there for a moment, silently taking it all in. The mountains, the floral arrangements, the flickering candles, the blanket, the pillows, the huge wicker basket—it's all so romantic.

Everything from soft hydrangeas to spiraling morning glories to tall irises to fernlike periwinkles and sky-blue forget-me-nots is here. I know what's in every one of those wide planters sitting beside the picnic because blue flowers are my favorite. "You remembered," I whisper.

Greg nods.

"They're from my village," he says when I reach down and trace the delicate stitches of a floral pattern on a pillow on a chaise beside me. "The people in my community are famous for their embroidering."

"It's beautiful," I whisper, so overwhelmed my voice has all but left me. "All of it."

"Nothing is more beautiful than you—in this lifetime," Greg says, coming to stand before me. He is so close I can feel his sweet breath caressing my cheeks as he speaks.

Perplexed more than flattered, I stare at him.

"What an odd thing to say," I tell him, when he looks at me expectantly. "I don't know what you mean, but thank you."

Greg's smile turns down a bit at the corners. I get the impression he is laughing at himself, though I don't quite know why. "It means I've never been happier. If I had to wait a thousand years for this moment, ten thousand years, it would be worth it," he says, taking my hand and grazing my fingertips with his soft lips.

I close my eyes and let the wave rushing up my arm wash over me. It courses through my body like fluid electricity, and, suddenly, I am warm—warmer than I've ever been in my life.

And when I open my eyes, the world has changed. *Thick, heavy snowflakes fall all around me, weigh down my lashes, blinding me. There is an icy breeze piercing my face, and, above me, the sky is dark and gray. Purple-blue, sanguine clouds swirl overhead, and the mountains feel like they're closing in around me.*

Beside me is that other Greg—the beautiful Greg with the long hair and the penetrating gaze, the Greg from my earlier vision. I look up at his sad face. Tears fall and freeze as they make their way down his taut cheeks, and he looks down at me, overwhelmed with grief.

His wails of lament give me goose bumps, and I feel his sorrow all the way down to my bones, penetrating my soul as they leave his lips. I want to touch his face, to tell him I'm okay, that nothing's wrong with me, but I can't. I'm so cold. I'm frozen solid, in a way I can't comprehend. How did this happen? Where am I? Who am I?

"Blanca?" I hear Greg's voice, see his lips move, but I am so cold. So, so cold.

I open my lips and cry out, "No!"

"Blanca? Can you hear me?" Greg's fingertips, tapping lightly on my cheeks, are real enough, but I don't feel at all like myself. It's like I'm in someone else's body, experiencing someone else's mortality. She's dying—this someone else—though I am aware it's not me who's dying.

"I'm alive," I whisper, shivering as Greg pulls me closer to him so that my face is tucked just below his neck.

"Yes." Greg sounds relieved as he pulls back to look deeply into my eyes. "Do you know where you are, notlazohtzin?"

I look around at the world as I had left it, before I went to that other place. Greg's arms slacken, and I realize he's holding me as if I've just lost my balance. "Yes," I whisper. "I'm at Grinnell Glacier. What happened?"

"You looked woozy," Greg explains, his arms still around my shoulders and waist. "I thought you might faint."

"That's new," I tell him. "I've never fainted before."

Greg releases me, though he keeps a hand on the small of my back. "We should go," he says. "The high altitude might be affecting you. The air is too thin up here."

"No. No," I tell him, because my head has cleared, and I am back to feeling like myself again. "It's probably my blood sugar. All I've had today is that glass of orange juice in the jet."

Greg lets out a loud sigh of relief. "Then we should eat," he says. "Stilson prepared a basket. A total feast. I'm sure you'll find something you like."

"I'm not picky," I say, as he guides me around the embroidered cushions on the ground, and we sit on the blanket.

After we have our fill of cheeses and fruits followed by the most delicious roasted chicken and corn, we follow the trail up and over the rocky moraine. We stop to view the glaciers and Upper Grinnell Lake right as the sun begins to set. The whole world is aflame with that resplendent sunset. Even the tiny snow flurries look like fireflies in that gorgeous light.

Greg puts his arm out, and I sneak in under it. We stand like that, huddled together, as we watch the sun turn the mountain peaks a blazing orange. Just before it descends, Greg squeezes my shoulder and I look up at him. His eyes are ablaze with the same amber light as that orange sun.

"Blanca Rosa Montes, would you be my girlfriend, officially?"

I blink because there are tears warming my eyes, threatening to spill over, overwhelming me with something that I can only describe as happiness. I pretend to think about it, or maybe I am thinking about it. I don't know. I'm a bit stunned by his request.

"Well?" Greg asks, when I don't answer right away.

"I thought I already was," I say, giving him my most impish grin. "But sure. Okay."

Greg throws his head back and laughs, a throaty, rich sound that sends a delicious tingle up my spine. I want to kiss him so bad, but I don't. I want him to lean in for it—to want it as much as I do.

It's cool. I can wait.

I think.

CHAPTER

21

The following week brings Blanca and me closer together. No matter how incredible our relationship feels, I try to go slowly. I'm waiting for something long-lasting to blossom.

I want her to fall in love with me.

Okay, I also literally *need* Blanca to fall in love with me. Teresa says that neither of us—nor any of the others whose destiny is entangled with ours—will be free unless she does.

And Little Sister believes she's figured out which people are likely reincarnations of friends, family, and enemies from Tollan.

"We bound them to Iztac's soul," she tells me in the library that Wednesday, "so they'd return when she did. They're here in Reno. Some of them in this school."

I've been sensing something. "It's AP English Lit, right? You four thought Tina might be Iztac because she's one of the Returned."

Sofía nods. "Seems that way. Maybe the sister? One of the mothers? We think the teacher's reincarnated, too."

Tapping my fingers against the tabletop, I raise my voice excitedly. "Tony might be Meconetzin! No wonder he feels like a little brother to me!"

"SHHH! Ahem. This is a library, young ones."

It's Tony, winking as he taps a finger against his nose.

"You're in a good mood," I mutter. "He hasn't bugged you anymore?"

Tony gives a sheepish grin as he sits. "The bookie? Nope. Guess being *like a little brother* to you really helps."

I'm about to ask how much he's overheard when Sofía interrupts.

"Wait. You told them Greg gave you the money?"

Tony shakes his head. "Nah, they already knew. Must've been, I dunno, monitoring my bank account or something."

Sofía sighs. "I'll see you dudes in class. Got to make some phone calls."

As she wanders off and Tony bombards me with the latest in gaming news, I keep running the roster of our English class through my mind, trying to fit the faces of the departed onto the students. Is one of them the emperor, too?

And Jackson? Could he be Tzinacan returned? He shares the same haughty jealousy.

If so, are we destined to fight again? What will his trap be this time?

———————————

On Friday morning, Blanca whispers to me toward the end of class. "It's my turn tomorrow. Be ready by noon. I'll pick you up."

I can hardly sleep, tossing and turning with excitement. I'm ready, dressed, and waiting for her a good thirty minutes early, standing just outside the front door.

Careening around the curves comes a sky-blue Jeep. It pulls up under the portico alongside me, its knobby tires coming up to my waist. A serious off-road vehicle, despite looking pretty. Like its owner.

"Hop in," says Blanca, looking over the tops of her sunglasses. "Let's go for a little trip."

She heads west on Mount Rose Highway, climbing into the mountains, using her stick shift like a pro on the steep inclines. As we pass a resort, she points.

"There's a ski run there called Greg's Gamble. Steep and full of trees."

I have to laugh. "Sounds about right."

Soon we pass Mount Rose herself. Blanca makes the sign of the cross and kisses her thumb.

After a half hour, we exit onto Highway 28 and drive into Incline Village, pulling into the parking lot of a little café that overlooks the still water.

Inside, a middle-aged Washoe woman looks up at Blanca. We head to her table, where the two of them hug.

"Blanca, it's good to finally meet you face-to-face!"

"Likewise! So sorry about the mix-up with the invite. I really wanted you to come to the grand opening."

The woman waves this away. "No worries. But tell me, who is this handsome young man?"

"Gregorio Chan," Blanca explains. "He's . . ."

"Your boyfriend?"

Blanca smiles. "Yup. Greg, this is Lorraine Fillmore. I've told you about her."

"Hunga mi' heshi," I say in Washoe, dipping my head.

Ms. Fillmore gives an appreciative nod. "Hello to you, too, Greg. Wait—Chan, as in Tolchan, the corporation? I hear we've received a substantial donation from your father."

Blanca glances at me, surprised. "Greg?"

"I want to be a good ally," I explain. "After talking with Blanca and Tina Gorena, I asked my dad to look into ways to help you achieve your goals. The most obvious choice was funding."

Lorraine gestures at the table. "Have a seat, please."

We order burgers before Blanca and Ms. Fillmore discuss proposed legislation that will give the Washoe Tribe of Nevada and California more land management control over the lake's eastern shore.

"I think we've got the governor and key lawmakers in Nevada on our side. But California is a little thornier," Fillmore explains. "We need to push harder. Have you seen the water level out by the dam? These brutal summers are making it hard for conservation efforts. And things are complicated by the pollution and diverting up and down the Truckee River."

"Like Carrizo," I suggest.

"Yes," Blanca says. "Their water supply is almost as bad as Flint. Corroded lead pipes everywhere."

"Our legal advisors have been digging into the culprits," Fillmore adds. "Most of them have bought land from a little-known real estate agency called Hibernaculum Land Company, which has spent decades snatching up big tracts of land along the river from Native and Chicano families."

"And reselling them to corporations for a big profit?" I guess.

Lorraine nods. "But it's a paper company. A shell of a shell of a shell. Our people can't get through all the layers to find out who controls it."

Blanca turns to me.

"What about Grupo Tolchan? Could your father get someone to dig deeper?"

I nod. "Sure."

"I know I'm asking for a lot," she continues, "but what about California? Any subsidiaries of Tolchan? Any influence on state legislators at all?"

Her eyes burn with purpose and determination. I'm impressed.

"Let me look into it."

Lorraine Fillmore stares at me for what seems a full minute. "Take him down to Skunk Harbor," she suggests to Blanca. "Let him see what Da'aw looks like in its pristine state, cleaned up and managed by the people who have lived here since time immemorial."

"Da'aw," Blanca says. "The lake. It should be theirs. All of it. To share or not as they see fit."

"I agree," I say, gazing over at her.

It's amazing to see Blanca in her element, getting things done, fighting for what matters. Even if she weren't the incarnation of Iztac, I'd be dazzled by the largeness of her heart.

———————————

After lunch, we drive south till we come to a trailhead and park. Blanca leads me along a dirt path that ends beside the startling blue of the harbor. There are a few stone-and-wood buildings that fade into the foliage. Beyond that, we might as well be standing in an area untouched by Westerners.

"Wow," I say, taking Blanca's hand. "I can see why you want to preserve this place."

Her smile crinkles her face in what I now recognize as true joy.

"Yeah, I love the lake and its people. I'd do anything to save them."

We walk up the strand together, past a tumble of boulders. The beach narrows to a sliver as it approaches a forested spur that thrusts out into the clear water.

As we stand in the shade of those trees, Blanca shivers. Though it's early September, the air at this end of the harbor must only be in the upper fifties.

I pull her hand closer, sliding it into the pocket of my light jacket. "You're so cold," I mutter.

She turns to face me, takes my other hand in hers, and thrusts them into my other jacket pocket, stepping so close our bodies lightly touch.

I feel fire creep along my nerves and veins as she looks up at me, eyes half-closed, cheeks flushed. She begins to lean into me, and I can feel her every curve. Her lips part slightly. My heart beats faster.

She's so beautiful. I want to kiss her more than anything.

Instead, I lean in. Her eyes close, expectant. Then I whisper.

"The beautiful view has given me an idea. Can we visit Mount Rose?"

Opening her eyes, she arches an eyebrow.

"You want me to drive you up a steep, snowcapped mountain instead of . . . hanging out with me here?"

I give her a big smile and nod like a puppy. "Yup."

She shakes her head and laughs. "All right, Greg. But we're going to need some dinner first. And probably a thermos of coffee."

After steaks in the same diner, which happily fills an aluminum carafe full of their "joyful joe" for us, Blanca drives along the Mount Rose Scenic Drive to a high pass, where we take the detour that leads to the Winters Creek Base Lodge. A few hundred yards from the Mount Rose Ski Area, Blanca pulls off the road into a pine-ringed clearing near a sheer drop. Opening before us is an amazing vista:

another lake at the heart of a valley below, the glittering water being slowly dimmed by the shadow of the mountain, which stretches east as the sun sets behind us.

"Amazing," I mutter as she turns off the car. "What are we looking at?"

"Washoe Lake, in the Washoe Valley. It's not Tahoe," she adds, "but it sure is beautiful."

I reach over and pull a strand of hair from her face.

"As beautiful as you, notlazohtzin."

She eases closer. "You keep calling me that. What does it mean?"

"Many meanings. *No* means *my*. *Tlazohtzin* can be *precious. Cherished.*" I look away for a second, pausing. "*Beloved.*"

She says nothing, just leans her head on my shoulder and puts her hand in mine.

Without speaking, we stare out at the valley as dusk swallows it up and lights fill the twilight below like the millions of stars emerging above.

The only sounds are the muffled calls of animals and our breathing, which has synchronized as the cosmos enchants us.

There's no cell service at this altitude. No dings or rings or chirps. No way for anyone to interrupt this moment.

Blanca shifts, moving closer, her face against my neck. Her warm breath contrasts with the cool of her skin.

I can feel her, expectant, waiting for me to kiss her. But I don't.

I wish this magic moment could make her speak. That she would say she loves me.

It's the only way we can escape.

Instead, she begins to tremble from the cold. It's below freezing now, the windows frosting over.

Through some instinct I can't explain, I reach out and draw heat from the magma far below us, easing it into the air around us. Just enough to make her comfortable.

Mumbling words I can't make out, Blanca falls asleep, nestling like a bird into my side. I ease the seat back just enough to make her comfortable, moving her head slightly so it fits in the crook of my arm.

Where my hands happen to touch her skin, electricity sparks through my fingers. Wincing, I plant a kiss upon her forehead. Then I spend hours looking down at her, breathing in her scent.

As the moon rises above us, I drift off into the unknowable realm of sleep.

In every dream, she smiles and says my name.

CHAPTER

22

I wake up, open my eyes, and blink, disoriented because I don't know where I am. *What happened?* I ask myself as I look around the cabin of my Jeep. My body feels lethargic, like I slept too long.

I look over at Greg, still asleep beside me, his beautiful face at rest. Suddenly, I remember everything. *Lorraine. Skunk Harbor. Mount Rose. The lake. And stars . . . so many stars. Snuggling with Greg . . . such warmth.*

"Oh my God!" I shake Greg, because it hits me how much trouble I'm going to be in when I get back home. "Wake up, Greg."

"What?" Greg wakes, looking as disoriented as I was a minute ago. "What's going on? Are you okay?"

"No," I tell him. "I haven't been home all night. My padrino's going to flip!"

"I'm sorry," Greg says. "This is my fault."

"No faults, okay? It was a beautiful moment, and we can't regret it," I say, as I turn the engine and start driving down the mountain. When we're almost to the highway, my phone starts pinging in the cupholder.

At the solitary intersection, I pick up my phone and check my notifications. I don't want to panic, but it's hard not to because I have a series of missed calls from my padrino and Jackson, as well as several texts from Tina. All of them concerned.

TINA: *Dude, where are you? Everyone's looking for you.*

TINA: *Call me back. I'm worried.*

TINA: *Blanca, please call me. Your padrino, Jackson, Sofía, everyone's freaking out.*

"Is it your padrino?" Greg asks, giving me a moment to finish reading. "Do you need to talk to him? I could drive."

I shake my head and shove my phone in my pocket.

"No, thank you. I'd like to get home as soon as possible," I say, grinning as I put the Jeep into gear and hit the highway.

Greg throws his head back and laughs. The soft sound makes me all warm and fuzzy inside, and I'm glad we keep our cool, even though we both know this is not going to end well.

I pull up in front of Greg's house, the Jeep's engine idling quietly, as he steps out. "You sure you don't want me to go with you? Explain things?" he asks.

I look out the glass door, beyond the trees, to where the roof of my house peeks out, clearly visible in the moonlight. "Oh, trust me," I say. "It's better this way."

"Okay," he says, his eyes concerned, a slight frown overshadowing them. "But call me if you need . . . anything."

"See you soon," I say, waving as I drive off.

Because it's almost 5:00 a.m., I'm careful not to make any noise as I skulk into my house through the back door. My efforts, however, are for naught, because my padrino is already awake and waiting for me in the living room. Worse yet is the fact that he is not alone. Jackson and DA Flowers stand up as I walk into the well-lit room.

"Oh, thank God you're okay!" Jackson says, walking over and putting his arms around me, like I'm a child. I slip out of his arms, avoiding the kiss on the forehead he was about to plant on me.

"What are *you* doing here?" I ask him, as I step back and pull my cardigan close, stuffing my hands under my arms self-consciously.

"I called him over," my padrino says. "We've been desperately looking for you for hours, all night, actually. Where were you? Do you know what we've been through—how worried we've all been? The police just left, but this woman—this individual"—my padrino gestures at DA Flowers—"she wanted to make sure I hadn't killed you and had you buried in the desert."

"That's ridiculous," I say, glaring at DA Flowers. "I'm fine. He wouldn't . . . he's always taken care of me."

"It's just common." DA Flowers shrugs and takes a pencil and small pad out of her pocket and starts writing something. "The parents are always prime suspects when a child goes missing."

"I'm not a child," I tell her, shrugging because Jackson is trying to put his arm around me again.

Jackson side-eyes me. "Where were you?" he hisses.

"Stop it. You have no right to ask." I push him away, a little too hard, and he teeters back, exaggerating my actions.

"Well, I can see that everything is back to normal here," DA Flowers says, shoving the pencil and pad back in her pocket and grinning at my padrino. "I'll see myself out. Unless, of course, you need me, Ms. Montes."

"I'm fine," I tell her, forcing myself to stay quiet until the nosy woman leaves because I don't want to make the situation any worse.

"Well," my padrino asks. "Where were you? Security assures me you drove out of St. James Village in the early afternoon."

"You were with him, weren't you?" Jackson demands. "You were with that *Mexican!*"

Jackson's vileness infuriates me. "You're Mexican too!" I tell him. "Or did you forget?"

My padrino cringes. He presses the bridge of his long, curved nose with the fingertips of his thumb and index finger and lets out a long, deep breath.

"Listen," he says. "It doesn't matter who you were with; I just want to make sure you are being safe. That you are doing good things out there, things that don't jeopardize us—you, me, our position— who we are and what we stand for in this community. Do you understand?"

"Yeah, you shouldn't be staying out all night with some greasy guy you don't even know," Jackson says, glaring at me.

The words send me over the edge, and I take a deep breath and try to slow my heart rate, to push back all the anger that is roiling up inside me, like a dormant volcano rumbling and roiling as it wakes. Ready to explode. Surprise everyone around me.

"Jackson's right," my padrino says. "You shouldn't just disappear like that. You didn't do anything to embarrass us, did you, Blanca? Because if you think you might have . . . you should tell me now. I'll find out anyway."

"Everything comes out," Jackson says, nodding. "Eventually."

"Augh!" I roll my eyes and push past Jackson, rushing out of the room and running up the stairs. Once inside, I lock the door and fall on my bed, emotionally exhausted. Tears rolling down my face, I pull my phone out of my pocket and call Tina.

"Dude!" Tina says, mumbling into the phone. "What are you doing? It's five-thirty in the freakin' morning!"

"I need to talk to you," I say, hiccupping, because I can't control the emotions coursing through my body, chilling me, making me want to scream in rage. "*Now.*"

"Now?" Tina is suddenly alert. "What's going on? Did something bad happen—with Greg?"

"Yes. No. I don't know," I whimper, wiping my runny nose with a tissue from the box on my nightstand, because I've lost complete control of myself.

"What is it?" Tina asks quietly. "What's wrong?"

"I just . . . I wish . . ." I hiccup a few more times and blow my nose before I say what's gotten me so unhinged. "I just wish my mom were still here."

CHAPTER

23

I wait as long as I can stand before texting her.

ME: *Are you okay? I hope you weren't too startled, waking up in the Jeep like that.*

BLANCA: *I'm fine.*

ME: *You handled the fallout?*

BLANCA: *Yup! All good. Call you tonight.*

To distract myself, I spend a few hours exercising. But during my routine, I can't help but review yesterday scene by scene. I'm once again struck by Blanca's admiration for Lorraine's work, as well as her own determination to ensure clean water in nature and for people.

It's inspiring. I find I also want to make a difference. Blanca is my new role model, I realize. How can I show her my devotion, not just to her, but also to the noble cause she champions?

When it comes to me, the idea takes my breath away. I towel off and grab my phone, tapping "Papá" in my contacts list.

Blanca's going to flip when the project's done.

My phone rings at exactly 10:00 p.m. It's Blanca, and she fills me in on what was waiting for her.

"I'm so sorry," I tell her. "I should've woken you up."

"No, no," she insists. "This is *not* your fault, Greg. And I don't regret spending the night with you. My choice."

"I love," I begin, sensing tension at those words, "your integrity and self-determination."

We chat about all sorts of things—water conservation, the history of the area, Blanca's first trip to Lake Tahoe, what it was like growing up under Rafael's tutelage. I lie back on my bed as the talk turns slowly toward us, the adventures we've had together, what we might do the next time we go on a date.

Hours pass this way, till her voice grows drowsy. I suggest we hang up, but she refuses.

"Just another few minutes," she whispers, and I'm reminded of a different voice muttering the same words in a different language, in a garden far from here, when I had so many bright and beautiful dreams for the future.

"Whatever you want," I say again, my entire philosophy in three words.

My alarm goes off. I jerk awake, realizing I fell asleep with my phone beside me, spending the night without a single dream as Blanca's slow breathing spilled from the speaker.

It's now interrupted by a long yawn and a yelp of surprise.

"Greg? Oh, we fell asleep talking to each other, didn't we?"

I lift the phone to my ear.

"It's becoming a habit. Good morning, notlazohtzin. Get some breakfast. I'll see you at school."

A pause.

"Could you . . . pick me up? I'd love to ride with you."

My heart skips a beat. "Absolutely. In an hour?"

"Yes. See you soon, Greg."

When she slides into the passenger seat, she's wearing just a simple pair of jeans and a powder-blue T-shirt, but she looks stunning.

"Morning," she says, reaching her hand out to squeeze mine.

I smile as I hook her fingers with mine and don't let go.

"Beautiful woman, beautiful day."

The drive is short but sweet. We hold hands from the car all the way to her class. It's nothing new—it's become our routine over the last two weeks—but something feels different today.

There's a shift in our feelings, like we've crossed an emotional divide. It takes every ounce of my willpower to let go of her hand outside the classroom.

I want to cling to her. I'd use my power to reshape the world if it would keep her forever by my side.

We're eating lunch with the girls and Tony when my phone vibrates. It's the foreman Grupo Tolchan hired to oversee the project.

"Your father said I should call you, sir. We've moved everyone to hotels. Project's underway."

"You've got enough workers to keep shifts going around the clock?"

"Yes, Mr. Chan."

"Perfect. Let me know if anything unexpected happens," I add before hanging up.

Blanca tilts her head at me. "What's up?"

"You know how you look forward to taking the reins of Montes

Realty? To do some *real* good with it? I feel the same way about Grupo Tolchan. My dad's let me take charge of a special project."

She leans forward, excited. "What?"

I make a lip-zipping movement. "Top secret."

"I wouldn't tell anyone." She gives me a disappointed look, eyebrows beetling together.

I laugh. Her eyebrows bunch together even more, making me laugh harder.

"If I told you, it wouldn't be a surprise. For *you.*"

Sofía leans forward and pats Blanca's reddening cheek.

"Must be some surprise," she says, "if men are working around the clock."

Tina almost spits out her juice. "I'm afraid to even ask."

"An elaborate setup is required for our next date," I explain, winking. "Actually, Tina, I could use your help."

Smiling, Tina scoffs. "Hey, I love planning surprise parties, but I prefer to keep the person being celebrated, you know, *in the dark.*"

She's not expecting it, but I plan to make her star rise at the same time I make my date with Blanca a dream come true.

Blanca gives an exaggerated sigh. "Great. Now I'm going to be obsessing about this all week. You've set the bar pretty high, Greg. Hope you can live up to the hype. Just sayin'."

I grin. "Oh, you will *not* be disappointed."

That evening, my father video-calls me, his face serious.

"After our chat yesterday, I had Legal dig into that company Lorraine Filmore mentioned. Though it's cleverly hidden," he explains, "Hibernaculum's real owner is . . . Blanca Rosa Montes, who on paper controls a majority of the shares through a holding company."

I suck in air. "Which means Rafael Montes is behind the land deals. Causing the very pollution Blanca wants to combat."

"Yes. And Hibernaculum has been a generous donor to conservative political campaigns for legislators and judges who have turned a blind eye. But that helps us. Grupo Tolchan is going to start acquiring the companies to which Hibernaculum has sold land. We'll shut down whatever they're doing to pollute Nevada's potable water."

"Thanks," I mutter, my mind reeling. "I wonder how much deeper Rafael's corruption goes. And if he's using Blanca's name this way, he must plan to keep controlling her for many years to come."

My father nods. "We'll keep digging. I'll loop you in the moment we learn more."

"Okay. Be well, kid."

That makes him chuckle a little. "You too, old man."

Blanca pesters me over the phone that evening and during our shared classes on Tuesday, but I refuse to spoil the surprise.

As we're walking hand in hand in the parking lot after school, she tries one last time to weasel more information from me.

"Greg! Come on. A hint?"

"Let's just say it's the sort of gift that a woman as brilliant, tenacious, and compassionate as yourself deserves."

Her eyes water up a little.

"Aw," she says, pulling me to a stop. "Qué lindo."

Then, standing on tiptoe, she plants a kiss on my cheek.

Jeers and oohs go up as a knot of football players walk by, Blanca's ex among them.

"Damn, Jackson, that's cold!" shouts Mark Montoya, the team's tight end. "Brown Jeff Bezos not only stole your girl—now he's kissing her in front of the school! And you're just standing there like a menso."

Jackson goes red, his hands balling into fists.

"Don't," Blanca mutters, feeling me tense up. "It's what he wants."

I kiss her hand, then let it go.

"You douchebag," he spits. "Come into my town, seduce my girl, keep her out all night—did you think I was just going to sit there and take it?"

"Aside from the lies you just spouted? Yes. I hoped you'd be smart enough to see that Blanca can make her own choices. But you're a twisted, paranoid little fool who needs to learn the hard way."

Howling, he rushes me, swinging his right fist.

A thousand years of muscle memory take over. I take a single step back before pivoting aside. He misses my face, his wild momentum throwing him off-balance and sending him thudding to the blacktop.

The gathering crowd explodes with guffaws.

Jackson scrambles to his feet, his palms and right cheek scraped, bleeding. I rush at him. He raises his hands in a defensive gesture, but I stop just inches away. He takes a step back, but his foot bangs against the curb.

As he loses his balance, I flick my fingers. He jerks away and goes sprawling, his back slapping against a tree root.

Furious, growling with pain, he jumps up and aims a kick at my head. I lean back, lifting my hands, and as his foot passes a few inches from my face, I yank on the hem of his jeans.

He spins around, taking hopping steps to try to retain his balance.

The crowd howls with laughter at how awkward he looks.

"Stand still and fight me!" Jackson screams.

I shake my head. "No. If I did, you'd end up in a hospital. I won't dirty my fists or future on someone like you."

"You're just a wuss," he spits, assuming a crouching stance. "Always avoiding conflict. Probably can't throw a punch."

I also crouch, extending my hands as if inviting him to grapple. "Come, then, brat. Find out for yourself."

Enraged, he rushes me, head down. I leap into an aú giro sem mão, a sort of flying cartwheel. I let the fingers of my right hand brush his back lightly as I spin through the air above his passing form.

He can't pull to a stop in time. He slams into a parked car, dropping back onto his rear with a pained gasp.

I land at the same time. Cheering comes from those students wise enough to root for me. Carlos Sáenz pumps his fist.

Jackson drags himself to his feet. Blood is running from a cut on his scalp down over the scrape on his cheek.

Slowly, deliberately, he comes toward me, fists up. He doesn't intend on losing his balance again. Rather than back away, I start my balanço, a snaking movement back and forth, unpredictable. He can't keep track of me or predict my position. He flings punches, but they never land.

"Now you're dancing?" he barks through gritted teeth. "What the—"

A whistle cuts him off as security comes bouncing toward us on a golf cart. I make one final move, a macaco em pé. The back handspring brings my feet so close to Jackson's face that he stumbles back and once more loses his balance, crashing into the asphalt.

"You can't touch me, Jackson," I call loud enough for everyone to hear, "and you're too insignificant for me to bother touching. So keep your distance, boy."

Despite what I've said, Jackson is important enough for the

security guards to leave him alone once he tells them he's heading home. I answer their questions politely, and several dozen students confirm that I never actually hit him.

Blanca isn't pleased about the confrontation, but she gets my logic. Jackson wouldn't leave us alone if I didn't defeat him publicly.

I cross my fingers he isn't one of the Returned.

Especially not Tzinacan.

CHAPTER
24

"Oh, that's Tule Peak!" I yell, pointing at the snowcapped mountain outside the car window. I've been through here, on road trips with my parents, when I was a child, but we never stopped. "Are we going hiking again? No. Wait. Camping. We're going camping, right?"

Greg smiles and shakes his head. "Nope."

My phone pings, so I pull it out of my back pocket.

"It's Sofía," I say. "She wants to know what the surprise was."

He gives a soft chuckle. "Don't look at me."

"*A weekend getaway, I think*," I say, putting the phone face down on my lap after texting this revelation to Sofía. Like me, she's been dying to know what surprise Greg has been hinting at all week.

Greg raises an eyebrow at me. "So that's it?" he asks. "You're not giving her any additional information?"

I make caras at him. "How can I tell her when I don't know where we're going?"

Greg grins. His perfect teeth gleam in the sunlight, and, suddenly, I want to kiss him. "North," he says.

"Uhm, yeah," I tell him. "But north could lead to a hundred thousand different places, and that's just in the United States. Wait.

We are staying in the country, right? Because I didn't bring my passport."

"We're not leaving the country," Greg says. "We'd take the family jet for that. Today we're going a little bit down the road. To a very special place. You're going to love it there. It's very much *your thing*."

"Very much my thing . . ." I think about where that could be. Not Vegas. I don't like Vegas. Does he know that? I pull up a map of Nevada on my phone. "Okay, twenty questions. Number one. Are we staying in Nevada?"

"Twenty questions?" Greg looks confused.

"It's a game," I say, pushing my hair out of my face and turning on my seat so that I'm facing him as he drives. "I ask questions and you tell me when I get it."

Greg laughs. He points to a green marker on the road and says, "We're five miles away. How's that for an answer?"

"Carrizo?" I ask, reading the sign as it whizzes by. "What's in Carrizo?"

Greg's eyes twinkle as he gives me a side-look. "Your heart, not-lazohtzin. Only your heart."

I cock my head and stare at him for a moment. "Awww . . . well, as much as I love that place, I don't understand why you'd book a weekend getaway there. Unless there's been some development I don't know about. Wait. Is this about the lead pipes?"

I start to search for recent news articles on Carrizo, but Greg gently takes the phone from my hands, shutting off the screen and passing it back to me.

"Lead pipes are just part of the problem. You told me their local water supply has been diverted. It's a tributary stream of the Truckee River. I . . . looked into the corporation responsible and discovered its terrible standards, which have left the people of Carrizo with no access to fresh water. I know how important that is to you. That's why we're here today."

As we drive into town, the place is all but deserted. I see a bus sitting on Main Street, but no one's inside it. The picturesque little storefronts are all closed. Decorative Out for Lunch and Be Right Back signs are hanging on doors, and, except for a stray dog scratching at his long, floppy ear, there is nothing else going on in the streets. The whole thing gives me chills, and I rub the goose bumps on my forearms lightly.

"It looks like a ghost town," I whisper, trembling, because I'm afraid of what this means. "Where is everyone?"

"It's okay," Greg says. "You'll see."

When we turn the corner, things change. There's a row of cars sitting in the angled parking spaces in front of city hall. Greg takes the empty spot at the far left and stops the engine.

"We're here," he says, and he gets out of the car and stands looking around, as if trying to figure out where to go.

I'm about to ask him what we're doing here when two well-dressed women and a man wearing a navy-blue suit come out of city hall. They smile as they climb down the short set of stairs.

"You made it!" the woman says, and she offers Greg her hand. "Is this our special guest?"

Greg shakes her hand. "Ms. Longoria, this is Blanca Montes. She is the inspiration for all this."

"Welcome, Blanca," the woman says, smiling and hugging me warmly, the way a tía might hug her favorite niece. "I've heard so much about you, from Mr. Chan and others. I am Margie Longoria, the mayor of Carrizo. This is José Robles, my assistant, and Alicia Rodríguez, head of our city council."

"So nice to meet you," I say, because I have no idea why I'm meeting them. Unless, of course, Greg is trying to help me network. That is what I'm trying to do, after all—build a community before I step into my position as CEO of Montes Realty.

"Well, we're certainly honored to meet you," Mayor Longoria says. "Greg has told us all about your desire to use your resources to serve our cause. Helping small towns like ours get access to clean water is an admirable objective."

"Mr. Chan." Alicia Rodríguez turns to Greg. "We thought we would start by giving you a tour of our small but beautiful city."

"A tour would be a great way to start," Greg says. "My dad's people tell me we're on schedule for the day's events."

"Events?" I ask, intrigued, because I still don't know what I am doing here. I won't have access to my parents' company funds for a while. And because I have to go to college before I run the family business full-time, it will be years before I can do anything to help the people of Carrizo. So, I am having a bit of imposter syndrome as I look at the excited faces around me.

"Trust me," Greg says as he takes my hand and kisses it. "You're going to love this."

I nod, and we follow the mayor and her associates around, listening and smiling as they describe each of the sites. We learn all about city hall, the bank, a small clinic, and after a late lunch we visit the historic district and two churches, including Santa Rosa Catholic Church, which used to be a mission in the 1700s.

It's all very interesting, but not as interesting as finding out that Grupo Tolchan moved the entire town, all 10,364 residents, to hotels in nearby cities, Spanish Springs, Patrick, McCarran, Lockwood, and flew in dozens of work crews—hundreds of men and women—to replace the pipes in town.

"All of them?" I ask, flabbergasted by what Mayor Longoria is saying. Turning to Greg, I lean in and ask, "You asked your parents to do this, didn't you?"

"Let's just say you've inspired me to effect change now, when it's most needed," he whispers back, and my heart soars. "Why wait, why make people continue to live in such deplorable conditions, when we have the means to fix it?"

"Exactly the way I feel!" I say, because I still can't believe how much Greg and I are vibing—how well matched we seem to be. He very well could be my media naranja! "A week, huh?"

"Less than that." Mayor Longoria grins. "Six and a half days, wasn't it, José?"

José Robles nods. "They worked twenty-four seven, rotating crews every few hours, but they got it all done. It's just amazing how much human power we had working out here."

The sun is setting as we walk out of the small hospital and take a right, heading in the direction of the town square, with its park benches surrounding an old mission fountain carved from cantera.

"Oh, that's beautiful," I say, when I catch a glimpse of its decorative multitiered stone design.

"Yes. It's a shame it's been unused for decades," José Robles says.

"Decades?" I ask, horrified. "That is an absolute travesty."

Mayor Margie Longoria sighs and looks at the top tier, with its innocent angelito statue looking down at us as if imploring us to do something. "Ever since the creek was diverted, twenty-four years ago. But we weren't the only ones affected," she says. "That travesty, as you call it, cut the water supply to several nearby Native American communities. It changed the entire ecosystem."

"So, replacing the pipes is not enough?" I ask, turning to Greg.

"That's why Grupo Tolchan bought the offending corporation," he says.

"What?" I ask.

Alicia Rodríguez grins at me. "Grupo Tolchan redirected the creek to its old course, and now we can start using it again."

"That's why you're here," Greg says, pointing to a switch on the side of the fountain. "To do the honors."

"Really?" Tears start to brim my eyes, threatening to spill over.

Greg squeezes my hand before he lets it go. The setting sun inches down a bit more on the horizon, and I catch the last rays of its light as they fall over his face before the darkness starts to descend on the square.

"Go on," Greg says, and he steps back to watch me.

I put my hand on the long, angled handle. It's big, so I use both hands to get a good grip. And when I pull, something extraordinary happens. The whole plaza lights up, and the water shoots up, arching over the fountain, creating a dazzling, magical display that takes my breath away.

Bright, upbeat music begins to play, and I turn to see a spectacular surprise. Con Cariño rolls into the plaza on a flatbed truck with a built-in stage and Tina crooning her original song, "Agua Es Vida," in that unique contralto voice of hers, and she waves to me excitedly.

"So that's what you were teasing her about!" I say.

Greg smiles and bows his head. "Yup, it was harmless fun . . . and a good gig for her."

"She looks like a rising star," I whisper as I watch Tina dominate the stage with her resplendent presence.

"She was made to sing," Greg agrees, as droves of people start pouring out of the buildings around us. They emerge from their businesses and homes, cheering and laughing as they form a circle around us. In their arms, they carry baskets, pots, and pans. Everything

197

from dishes to tablecloths and cutlery is set up as they throw a huge fiesta to celebrate the renewal of their town, the beginning of a new age for themselves and future generations.

There are so many people coming over to thank us, I am overcome with emotion. I look around and realize there is no fanfare here, no media, no paparazzi. We are surrounded only by genuine, honest, hardworking people, gente buena who deserve a good life. And my heart swells with love for them, and for Greg, who made all this possible.

"You did this," I whisper to Greg when we have a moment to ourselves. "For me."

"Yes. For you and for them," he says. "This is what we can do with our wealth, Blanca. Once you take over your family's business, you can improve people's lives. I know you'll make the world a better place by leading others to change."

The hope in his eyes, the wisdom in his words, the faith in my potential, is all so much more than I was expecting that I do the only thing I can do to show him how much this means to me. I jump up, wrap my arms around his neck, and plant a long, lingering kiss on his soft, full lips. He tastes like he smells. He is earth and rain and fire in harmony with mint leaves.

As I cling to him, Greg puts his hands around my waist and kisses me back sweetly. When I open my eyes, I see that all around us, people are clapping and cheering, though I couldn't hear them before, because that kiss was *everything*. It was all that existed between us and around us.

CHAPTER
25

I can't stop thinking about those kisses.

The first, in Carrizo's plaza. The second, later that night when I walk her to the door of the little cabin I've rented for her.

The third in the morning, before we head to breakfast with Tina and her bandmates.

Sensations linger. The sweet warmth of her mouth, like a non-ochton fruit plucked from ice-laden branches. The feel of her hands on my face, soft and cold like powdered snow falling from heaven.

I've braced myself for Jackson's angry stares, but Monday morning he posts on social media that he's flying to Belgium for some "me time with European cuties" now that football season is over.

It figures he would run to his mother.

I don't feel bad for him, though. Not after what he got Tony caught up in.

As the week progresses, I enjoy more and more of Blanca's kisses. In my car before school. In the alcove near the gym. In an empty classroom she pulls me into.

Everyone notices that we've gotten closer.

"It's getting serious, huh?" Tony asks me, floating in my pool on

Wednesday evening. "The two of you were pretty flushed when you hurried into class late. Better be careful."

It takes me a moment. "I'm in no hurry. Plus, I'm a gentleman. And responsible, always."

"Well, the heat of the moment can make all that chivalry stuff go poof!" He makes an exploding motion with his fingers. "You're my bro, but I've known Blanca for years. Feel me?"

He *must* be Meconetzin. Or a really good friend. "Totally. No worries, Tony."

Most of the week, my dreams are about that distant garden. They begin as sweet memories, but then sour into nightmares. All *those* kisses were glimpsed by an unknown rival. One who turned her father against me, setting tragedy in motion. I try not to dwell on the sound that greeted me after I'd run for almost thirty-six hours: conch trumpets announcing her death. I try not to see Xochitzin in Iztac's chambers, clutching the lifeless form of her stepdaughter, noose still round her neck.

When I wake up on Friday, I begin to doubt that Iztac will ever awaken within Blanca. Over breakfast, I look into Teresa's gentle eyes.

"Teicuihtzin," I begin, reverentially, "how do we make it happen?"

"There are two ways to awaken the other five," she explains, "so we can begin the process of redemption. We picked the slower one: nudging the Returned toward remembering. At the right moment, we tell them, and their identities crack, allowing who they *once were* to seep through. It's less traumatic, like a smaller and smoother version of the way your memories have been restored."

I tap the table. "So that's why the other three came here. To prepare the way. Daniela, looking for the sort of corruption Tzinacan would be involved in. María, overseeing the school attended by the richer teens that might be likely candidates for Toltec nobility."

"Yes, and Sofía, befriending the girls we believed might be Iztac. Then encouraging Blanca to break up with Jackson and get closer to you. The goddess of fate couldn't leave things to chance, not this time."

"It's already the right moment for Blanca," I say. "I want to tell her."

"Has she said she loves you?" Teresa asks, leaning toward me.

"No, but her feelings are pretty clear. The right setting will help her confess."

Teresa takes both my hands in hers. "And do you love her? Blanca, I mean, not just Iztac. Because she will be both at once."

"Yes," I admit. "And if there were no other way, I think I could spend the rest of my days with Blanca. I certainly will love her when she and Iztac are combined."

Teresa goes quiet, perhaps musing or communicating with her sisters.

"I'm not sure she's as ready as you think. Unlike the others, her soul has been in paradise. Though Iztac agreed to this course of action long ago, it might take more than just telling Blanca the truth. You may need to make her wield her power."

Wincing, I think of the incident in the science lab. "Okay. If necessary."

"Are you sure you want to try this, Goyo?" she asks, looking concerned. "We can cut to the chase and use a ritual to awaken them all at once."

I grimace. "Seems a recipe for disaster. Better to go one by one, even if it's harder."

I arrive at school later than usual. Blanca must be inside, but her godfather's car is still idling at the curb. The window rolls down. Rafael Montes leans toward me.

"Gregorio Chan. May I have a word?"

His driver hops out and opens the opposite door. I slide into the back seat.

"What did you want to talk about, Mr. Montes?"

"Several issues. First, while you have chosen to enjoy the company of my goddaughter, I'm certain that all of us—your parents, you, and I—can agree that she is not at your level. For men like you, royalty is typically the next step. And there are many lovely, eligible princesses in the world right now. No, Blanca is fated to spend her life with a boy like Jackson. I understand my place in the global pecking order. I'm certain I can make her acknowledge hers."

I'm caught off guard, but I shake my head. "All due respect, Mr. Montes, but that's nonsense. Blanca is a brilliant, beautiful girl who is at the same level as any aristocrat. Besides, we care about each other."

Rafael arches an eyebrow. "Such naïveté. You are quite mistaken, Mr. Chan. It is difficult to bow my head to you, but I do so now. I am so far beneath you that I was quite shocked to learn of recent inquiries into Montes Realty."

"I don't understand," I say.

"By Tolchan corporate lawyers and the district attorney's office. Quite discreet and competent. But a series of acquisitions by your father's company and the renovation of an entire town have drawn my attention. Looking into the matter, I've discovered your family's unwarranted interest in my affairs. Disappointing. As for myself, I have chosen till now to leave you and your handful of local friends alone. Let's avoid unpleasantries, shall we?"

Beneath the refinement and deference, I hear the venom on his tongue. And I understand. Rafael Montes won't let anything put his plans at risk—especially Blanca making her own choices.

"You think," I tell him tersely, "that you've calculated Blanca's worth. But you're wrong, Don Rafael. She is more capable than you give her credit for. Good day, sir."

When I meet Blanca, I don't mention my encounter with her godfather. Instead, I invite her to come over for a picnic on Saturday.

"In the woods?"

"No," I tell her. "On the island in Joy Lake. It's part of our property."

I set up everything myself. Prepare the food, spread the blanket, organize the basket just so. I planted forget-me-nots the first week of school, and they've now blossomed all over the isle, carpeting it with celestial blue petals.

Blanca arrives wearing a summer dress over her bathing suit.

"Let's walk down to the boat," I say, taking her hand.

Just north of the Glass Castle, a spit of land juts into the lake. There's about twenty-five feet between it and the isle, but I have a rowboat. I help Blanca in, then push the small vessel into the water, jumping in and crossing the short space with a few oar strokes.

"Oh my God, Greg," Blanca whispers as the rowboat comes to a stop. "How did you do this?"

I help her out, and we step carefully through the throng of flowers.

"I wanted today to be perfect," I admit. "I've been planning this for a long time."

We ease down onto the blanket, and I begin to set out the spread

I've prepared—diced fruits and sliced vegetables, artisanal cheeses, delicate hors d'oeuvres, small skewers of meat, dainty tarts.

Blanca tries a bit of everything, smiling with contentment. Beyond a slight chill in the wind that she hardly notices, the weather is perfect. A cloudless sky, sun golden and bright, breeze soft and playful.

We're sipping on mineral water when Blanca announces, "I want to go swimming." Without waiting for an answer, she pulls her dress off, kicks her sandals aside, and runs toward the lake.

I'm halfway done unbuttoning my white linen shirt when she dives in. Seconds later, I'm in the water with her, twisting and splashing in pursuit of her, like two otters in other lakes in a distant place where we once played joyfully, before Chaos took our happiness in its claws and twisted cruelly.

Birds sweep through the air above us, chittering spirals, echoing our own teasing pursuit. My fingers slip across her skin as she escapes, giggling, and my heart swells with joy. At last. After so much time, so much sadness, I've found the right girl. My girl.

When the moment comes, I can no longer tell who's caught whom, but we look into each other's eyes, panting from the chase. She gives a little nod, and we begin to kiss. Then I lean back, sustaining her weight as I kick us toward shore.

I barely notice how we stumble our tangled way to the blanket, where I press my lips to hers again. Her hands slide down my back. But I pull away, slow and gentle, staring into her eyes, which are unfocused with excitement.

"What's wrong?" she rasps.

Those eyes. Everything else has changed, but the gods gave her the same eyes. I could drown in them, happy to lose myself forever. But first I've got to speak the words.

"I love you, Blanca."

Her hand comes up to cup the back of my neck, drawing me down toward her.

"And I love you, Greg. Pero ven. Ven a mí, amor."

It's time.

I give her another deep, lingering kiss. Then I pull aside, sitting up on the picnic blanket.

Her face flushed, Blanca props herself up on her elbows. Her perfection is breathtaking.

I almost falter. Couldn't I just love Blanca Montes? Couldn't I be happy to live as Greg Chan? But I've come too far. Suffered too much. Watched too many people be born and die, nations rise and fall, nearly losing myself to madness and despair.

And Iztac agreed to be reincarnated, the Four have assured me. She wanted to put an end to this cycle, seek redemption for me and the others.

There's no choice. I have to shatter Blanca Montes.

"What's wrong?" she manages to say, catching her breath. "Did I do something wrong?"

Tears spring to my eyes.

"Never. You are faultless, blameless, perfect in my eyes and in my heart."

"Then—why? Talk to me, Greg." She sits up, her hair a nimbus full of blue blooms.

I take a deep breath.

"There's something you need to know. Gregorio Chan Ihpotok? That's just a name I use to move through the world. The most recent of many. A new identity, replacing an older, long-discarded one."

Blanca shakes her head. "What? Are you on the run or something?"

"Not exactly. I'm Popoca, son of General Zacametzin. Born on day One Flint of the year Two Reed, the last of the reign of Toltec empress Xihuiquenitzin. The eighth of August, 832, of the Common Era, by European reckoning."

She puts her hands up, hurt and anger twisting her features. "What are you doing? Are you recording this? Do you enjoy freaking girls out or something?"

"No, beloved. It's the truth. I'm the Popoca of the story from English class. And you—ah, notlazohtziné—you are Lady Iztac. I've waited twelve hundred years for you to return. Now you have. Reincarnated as Blanca Rosa Montes, whom I love as much as I loved you centuries ago, in the palace gardens of Tollan, before your father sent me away to do battle with—"

"STOP!" Blanca shouts, following that single word with a scream of frustration. She stands, her eyes casting about till she finds her discarded dress.

"Notlazohtzin. Beloved," I say, my voice quavering.

She pulls the dress over her head and wheels about to face me.

"Are you trying to ruin what we have? If you're into role-playing, springing it on me like this, in the middle of"—she waves her hands at the flowers and blanket—"this kind of moment *really* sucks, Greg. And if you want *out* of this relationship, this is a horrible way of breaking up. You and I are Iztac and Popoca, reincarnated? Whatever."

"You're the one who's been reincarnated. I lived through those centuries."

She sneers. "So now you're immortal? Don't tell me—a vampire, right?"

I sigh. The revelation is going worse than I had expected.

"Mockery doesn't help. I screamed at the gods to return you to me. And they agreed to my demands, but after their own inhuman fashion. They made me a tepictli. A mountain demigod. Said you would return once they were satisfied with my service."

Blanca bursts into hysterical laughter, tears running down her cheeks. "Ay, no manches, now you're a *demigod*? Talk about delusions of grandeur. Row me back, Greg. Now."

"I need you to believe me. My heart is bound to Popocatepetl. Wherever I go, magma responds to my moods. All the recent activity at Steamboat Springs? That was me. I can wield that heat."

The crystal glasses we just drank from lie tumbled before me. I reach out a finger.

"Ma chinolo," I whisper.

In seconds, it melts to slag, burning through the picnic blanket and fusing with the soil beneath it. Her eyes go wide, but she shakes her head.

"No. You're filthy rich. You renovated a town in less than a week. Who knows what tricks you've got set up?"

Leaping to my feet, I grab the bottle of mineral water and lift it into the air.

"You *must believe me*," I moan. My hand erupts into flame. The bottle melts, raining liquid glass all around me.

Blanca screams.

"I'll set this isle on fire to prove that what I say is true!" I shout above her horror. I want to stop, want to let her go.

But she has to crack. Has to let her old self through.

Lifting my other hand, I let flames erupt upon my skin and take a step toward her.

"No!" she gasps. "Don't!"

Shuddering with sobs, I scream back at her, "Then stop me! You're the only one who can! Remember what you did in AP Chemistry class? You smothered that flame, by instinct. I'm so sorry, Blanca. BUT YOU MUST PROTECT YOURSELF NOW!"

I shove at her with living fire, enough to burn any human to an instant crisp.

Howling in terror, Blanca raises her perfect white arms, crossing them in an X.

And dead cold winter slams against me, extinguishing my flame like a sputtering candle, knocking me on my back.

"Yes!" I shout. "Unleash the chill that stifles your soul! Your heart is bound to the dead volcano of Iztaccihuatl. Just as fire burns in my heart, ice creaks in your own!"

I clamber to my feet even as a groaning blizzard continues to swirl around us.

Then, I stop holding the magma back. I become a raging bonfire.

"Hold me!" I beg. "Hold me and be broken. Hold me and remember."

But Blanca shakes her head as pummeling waves of cold flow from her, shoving me aside and freezing the lake all around the isle.

When she realizes she no longer needs the boat, my beloved steps onto the ice. Seeing that it holds her weight, she begins to run.

Fleeing from me.

"Blanca?" My padrino raps lightly on my door. "Blanca? Are you in there?"

I open my eyes and look around my bedroom, disoriented. My lids hurt, and I reach up and press my fingertips against them. They *are* swollen, and tender, and that's when I start to remember things. We were swimming, Greg and I. And kissing. Yes, we were kissing. But then, things got strange. And weird. And I ran. I ran through the wilderness, trampled on weeds and brush, climbed rocky hills, and fell once or twice, until, finally, I ran up here, to my room, and fell on the bed and cried myself to sleep.

"Open the door," my padrino insists, knocking again. "You have visitors."

"Visitors?" I reach for my phone. It's 10:00 p.m. Saturday night. Then, because he knocks harder, I call out.

"Blanca, are you okay?" It's Tina, and she sounds worried.

"We need to talk to you," Sofía says.

"The girls are worried about you," my padrino says. He must be desperate, to give the girls such importance over his own desire to dictate what goes on in my life.

Sofía sounds more cautious than worried when she says, "Blanca? Can we come in? You said we were going to study tonight. Remember?"

Study for what? I'm about to contradict the comment when I realize what Sofía is saying is code—for whatever reason they're really here.

Could it be they heard from Greg? No. He couldn't—wouldn't have called them. Not after . . .

"Blanca?" Tina calls again.

"I'm coming," I say, and I crawl out of bed, check my face in the mirror, and rub the dried tearstains away, before I open the door.

The girls look relieved when I stand aside to let them in. They both peck my cheek as they walk into my room. My padrino is standing a few feet away, half turned, as if he doesn't know whether to leave right away.

"Everything all right?" he asks. His eyes narrow as he takes in my disheveled hair and crumpled clothes.

"Yeah," I tell him. "I just . . . lost track of time."

"Girl, what's going on?" Tina hisses when I close the door and lock it behind me.

"What do you mean?" I ask, as I walk past them and fall onto my bed, covering myself up to my neck with my colcha.

"Greg's freaking out," Sofía says. "He called me, all torn up, saying he'd ruined everything with you. What did you do to him?"

What did I do to him? I grab my favorite purple pillow and hug it against my chest. Then I remember . . . "I didn't . . . I couldn't . . ."

"Blanca?" Sofía's voice is gentle, almost motherly as she moves a strand of my hair away from my cold cheeks. My lips start to quiver, and she soothes me. "Shh . . . You're all right."

"What happened?" Tina asks, shaking me as I close my eyes and try to slip away from the memories. "Did Greg hurt you? Because if he did . . ."

"No," I say, putting it all out of my mind, tucking it away where I can't see it again. "No."

"So . . . you're okay, then?" Tina asks.

"I'm so cold," I say and pull my blanket tighter around me. "I just need . . ."

"To rest," Sofía whispers. "It sounds like you might be coming down with something."

I nod. "Yes."

They sit quietly by my side, and I get the impression they don't quite know what to do. At that very moment, someone taps on the door. Tina opens it and smiles at Rosario, who walks calmly into the room holding a tray in front of her. "I've brought some refreshments, at your padrino's request, but also some caldito de pollo, because you missed dinner."

"Thank you, Rosario. That smells delicious," I say, sitting up as Rosario puts the tray on my nightstand, but I am so tired I can't fathom the idea of getting out of bed to eat.

Rosario leaves the room quietly, and the girls watch as I settle back against my headboard and close my eyes.

Tina and Sofía look at each other earnestly. "We should go. Let you get some rest," Sofía whispers. "We can talk more tomorrow, when you're feeling better."

"Yeah, we just wanted to make sure you were okay," Tina says.

"Forgive me," I say as they scoot in beside me after Rosario moves away. "I'm just . . ."

"It's okay," Sofía says. "No need to explain."

Tina leans over and hugs me. "It's okay to do this, you know. You gotta do what you gotta do to protect yourself. We'll talk later."

Yes. Yes, my mind whispers, as the door closes behind the girls. Nestling into my pillows, I close my eyes and force myself to take slow, shallow breaths to stop my heart from beating so fast.

You must protect yourself now. That is exactly what Gregorio Chan said before he turned into a volcano, before he caught on fire and scared me half out of my mind. That he's some kind of divine entity—a demigod, the warrior Popoca. And me? He said I am the chick from the Nahua myth, Iztac.

Only I know I'm not her. I can't be. I'm Blanca Rosa Montes.

I remember now.

Once my head stops spinning, I curl up under my blanket again and fall asleep. In my dreams, Greg is a flickering flame, burning bright, reaching out, scalding me with his breath, searing me with his touch, and because he demands it, I protect myself. I cross my arms in front of myself and freeze him out.

When I wake up the sun is so bright in my room, and I know I've slept too long. I roll over in bed and cover my eyes with the back of my hand. At least, the world isn't spinning, and I'm not disoriented anymore.

I touch my eyelids.

Nope. Not swollen anymore. And my cheeks feel cool to the touch. Too cool, for someone who's been lying in the sunlight for hours. That's when it happens. Greg's words drift out of the shadows of my mind and linger in my thoughts: *Remember what you did in AP Chemistry class? You smothered that flame, by instinct. You smothered that flame, by instinct. By instinct, by instinct, by instinct!*

The words unfurl themselves from the shadows of my memory and swirl around me, like old maple leaves caught up in a windstorm, repeating themselves, over and over again in my head, until I open my eyes, sit up, and admit it myself.

I didn't just protect myself.

I created a shield of ice.

I have powers?

The thought is unnerving. I get dressed and leave my room, because I need time and space to think, to breathe, to make sense of it all. I forgo the brunch Rosario offers to put together for me and walk out of the house, escaping quietly through the French doors in the family room. Before I know it, I am walking along the garden path in our backyard, heading toward the floral hedge maze beyond the pool.

I used to play here with my mother when I was a child, and I know just how to get lost so my padrino won't see me trying to re-create that thing I did in chem class. The rambling rosebushes growing on tall trellises are thick enough to keep me from being seen, and I make sure I'm behind one when I take my first shot at unleashing the chill that *stifles my soul*, according to Gregorio Chan.

Readying myself, I take deep breaths, until my heartbeat slows down enough that I am confident I can do this . . . I can release the coldness I feel deep inside. Then I lean forward and breathe onto a blushing, fresh rose. The delicate pink petals flutter, quivering at the assault. But when I lean back, I see that nothing has happened. The rose is as fresh and unchanged as it was before.

Refusing to give up, I yank on a leaflet and pull it off the vine. The three small leaves on the sprig tremble in the wind, and I pull it close to my lips, repeating the experiment by taking a deep breath, concentrating, and deliberately breathing coldly, dispassionately, over it.

That's when it happens. The leaves look completely different, frosty and cold. I am enthralled by the icy sprig at my fingertips, trying to figure out how this happened, how I can do this, when I hear footsteps on the other side of the trellis.

"Yes, of course you have my permission," I hear my padrino hissing, and I freeze. He is clearly upset with someone. "I already told you. I don't want him anywhere near her. Do whatever you have to do to get him out of the picture."

Who's he talking about? I wonder, as I stand there, eavesdropping on my padrino's conversation. I know he comes out here often, to walk while he takes care of social things on the phone, catching up with investors, setting up golf games, stuff like that. However, this doesn't sound congenial at all. This sounds intense. Serious. Hostile.

"I don't know! You did it once before; I'm sure you can find a way now," my padrino continues. "Yes, yes, but whatever you do don't touch Blanca. She is the key. She is the kingdom. Without her, I have no power. Understand?"

The words *You did it once before* stab at my side, like a spear pushed under my rib cage, but I push the pain away because other words are swirling around in my head, overshadowing my thoughts.

She is the key. She is the kingdom. The words bounce off the recesses of my mind, reverberating inside me, amplified by the blood rushing to my head, beating against my eardrum, and I close my eyes.

She is the key. The key. The key. The key.

Without her, I have no power.

As they spin and swirl in my head, the words trigger a memory, and I have a vision . . . *a shadowy figure, a broad-shouldered man dressed in ancient garb, dark robes with glinting metal ornamentation from a place and culture I do not recognize.* Instantly, I know this happened in an ancient world, way before my time. How or why I am there, listening in the darkness, I don't quite understand. But I stand frozen in place, trying to comprehend, to recollect, to grasp the wisp of what is rising like a nightmare out of the darkness of my mind. I feel faint, and I reach up and grab on to the vines of hearty rose-bushes clinging to the tall trellis for support.

She is the kingdom. The kingdom. The kingdom.

Without her, I have no power.

The words are the same, but the voice is different—deeper, darker. More sadistic. *The shadowy figure is standing with his co-conspirators, dark, skulking figures who look at the ground and nod. I want to step forward, come out of the darkness, but I have to be quiet. I have to find out what he is plotting.*

Suddenly, as quickly as it came, the vision dissipates.

I open my eyes, and I am back in my time. Only I am not gripping the rose vines in front of me, eavesdropping on my padrino. I am alone in the garden maze, looking down at my numb hands, alarmed by the coldness of the frozen noose I am holding before me.

Horrified, I scream and drop the loop of ice. It shatters on the brick walkway, like an ancient crystal artifact, sending a thousand shards of ice flying around my feet. I step back from that malevolence, turn, and run.

As if in slow motion, I run through the maze, twisting this way and that, my breath leaving my lips in tiny puffs of air that crystalize as I rush, rush, rush—until I break through the thicket and stop. There, at what feels like the edge of time, I stand still, arms outstretched, balancing myself so as not to fall into the deep end of the pool in our very own backyard.

As I teeter there, on the brink of tumbling over and plunging into that resplendent pool, another vision comes into my subconscious. *A dark image wavers and unravels, becoming more and more tangible, until it is superimposed on my sight, and I realize I am on the*

*verge of plummeting into a roiling river, where a fearsome jaguar
awaits my fall.*

My phone pings, and the sound pulls me back, back, back from
the vision. My eyes refocus, and I stand as disoriented as if I were
waking up from a terrible nightmare. Horrified, I step away from
the edge of our pool. I have no recollection of how I got there. Standing a few feet back now, I look at the text message. It's Tina, checking
up on me.

TINA: *hey, feeling any better?*

ME: *Yes. No. I'm not sure.*

TINA: *what do you mean you're not sure?*

ME: *Something's happened. Can you come over?*

When I tell Tina what I overheard in the garden, she freaks out,
which is the reason I didn't tell her what I was doing out there. That
would send her over the edge, and I need her to focus on what my
padrino said.

"So you think he killed them?" she asks, sitting beside me on my
bed, whispering so low she's almost mouthing the words.

"I don't know. It's all so . . . foggy."

"Sure," Tina says, gently stroking my arm. "I mean, you've had a
rough few days. Hallucinating, well, I'm not sure, but it might be
a symptom of dehydration. I'll have to look it up . . ."

"No, I don't think I imagined it. I'm pretty sure he said it. Whoever he was talking to, he told them to get rid of him, and then he
reminded them they'd done it before. I mean, who else could he be
talking about? Who else would he want dead before, except *my
parents?*"

"I knew it," she hisses, as we sit huddled under the canopy of my
bed, "I knew something was up. When he wouldn't invite Ms. Fillmore to the grand opening, I knew something was going on. It made

no sense to keep them away, except, of course, to make sure you don't give away your parents' fortune, the fortune he worked hard to control."

The horror of it strikes me, and I cry out. "By killing them!"

"That's like straight out of a crime drama," Tina whispers. "And who would do this for him? What kind of psycho is he involved with?"

"I don't know," I say. "It was all so vague. It could have been anyone, maybe even someone I haven't met."

"If you ask me, this is all connected to you taking off with Greg. Maybe he's the target," Tina says.

"Greg?" I ask. "Okay, but what would make Greg a target like that? I mean, to order a hit on him? That's just . . . insane!"

Tina takes my hands and holds them tightly between us. "There's got to be more to this than your amorío with Greg. And we have to figure things out before it's too late."

Thinking about everything that's happened, how connected Greg is with the local authorities, and especially the powers he showcased for me at the lake, I am sure he has nothing to worry about.

"Do me a favor," I tell her. "Let's keep this between us. Just until I figure out what my padrino is trying to do."

"But don't you want to warn Greg?" Tina asks.

"Trust me," I tell her. "Gregorio Chan can take care of himself."

CHAPTER

27

Sitting across from me at the table are Sofía Cisneros and Teresa Segundo.

Their eyes shine with the same mischievous light. Their disapproving frowns threaten to become smiles.

"We tried to warn you," Sofía begins, "that it's hard to wake them up."

"One by one," Teresa continues. "Their present selves are too strong."

I've been wallowing in self-pity since yesterday afternoon. Blanca is ghosting me. Little Sister and Tina visited her, so I know she's confused.

I've ruined our reunion. Twelve hundred years, and I've learned nothing. I'm still the impatient warrior willing to risk everything for love but lacking whatever's needed to hold on to it.

Tears on my cheeks, I push my chair back and fall to my knees.

"Lady Cotton, Weaver of Fate, Goddess of Vice, and Eater of Sin, help me. Restore my beloved's memories so that we can finally be reunited."

Sofía stands first, looking down at me with compassion.

"We can do that, Goyo, but you know the deal. We tangled their souls in a skein."

"To open Blanca to her previous life," Teresa reminds me as she stands as well, "is to open them all. They'll even remember what happened to their souls after their deaths."

Sofía picks up the thread. "Our plan was to redeem them together. We've got a pretty good idea who's who, but we're not positive. It's going to get messy. Are you ready for the fallout?"

I touch my head to the tiled floor. "Yes, Dear Lady."

Teresa nods. "All right. We'll get to work. Expect big changes, Popocatzin. All hell's about to break loose."

"In the meanwhile," Sofía adds as both close their eyes and shudder, "you'll have to return to Mexico. You'll be gone about a week."

"What? Why would I—"

"Three," they say in unison, "two, one."

Stilson bursts in, chest heaving. "My lord. It's Roberto Chan. Your *father*. He . . . has just suffered a massive heart attack."

No matter how many loved ones you lose, the anguish is always bright and biting. I stand so suddenly that I feel dizzy.

"Get the jet ready. I want to leave as soon as possible."

That evening, I'm sitting in the VIP visitors lounge of Médica Sur Hospital in Mexico City, consoling Dolores. Though the world knows her as my mother, she was a teenager when I returned to my volcano. We haven't spoken in person since I left for the US.

Still, while she never got a chance to mother me, my affection for her endures.

The decades have only brought her beauty and wisdom into sharper relief.

"This operation," she manages to say. She turns red eyes on me. "Please, do whatever you can to intercede. We were looking forward to a decade or so of peaceful retirement. Fifty-two years he dedicated to stewarding your business empire."

"Yes," I say. "I've remembered your families' long dedication to my cause."

Dolores averts her gaze. "And we are not ungrateful, Gregorio. But I am greedy for his love. Every moment, until we breathe our last."

I think of Blanca, whose heart I have so broken she cannot bear to speak or write to me. How did I teach Roberto to treat his wife better than I have my own love?

"I promise he'll be fine. You will have your happy ending. Nonantzin."

She smiles when I call her *mother*. Wiping her eyes, she puts her small hands on mine. "I can see your anguish. It isn't just Roberto's health that worries you. It's Lady Iztac, yes?"

It's my turn to look away. "I was arrogant. Believed I knew precisely what to do when I found her. But I've ruined everything."

"I doubt that, Gregorio. Be patient. Often, that's all we mortals can do. Step away for a moment from those we've hurt, giving them space and time to heal and forgive us."

Wise words. I kiss her forehead and settle in for my own long wait.

Once the doctors awaken us to report that the operation has been a success, I leave Dolores to sit beside my unconscious father while Stilson drives me to our mansion in nearby Bosque de Tlalpan. The estate sprawls amid the pine forest, reminding me of many other homes, especially the Glass Castle. For a moment, I imagine Blanca, emerging at a run from the tree line to greet me with a tight embrace. Amazing how my pulse quickens even at the thought of her.

The mayordomo is leading me to the room they've prepared for me when I bump into myself. My double. My doppelganger. Aside from slight differences in height, bone structure, and eye color, he could easily be mistaken for me.

"Oh," I say. "You're the other Gregorio Chan."

"No," he mutters in English, irritated, "I'm the *real* Gregorio Chan. Mother and Father changed my name when they adopted me. I've lived my entire life as their son."

I understand his resentment. I just don't have patience for it right now.

"And I assume you were told many times *why* you were adopted, *why* you bore that name, *why* you went to the best schools in the world, *why* you enjoyed such riches."

He gives a curt nod. "Yes. And for the longest time, I was smitten by the idea. By your romantic quest. By the chance to play the part of a literal demigod. It got me through the homesickness I felt when I was at school in Europe, through the multiple plastic surgeries over the years. But now you're awake, you've found your beloved, and the rest of us are screwed."

I sigh.

"In what way, Kevin?" I ask, using the new name he's picked.

"Every other time you've woken up, you've spent years easing yourself into a new life. Your double has had a chance to get used to the idea of losing his name, his friends, his life. He's had time to make the transition into a new identity. His adoptive parents, too. But that cycle's over. You have what you wanted. The rest of us are scrambling to find meaning as our system crumbles. Me. My parents. The villagers of Santiago Xalitzintla. All your faithful followers. What awaits us, Popocatzin? How quickly will you discard us?"

Tears are running down his face.

He's afraid. Of abandonment. Of losing everything that matters.

How have I let the ones I care about feel such existential terror? How did I get so wrapped up in my own needs that I forgot about theirs?

I don't want to be that sort of leader.

"My friend," I whisper, reaching out to grab his shoulders. "I'll never abandon you or any of the rest. I swore an oath to the Divine Mother to love you, to keep you safe, to make sure you never lacked anything. And that's what I'm going to do. As planned, you'll become my cousin, rising fast to sit beside me as vice president. Dolores and Roberto will retire comfortably to our island off the coast of Yucatan, where you and I will visit them often in their remaining years. And the villagers who've given me their sons and daughters, who've kept my secrets and guarded my slopes? They'll have all they want for as many centuries as my wealth lasts. My children, if the gods bless me with any, will protect Santiago Xalitzintla forever with every ounce of our power."

I pull him into an embrace. He resists for a moment, but then he hugs me back.

"You promised, dear cousin," he mutters against my neck. "With all the gods watching."

I loosen my grip enough to look him in the eyes. "Yes, I did, Kevin Chan. You've got a lifetime to hold me to it."

———————

A few hours later, once Roberto has awakened, I sit by his side, holding his hand.

"I'm so sorry," I say. "I put you in this position."

"Ah, nonsense," he replies. "How could my aging heart be your fault?"

I kiss his hand. "I almost ruined everything, Roberto. The gods had to resort to this emergency to pull me away before I caused irreparable harm. I'm sure of it. Now I can only pray that Ixcuinan's wisdom and power can set us back on the right path."

He chuckles, wincing at the pain of it. "So long-lived and yet so naïve. Is it because you slough off most memories during regeneration?"

"Sadly, much of my past wisdom is just written up for my future reference, rather than coming to me instinctively."

"Then let this old man set you straight. You haven't ruined anything, Popocatzin. The gods didn't give me heart failure. Some bad things just happen. And what do we do? What did you tell me a thousand times we do when the world goes wrong, my lord?"

I swallow heavily, tears in my eyes.

"We fix it," I whisper.

That night I send a text to Blanca, explaining that my father is ill and that I'll be back soon. Her response is brief:

Ok.

I'm relieved. Short and sweet is better than long and final.

I spend the rest of the week with family, both old and new. Kevin and I take turns keeping Roberto company in the hospital as he recovers, making sure that Dolores gets plenty of rest as well, despite her insistence on being at her beloved's bedside day and night.

By the weekend, he is released. The Chan family has a permanent table reserved at Tepeton, a renowned Michelin-starred restaurant in the Polanco neighborhood, and Chef Óliver Enríquez treats us to his latest dish.

As we're waiting for dessert, the pleasant conversation and joking winds down. I stare at Roberto for a while, happy to see him strong and smiling. He seems a man who can last another three decades, at least.

"What, Gregorio?" he asks. "You look somber all of a sudden."

"It's just that . . . I've been so selfish. I haven't thought about how my needs impacted the folks who have supported me over the centuries, and I didn't consider Blanca's feelings, either."

Roberto reaches across the table and pats my hand. "All you have to do is say you're sorry and change your behavior. That's another lesson you taught me when I was just a brat. It's okay to make mistakes. But then you have to do better."

I turn to Dolores with a smile. "He turned out pretty good, didn't he?"

Her chuckle chimes almost heavenly through the air. "Yes, he did, my lord. The best."

CHAPTER

28

I spend the first part of the week ignoring Greg's text messages. Mostly because I am still confused. I love him. I do, and I desperately want to see him, hold him, kiss him, but I also need time to process what happened between us and what Tina and I suspect about my padrino's true nature.

I've spent the last few days in my parents' room, pretending to linger there out of nostalgia and residual grief when, in reality, I'm looking for anything that might help me figure out if my padrino was behind their accident. I just wish I could find something— newspaper clippings, old photographs, a journal or diary—anything that might incriminate him.

But that's not all that's weighing on my mind. There is that other thing—the discovery that I can do things no other human can do— *supernatural things*. I haven't talked to Tina or Sofía about my so-called powers because, well, I don't quite know what to make of them.

To my surprise, Wednesday evening Tina shows up to dinner. After following Rosario into the dining room, she slides into the chair to my left, lets out a long sigh, and takes a sip of my water.

"Hello?" my padrino says, quirking an eyebrow at Rosario, who shrugs and shakes her head. "Did you need something?"

"Oh, I'm sorry." Tina places a hand over her chest. "Did I come on the wrong day?"

My padrino frowns at me.

Tina kicks my foot under the table, and, taking my cue, I fake a giggle. "Oh my God! I forgot to tell you. I hope you don't mind, but I invited Tina to dinner. Rosario? Do we have enough for one more?"

"Of course she does," Tina says. "You know what Mami says when you come over, donde come uno, comen dos."

My padrino shakes his head and motions to Rosario, and she rushes off to the kitchen. Within minutes, she comes back with a place setting, utensils, and a glass of water for Tina.

"And to what do we owe this honor?" my padrino asks me, forcing a smile.

"Honor?" Tina feigns bewilderment, and now it's my turn to kick her under the table.

"What's the special occasion? Surely there's a reason for this intru . . . *invitation*." My padrino gives his attention to the Niçoise salad Rosario sets in front of him.

"Her parents are busy tonight, so I told her to come over. I didn't think you'd mind. It's not like she's never eaten with us before," I say.

"That's right," Tina says, as Rosario puts our salads in front of us. "Like when I went with you to Mexico City. We shared many meals together then."

"We did," my padrino acknowledges.

"Where else have you all taken me?" she asks. "Utah. Arizona. Didn't we go to New Mexico a few times?"

"Well, now that we're done reminiscing, can we get on with the meal?" My padrino digs into his salad.

"We had such a good time. We went sightseeing with Rosario and ate together every day." Tina twirls her fork in the air and smiles before she stabs at the greens in her salad. "But only at dinnertime, because your padrino always had business meetings. You remember that?" Tina turns in her chair to face my padrino. "How you were always off to work?"

My padrino's eyes narrow.

"I fail to understand the purpose of this conversation. Why don't we just eat our dinner before it gets cold," my padrino says, and he cuts into the ribeye that Rosario has brought out.

"It's been a while since you took a real vacation with your padrino, hasn't it, Blanca? You know, one without all that business," Tina finally says, talking to me as if we are the only two people in the room.

I gaze over at my padrino, but he doesn't say anything.

"I guess it gets old," Tina mumbles, "dragging someone else's kids around every time you have to go out on business. I'm sure that's not what you signed up for when you promised her parents you'd take care of my girl here. Of course, you never expected them to die, did you?"

My padrino turns to look at Tina so quickly it startles me. "Excuse me?"

"I mean, how could you?" Tina shrugs a shoulder dismissively.

Tears spring to my eyes, and my voice trembles, when I look at him and say, "How could anybody?"

My padrino drops his knife and fork. They clatter against the fine china when he slams his hand on the table. Then, because he sees the tears in my eyes, he sits back and gathers himself, considers his words, before he stands up.

"Let me make this clear." My padrino leans over his plate and addresses Tina directly. "There was no business taking place during our vacations. I took you both skiing. White-water rafting. Hiking. I even rented a balloon and got sick for the experience . . . We went all over this country. And abroad. I don't know what you're implying here, but I will not have you tarnish every good thing I've attempted to do for my ahijada. In her best interest. To keep the promise I made to her parents!"

"I'm sorry," I whisper. "Tina didn't mean to imply anything. Did you, Tina?"

"No, of course not." Tina's big, innocent eyes and impish half smile do nothing to help the situation, and I kick her under the table again, because I just want this strange, uncomfortable dinner to be over so I can ask Tina what in the world is going on.

"I'll get you some gravy," Rosario says, stepping away from the table.

"Don't bother. I've lost my appetite." My padrino's phone beeps in his pocket. He pulls it and checks it. "I have to go. But, please, don't let my departure ruin your dinner. You two have a good evening."

"Oh, we will," Tina says, stabbing a slice of sauteed zucchini and popping it in her mouth with relish.

"What the hell's wrong with you?" I ask Tina when we go back to my room.

"Don't be mad," she says. "I needed to test my theory."

"What?"

"Just listen, okay." Tina plops herself on the chaise beside my bay window. "The night of the big fiesta in Carrizo, I got wind of something . . . and I think it's big."

"How big?"

"Huge. After you left, I hung back and talked to some fans. And that's when it happened. Some locals got sloshed—hasta las teclas—and told me it's ironic that you, the heir to Montes Realty of all people, should be the reason their water issues were finally resolved."

"I don't understand."

Tina sits forward in the chaise. "Well, they sort of implied that your family business is the reason they have water issues to begin with. I mean, they never said it. But they kinda said it."

"Montes Realty has nothing to do with Carrizo. We don't manage any of their properties."

"Don't you?" Tina arches an eyebrow. "Then why was your padrino so uncomfortable when I mentioned he had business in all those places? Do you know what else is in Utah, Arizona, and New Mexico?"

I gasp. "Indigenous communities with water issues!"

"Yes!" Tina slams her small fist on the bed. "Water issues that were brought on by builders and corporations encroaching on them."

"Yes. But this doesn't mean . . ."

"Think about it." Tina stands up, hands on her hips. "Why was he so flustered when I reminded him he was doing business in those states? Who sold those lands to those corporations?"

"My padrino?"

"It has to be him!" Tina punches the air. "Why else would he want to vacation there, if he wasn't selling Indigenous people out and making a bundle doing it?"

"Are you sure? How can we prove that? I mean, those are some serious accusations," I say as I start pacing the floor.

The more I think about it, the colder I get. Sure, my padrino lets me see the company's business reports, but it's not like I have full access to the company files, know the inner workings, the behind-the-scenes day-to-day dealings.

Tina flips her long, dark hair back. "Well, there's only one way to do that," she says, and she steps past me and opens the bedroom door. "Shall we . . . enter the lion's den?"

"His office?" I ask.

"Come on. He won't even know we were there."

In the office, we skim through files. My fingers fly through the rows of contract folders. I pull a stack of them, and we read through the pages, but we don't find anything tying him to sales in those communities.

"What is this?"

I jump and Tina screams, because my padrino's voice is a loud thunderclap that bounces off the walls. My hands tremble as I straighten up.

"Nothing," I say. "We were just . . ."

My padrino waits for me to finish my thought.

"Go on . . . ," he says.

"Pictures. We were looking for pictures," Tina says, stepping away from the desk.

My padrino's eyes narrow. "Pictures."

"Well, not just any pictures. We were reminiscing, and I remembered the time my parents took me to Africa," I tell my padrino. "I don't have any pictures of it."

My padrino comes forward and assesses the mess we've made on his desk. "And you thought for some strange reason they might be in my desk?"

"Well, one thing led to another and . . ." Tina shrugs, smiling at him.

"And you decided to snoop around in my business." My padrino's curt words send a chill down my spine. But it's not fear or discomfort that makes my blood turn cold in my veins. No. It's his word choice that upsets me.

"You mean *our* business, don't you?" I ask.

My padrino is silent as he taps a bunch of files against the dark mahogany and shoves them back into the bottom drawer. "That is what I meant," he finally says. Then he gives the drawer a hard push and slams it shut. "You may look at anything in this office anytime you want. Just know that I keep no mementos here. That is all in the family room. Where it belongs."

"Well, I'm sorry, but I have to go now," Tina says, breaking the tension in the room. "Walk me out?"

I walk Tina to the door, and she slips out sedately, because she knows my padrino has cameras aimed at the entryway. When I turn around and rush back to my room, I almost bump into my padrino.

"I know I can't forbid you to see that girl," he says, putting his hand on my shoulder. I freeze, waiting for the earlier vision I had in the garden to come back to me, but it doesn't. "Teenagers thrive on disobeying their parental figures, but I don't want to see her at our table ever again."

I nod, push past him, and run up the stairs to my room.

As I lie staring at the ceiling, trying to decide how to investigate this without my padrino finding out, my phone pings in my pocket. It's Greg, giving me an update on his father's condition. My heart tightens inside my chest, because I can only imagine what he's going through. And because I'm not there to support him, comfort him in his time of need, I press the heel of my hand against my lashes and wipe hot tears from my face.

I want to call him back. But I don't know what to say, how to talk to him, without letting what happened on that last awful date color our conversation. It's not every day that your boyfriend turns into a fiery monster and claims you are reincarnated lovers from an ancient civilization. Anyone in their right mind would have a problem with that . . . and the powers . . . Do I really have supernatural powers? How did this happen? Why? I can't understand, because everything Greg said, everything I've experienced, well, it's all too surreal.

No, this is something we have to sort out in person. But I can't ignore this text. So, I send him a quick "Ok" back, because I don't know what else to say. I suspect Tina is mulling things over too, because the rest of the week goes on without incident.

Friday afternoon, however, things shift. After school, Sofía and Tina come looking for me in Ms. Dresch's room. I'm supposed to take them home, but I'm busy reading through the script *Corazones de Fuego y Hielo*, the one-act play our principal wrote about the myth of the two volcanoes, because she wants us to perform it.

"Oh, that sounds wonderful!" Sofía's eyes glitter with excitement. "Wouldn't that be fun, Blanca? To work with me and Tina on a play? Oh, maybe we can get Greg and Tony to be in it! I can totally see Greg playing Popoca!"

Sofía's suggestion shocks me, because she has no idea how true that might actually be. Pushing the thought aside, I turn to Tina because I'm not sure we can get involved with this right now, not when we're trying to investigate my padrino. "I don't know," I say, giving Tina a meaningful gaze. "We have so much going on—especially outside of school."

Instead of Tina siding with me, her eyes soften. "Oh, okay, but only because you said you can get the guys to join us."

232

"Really?" I ask. "With everything we have to do?"

"Aww, come on," Tina says. "Look at her. Nobody can say no to that face."

I'm not sure how I feel about doing this, and I'm especially apprehensive about recruiting Greg. Not before we've had a chance to sort ourselves out first. Then, because I want to make sure we slow down and think about who we are casting, I turn to address Ms. Dresch.

"I don't know about Tony, but Greg's out of town," I remind her. "He had a family emergency. I'm not sure when he'll be back. Do we have to start tomorrow? Can't it wait till next week?"

"I'll text Tony." Tina pulls out her phone. "See if he can make it tomorrow."

"Principal Primo thought we might do a read-through with her at the parish tomorrow morning." Ms. Dresch nods at us. "It would give us an opportunity to get a feel for the space, before we start blocking."

The next morning, at 8:00 a.m. sharp, Tina, Sofía, and I drive up to St. Rose of Lima, on Bishop Manogue Drive. My stomach tightens when I see Greg is already there, standing with Tony in front of his Phantom. I should be furious at him—for putting me through that hellish experience. But I have to admit his absence created a hole in my heart. I've spent a week trying not to think about him and failing miserably.

One look into him, and I am undone. I want to run to him, wrap my arms around his neck, cover that beloved face with kisses. But I don't because, the truth is, I don't know how to react to him. I'm a tangled mess of emotions. And if he says something—anything—about the other day, I might just break down in tears.

"Hey!" Sofía grins and waves as we approach them. "You made it."

Tony waves back. "Yeah, couldn't let my man go at it alone. I'm no actor; that's my dad's thing. But moral support, I can do that."

"Greg?" My voice sounds small, warbled, and I clear my throat.

Greg looks at me expectantly. He makes a small gesture, extends his arm just slightly, a tentative invitation to hold hands. Warmth begins to build deep down inside me, filling me with an overwhelming desire to be close to him, to reach out and put my hand inside his.

For a second, I can almost believe his fantastic story. How else to explain our connection, so much stronger than should be possible for a high school fling? So, I take strength from love and take his hand. He leans in and kisses me lightly, before he whispers, "I missed you, notlazohtzin."

In that moment, my fear and resentment fade. I know that we will sort our problems out, in our own time, at our own pace. Suddenly, I remember that he was gone for such a long time because his family needed him.

"What are you doing here?" I ask, pulling back to look at him. "I thought you were staying in Mexico for a while."

Greg's eyes soften, and he gives me a crooked smile.

"And miss an opportunity to play Popoca to your Iztac?" he asks. "No. Father's better, and I couldn't pass this up. Not in this lifetime."

My heart feels full, though I'm nervous. Blanca has forgiven me. I steal glances at her as we follow Ms. Dresch inside the church. We walk through a waist-high gate near the baptismal font, then down the aisle and into the broad space before the altar. Above it, behind the crucifix, hangs a stained glass representation of a mountain. Golgotha, though it could be Mount Rose. Or one of Iztaccihuatl's peaks.

"It's a good space," Blanca says, nodding. "Not much more scenery needed."

Ms. Dresch appears to agree. "All that's left is to set the tone. Sofía, I got your text this morning. There's something you wanted to read first?"

"Yes, ma'am. I translated 'The Idyll of the Volcanoes' by José Santos Chocano. A famous poem. The final lines could help the mood."

Our teacher gives a thumbs-up. "Go ahead."

Sofía walks up the steps to stand behind the altar. Blanca sucks in air, shocked at such sacrilege. Little Sister winks, then lifts her arms. The lights in the sanctuary flicker as she begins to declaim.

"And Popocatzin broke his quiver
across his knees and howled, full wroth,
conjuring the shades of his ancestors
against the cruelty of impassive gods.
His life was his, bought dearly
by defeating once certain death:
his the triumph, the wealth, the power
but not his love, now still of breath.
In his arms he took his cold bride
and into the heights did he stride
to light a fire there at her side
and await in a sarcophagus of pain
for his beloved to return again."

Then Sofía's voice doubles, trebles, becoming a chorus of four as she ends the poem with divine words no mortal man has ever set to paper, a convocation that pulls at our souls.

"Sleep no more, Iztaccihuatl,
shake off your mantle of snow
and see who stands vigil beside you,
like a torch that forever glows.
Awaken, dear princess of Tollan—
help us heal with your frigid hands
all the wounded hearts
that fate has torn apart."

Energy crackles through the air as the lights dim and clouds obscure the sun outside. Tina murmurs something. Tony stifles a cry at the strange flickering and deep groan that begins to thrum along the walls and floor, as if the cosmos itself were about to split open.

Then all falls quiet and still.

Ms. Dresch gasps, leaning against a pew, eyes unfocused till they lock on to me, tears trembling. Around me, three other heads turn, compelled by the shock of understanding to look at the one face they all remember, the one that in twelve hundred years has never changed.

Tina. Tony. And my girl, Blanca.

Lips trembling. Joy and horror mixing in their features.

I clear my throat and mutter, "Hey, friends."

Ms. Dresch drops to one knee, bowing her head. "Lord Popocatzin."

Sofía bounces on tiptoes. "It worked!"

I stare at Blanca, waiting for the war in her features to resolve itself. Then her eyes soften, and I address Iztac for the first time in twelve centuries.

"Beloved."

She gives a shaky nod, a smile spreading across her face. "It's me, notlazohyohtzin. Us. Both Blanca and Iztac."

I hurry over and hug her tight. There is no hesitation. Her arms lock around me as she breathes, shuddering, into my shoulder. Then we pull apart, gazing into each other's eyes as once we did in the palace gardens.

"I've spent a millennium," I whisper, "searching the world for signs you had returned."

"Looking down from paradise," she answered, "I also longed to return, to still the roiling of your molten heart and live a new life by your side."

Then our lips come together in a kiss that transcends history.

The contact of flesh and spirit make the four walls of the parish fade as if we stood for a moment on the highest summits.

The real world gradually returns. As if he's been waiting for the right moment, Tony walks toward Annabel Dresch, anguish on his features.

"Which one are you?" he pleads.

She looks up, face full of hope.

"Huixachin. Oldest daughter of the emperor."

Tony sags for a moment, but then he crouches before her.

"Big Sister, it's me. The one you plotted with. Who stabbed your first husband by your side. The one who killed his own father and mother on the battlefield. Your half-sibling. Your Little Brother. Your husband."

Annabel's hands go to her mouth. She rocks backward, and for a moment I think she'll flee. But instead, she leans forward and takes Tony in her arms.

"Meconetzin, my dear! I wandered centuries as a shade in the Realm of the Dead, searching for you. Those trials couldn't release me from the weight of our sin, but I hoped that together we'd find a way toward salvation."

Sobs wrack Tony's body. "So did I. Roaming those infernal deserts for a thousand years, catching rumors and traces of you, but always a step behind, your form an unreachable silhouette on distant dunes."

Annabel takes his face in her hands. "A small price to pay for the crimes we committed."

Tony nods, putting his fingers over hers. "The loss of our sister. We should have borne it better, not let it corrupt our souls."

Together, they stand. Then they turn to look at Blanca and me.

"Forgive me, Sister," Annabel whispers, her voice breaking.

Tony echoes the plea in Nahuatl. "Xinechpohpolwia, noweltiwé."

Blanca lowers her head. "Whatever power I have to forgive, I pour it out upon you both. Feel no more shame toward me, Sister and Brother. Receive my full love."

Her mercy almost breaks me. I slide from her arms and go to them, dropping to my knees. For centuries I've shouldered the weight of my own sin, forgetting and then remembering.

"I need forgiveness as well, Huixachin and Meconetzin. When I awakened, made immortal by the Great Gods, I descended from the volcano and went to find you, Little Brother of my heart. But faced with the devastation you had caused, I lost myself. Entered the palace at Tollan. Wielded my sword against you. And when Huixachin here attempted to protect you . . ."

My voice breaks. I can't bring myself to say the words.

"You slew us both," finishes Tony . . . Meconetzin . . . my dearest friend.

"Yes. And that was not the end of my sin. Now I can beg your forgiveness. I've done penance, lived twelve hundred years bereft. Please, help me put an end to this suffering."

The boy who once worshipped the ground I walked on reaches for me then, and the three of us share a trembling embrace.

Our shells of sin and tragedy crack in one another's arms.

Tina takes unsteady steps toward my beloved.

"Iztactzin?" she asks.

Blanca nods, tears flowing.

Tina reaches for her. "It's me, my dear warrior child, who survived the battle of childbirth, though I could not."

Blanca's face twists with pain and joy all at once. "Mother?"

"Yes, sweetheart. Maxio. Upon my death, unable even to look into your newborn eyes, I was transformed into a sacred cihuateotl,

239

winging my way through the skies with fierce demigod sisters, protecting the sun as it descended each day. Oh, but I never forgot my precious jewel. And when the whispered promise of the Great Gods reached my ears, I swore to persevere until I might see you at last."

Blanca rushes to her, and they hug, weeping for a time before finally laughing at the strange relationship they've had for the past decade and a half.

"You've always tried to mother me," Blanca jokes, running the sleeve of her blouse across her nose. "Now it all makes sense."

"And I dreamed, in our former life, of having daughters who would be my friends. That wish, at least, the gods granted. Even if you still won't lend me those red Louboutin heels."

Blanca can't help but chuckle.

"Your feet are much too wide, Mother. Or Maxio? What do I call you?" She casts her eyes about the sanctuary. "What do we call one another?"

Sofía speaks up. "You are indeed those people whose memories have been restored to you. You share the same soul. But you're also not. You are Tony and Blanca and Tina and Annabel. It's important not to let your past selves dissolve who you are now, my children."

Tony nods, then does a double take. "Wait. Then who are *you*? It doesn't feel like you're my mother, but you're familiar."

"Ah, I am Xocotzin herself."

Their eyes go wide before they bow deeply.

"Timitzyectenehuah, tonantziné," they intone as if we stood before her altar in Tollan.

"Thank you, my children. But let me warn you. We've returned your memories so that these two can at last be together and you four can be redeemed. But the rite has also awakened the past self of three others. One is pretty dangerous."

240

I hiss. "Tzinacan."

Blanca clings to her mother. "Now we'll have to be especially vigilant. Will he be someone close to us?"

"Yes," Sofía answers. "Someone you all know. And he's a wily one, that Tzinacan. He will figure out your identities soon enough. Be your modern selves as much as possible. Don't slip into old rhythms. Don't use old names or Nahuatl. You need to catch him first so that we can undo your collective tragedy."

I nod. "I'll do anything to make sure we succeed."

"Excellent," says Sofía. "Now, three of you have done penance for more than a thousand years. It is time to let go of your sins. We shall devour them for you."

She raises her arms. "COME, SISTERS."

The door creaks open, and into the sanctuary come three more women:

María Primo, oldest aspect of the goddess. Teresa Segundo, her middle-aged form. Daniela Tercero, the young woman facet.

They walk past us, up the steps, and arrange themselves in a line behind Sofía Cisneros.

And, impossibly, the four *step into one another.*

Fusing, they become one goddess, so radiant that I can barely look upon her. Those same features, but ageless, eternal. An elaborate headdress adorned with dark feathers and a spindle of white cotton, the same color as her gleaming robes. Dripping from lips, staining her chin and the front of her robes is the dark residue of all the human sins she's eaten.

She speaks in an unearthly voice:

"You stand before me, your hearts opened, concealing nothing. I know well the tale of your sins, your trek along the twisted road I tempted you to trod. Upon your deaths, you admitted your grievous faults and accepted the punishment meted out to you, centuries of suffering. Now I—Tlazolteotl Ixcuinan, goddess of vice and forgiveness—declare you absolved. Come unto me, dear children. Let me devour your sins so you may go forth in humility to live better lives."

I lead Tony and Annabel to her looming majesty, and with arms that remind us of our loving mothers, she embraces us.

CHAPTER

30

It is strange.

I am at once Lady Iztac, exalted daughter of King Tecpancaltzin and Queen Maxio, beloved by the people of Tollan and adored by our courageous Popocatzin. But I am also me, Blanca Rosa Montes, orphaned in childhood and raised in solitude by my padrino, Rafael Montes, without the tenderness and warmth of familial love.

How to reconcile?

How to appreciate such a destiny?

How to abide by two lives melded together—forged by fire and snow—the two volcanoes we are bound to by the infinity of time and space and universal wisdom?

I am grateful, because I am not so alone anymore, so lost as when I was an only child. However, now that I am two in one, my heart is heavy as packed snow, my soul an iceberg buried under the surface of Sun Lake at the summit of Tzinacantepec, that other dead volcano we now call the Nevado de Toluca.

The goddess releases Greg, Tony, and Ms. Dresch—Popocatzin, Meconetzin, and Huixachin. Then she separates, becoming four women of identical appearance except for age.

We all stand there, staring at one another. Then the parish bell tolls, programmed as it is to announce every new hour, and I am reminded we are living in modern times.

Sofía smiles and speaks. "I'm sure your minds and hearts are swirling with confusion, memories, and questions, but you must sort through them alone. I know that a part of each of you—reunited at last with people you love—wants to cling to the others. But don't. Not yet. Go home, process your feelings, and find a new balance for your dual self. Call on me if you need help. I can be by your side in seconds. One of us can. Rest and remember. Tomorrow your lives begin anew."

Greg and I do as the goddess commands and leave the parish separately. When I get home, I wander through the empty halls of our house in Reno as I once wandered through the nine levels of Mictlan.

I stand with my arms crossed, hugging myself, in front of the immense windows overlooking our backyard. The sky above is starting to go gray, and the wind caresses the dark waters of our pool, sending tiny ripples that glitter and shine like hopeful fireflies. The last rays of Nanahuatzin, our beloved Lord Sun, kiss its surface before the rain begins to pour down on Reno, and I weep.

Because I remember everything.

I remember how I formed the noose and yoked myself to death because it was more honorable than to bind myself to Tzinacan, that traitor whose conspiracy had caused me so much pain, hell-bent as he was on taking control of Tollan, either through marriage or civil war.

I felt no protection from my father, who sent my beloved Popoca to his demise and, like a coward, was handing an empire over to

Tzinacan's mutinous clan. But I would not let the traitor have me. I would rather step off a cliff, plunge into a roiling river, be devoured by denizens of the Underworld, than allow Tzinacan to take me as his bride—his prize!

Even as I forged a path, moving past the myriad obstacles throughout the nine levels of Mictlan, I thought of him, my most cherished Popoca, whose soul is embroidered with mine in the tapestry of eternal love. That he's waited this long, that he's found me after all this time—when I had no memory, no recollection of who I am, who I was—is a mystery only the gods could have woven for us. And for that, I am grateful.

Though I've waited, too.

After I crossed the Apanohuayan River, my soul was almost crushed at the place where two massive mountains smash together. Though I pulled back just in time, I was trapped, waiting until the mountains moved back and allowed me to pass with my sweet canine companion, whose vermillion coat shone in the darkness, a torch that lit the way through that dark descent.

And when I was done, I made it to paradise. But even in my eternal rest, in my palace of stone and living wood in Tamoanchan, I stood on that celestial balcony watching over my beloved for the next twelve hundred years, trying to calm the volcano tied to his soul when it was on the verge of erupting. Time after time, I soothed his rage with my icy frost, the chilling wind that whistles through the aching place where my cold, dead heart used to reside.

Remembering the moment when the goddess embraced Tony, Annabel, and Greg, a troubling thought enters my mind. I was not absolved, and the goddess did not take Tina into her arms either. Was she already forgiven? At the time of my birth, did the goddess come to my mother and devour her sins? Or did a millennium of protecting our Lord Sun burn those faults away? There are so many things I want to ask her that I pull my phone out of my pocket and text her:

ME: Hey, how are you? Did you make it home ok?

I wait. Stare out into the backyard, and sigh.

But Tina doesn't answer. So, I text her again.

ME: I wanted to talk. About what happened. I know she said for us to be alone, but can I come over?

After thirty minutes, I get scared. Something dark and elusive is poking and prodding at the back of my mind, trying to resurface. It's the memory of those co-conspirators, plotting in the shadows of my father's palace in Tollan. How near they were, bees in the hive, poisoning us even as they fed us their sweet, insipid nectar, and we never saw it coming.

And now that the goddess has awakened Tzinacan's soul, I am in the same position. She says that three others have been reborn. This time, I can't let them win. I won't let history repeat itself. That's why I have to talk to Tina.

But how can I do that when she won't answer me?

So I place a video call to the man I love instead.

"Beloved," Greg mutters upon answering. "I hoped you'd call."

"It's good to see your face," I say. "I'm looking for Tina. Have you seen her?"

"I'm sorry, Blanca," Greg says. "But Tina's missing."

"What?"

"Tony dropped her off at Momito's, that club at the end of the strip, for an early rehearsal. But now he's worried, because the band leader called him. Apparently, she wasn't there when they showed up. We're looking for her right now."

That elusive thing in the back of my mind comes to the forefront, and I recognize it for what it is. *Fear.*

"Oh my God, what if something's happened to her?"

"Let's not panic," Greg says, after a moment. "Her phone could just be dead."

"Yes . . . but what if Tzinacan is behind this?" I shudder at the thought of what he might do.

"I will make him pay dearly, if he lays a hand on her," Greg vows.

"If only we knew who he was," I say, wiping the tears from my eyes and forcing myself to be strong. "In this lifetime."

"Hold on," Greg says. "I'm updating Tony."

In the moment of silence that transpires between us, I try to connect things, put it all together in my mind. Suddenly, I see it.

"Wait! Something happened. In the garden," I tell him. "I overheard my padrino give someone permission to get rid of a man. But then he told them not to hurt me, because I am the key, that without me he has no power. At that moment, I had a vision of a shadowy figure I didn't recognize. But now I do. It was Tzinacan, outside the garden in Tollan."

"You saw Tzinacan?"

I lower my voice to a whisper. "I was there that night, when Tzinacan met with his accomplices outside the imperial gardens where he began the final stages of his plan."

My body is quivering as I finish telling him what I know, what I can remember.

"And your padrino's voice triggered this vision?" Greg ponders my revelation.

"You mean his tone?" I ask. "No. It was what he said. *She is the key. She is the kingdom. Without her, I have no power.*' I mean, who talks like that?"

"Only Tzinacan would speak such treachery," Greg says. "We have to do something. Quickly. Before he figures out who we are."

"Oh my God!" I say, my brain working on overload. "He was angry at her, Greg! She confronted him, about my parents' death. And he was furious."

Greg's eyes glimmer with astute intelligence. "So, you think he was behind your parents' death?"

"That's what Tina and I suspect," I tell him. "Though we couldn't find anything to tie him to the *accident*."

"Why didn't you tell me?" Greg asks. "I would've told you I share your suspicions."

"Hello?!" I say defensively. "You scared me to death claiming I was a reincarnated princess and then disappeared on me. I wasn't necessarily thinking straight."

"Fair enough. But what exactly were you looking for?"

"Evidence that he's connected to the water issues in Carrizo," I explain. "Tina was convinced that would bring him to the DA's attention . . . and then we could go from there. You know, connect the dots."

He leans back from his computer monitor, startled.

There is horror on his face. And something else.

Shame.

"Oh, dearest one, I am so sorry. I've kept something from you, too." He swallows heavily. "Rafael is, in fact, the person behind Hibernaculum Land Company. When my father found out, he acquired all the corporations that had bought land from them. Then I . . . went overboard with my cleanup of Carrizo. Your padrino noticed and confronted me."

Dread wells in my chest. "What did he say, Greg?"

"That I should stop seeing you. He was disappointed that I would target him and said, *'Let's avoid unpleasantries.'* Those were his words."

"Unpleasantries," I whisper. "Do you think . . . could he have . . . ordered her disappearance?"

"Maybe." Greg rubs his face.

"We need to go to the authorities," I tell him. "To DA Flowers, since she's been investigating Rafael. Middle Sister can get us in."

"Meet me outside in five," Greg says, and we hang up.

I close my laptop and open the door of my room, almost fainting from the shock. Standing in the hall, staring at me, is my padrino. His eyes are hooded, half-closed, and his hands are shoved deep into the pockets of his suit pants.

"Oh God, you scared me," I say, pushing my hair back out of my face, as I look around for my purse. It's sitting beside my backpack, and I pick them both up.

"Rosario's setting the table," my padrino says as I haul my backpack and purse and hoist them over my left shoulder. "Dinner's ready."

"Oh, no thanks. I'm going over to study with my friends," I tell him. Gripping the straps of my purse and backpack, I start toward the hall.

My padrino moves in front of me. "Stay," he says.

His hand on my shoulder is more than a request. It's a command, and, suddenly, I am back there again, in that other life. *His fingers touch my skin as it peeks out of the colorful ceremonial gown, the dress I was to wear for our wedding rites.*

The dress that I died in.

The dress that was eventually covered in snow up in those lonely peaks while my beloved performed his painful vigil at my side.

"Let me go!" I say, pulling away from him and rushing out of the room.

"Blanca!" My padrino's voice roars behind me. "Come back here, young lady!"

"No," I yell as I start down the stairs. "You can't tell me what to do!"

I know I'm making him mad, but I can't let him stop me. I can't afford to waste even one more second without doing something to find Tina. The fact that she hasn't answered any of my messages for over an hour tells me she is in great danger.

When we arrive at city hall, Daniela Tercero meets us in the lobby.

"We figured you would ignore our advice," she tells us with a wry smile, "but I didn't expect things to get this intense quite this fast. Come on."

Daniela raps lightly on DA Flowers's office door, and when someone says, "Come in," she turns the knob.

DA Flowers is standing in front of a huge board.

"What in the world . . . ?" The words escape my lips before I can hold them back, because on the board are five-by-seven photos of Ted Caldera and my padrino. Above their photos are their full names, but, below them, the words "Toltec Identity Unknown" scream out at me.

How does she know?

Even as my mind races, my eyes are drawn to the center of the board, to a circle between the two halves, where Greg's school ID photo is positioned. Above his handsome face, the letters read, "GREGORIO CHAN." Below it, the letters say, "POPOCA."

DA Flowers turns around and looks at us. Her eyes are smart, knowing.

"Hello, Commander," she says, a crooked smile forming on her lips. "I've been expecting you."

CHAPTER

31

I glare at Daniela. But I know better than to ask why she didn't warn me.

Instead, I give a slight bow of my head.

"Which are you?" I ask Flowers.

The district attorney's eyes flit from me to Daniela. "Agent Tercero, you should leave."

"No need," Daniela answers with a grin. "I'm not who I appear to be, either."

Flowers taps her lip with the marker in her hand, contemplating the situation for a few seconds before nodding.

"Very well. I am Xochitl. Daughter of Papantzin. Former empress of the Toltec Empire. Are you also one of us, Ms. Montes?"

Blanca takes several steps toward Xochitzin, tears brimming in her eyes.

"Yes, Imperial Mother. It's me. Iztac, whom you raised as your own daughter."

The empress sets her marker down and crosses the remaining distance, folding Blanca's smaller figure into her arms.

"Ah, precious feather! My sweet gift from heaven! I've missed you so."

Blanca squeezes her back. "Me too. Forgive me. Perhaps I should have lingered, helped you fight."

Her stepmother pulls away, looks down into her eyes. "Feel no regret. You did what you thought had to be done. I'll never gainsay your autonomy over your own mind and heart."

I clear my throat. "Empress, that fight is not over. Maxio has gone missing."

She spins to stare at me. "Maxio? She's also returned?"

"As Tina Gorena," I explain. "A student at Galena High School."

Grabbing her marker, she begins scribbling on her board, filling in missing pieces. "Who else have you confirmed?"

"Your son, Meconetzin. Tony Alsobrook, a student as well. And your daughter, Huixachin, in the form of English teacher Annabel Dresch."

The DA smirks over her shoulder. "Pardon me, but—how do *you* know, Tercero? What in the nine levels *are* you?"

I raise my hand in warning.

"She's one of the aspects of Ixcuinan. Tlahcotzin."

Flowers bows low. "I cry your pardon, Middle Sister."

Daniela waves this apology away. "What we ought to worry about is that Captain Tzinacan was also fully awakened to his true nature this morning. That makes the timing of the disappearance super suspicious."

"Fully awakened?" I ask.

Daniela sighs and pops her neck. "In 1994, we sensed that a soul had been connected to el Nevado de Toluca. So did your spirit. Popocatepetl even erupted in response. Soon afterward, we felt the tether shift here, to Reno."

Blanca gasps. "My padrino got his MBA in Mexico City. He graduated in 1994."

"Rafael Montes? You're saying your godfather is Tzinacan?"

My beloved explains the conversation she overheard and how her padrino's words echoed those of the traitor near the east entrance to the palace gardens in Tollan.

Flowers scrawls "TZINACAN?" under the photo of Rafael Montes.

"It seems," Daniela continues, "that Chaos somehow touched him when he was twenty-four. We don't know how much he's known these last thirty years, but it was enough to warp him. Now that he remembers everything, including his punishment, we're very worried."

Blanca shudders. "What do you mean?"

"Tzinacan spent the last millennium and change very differently from the rest of you. When Popoca killed him, the evil curdling in his heart transformed his soul into an ehecapol nehnemini."

Swallowing at the term, I venture, "And as an evil spirit wandering the world, he would have kept causing harm, yes?"

The empress's eyes blaze. "You let that creature be reincarnated, Tlahcotzin? Why?"

Daniela puts her hand on the shoulder of Christina Flowers / Xochitzin.

"Because he, too, deserves a second chance. And the rest of you can't resolve your guilt toward one another without him."

Blanca rubs a hand over her face. "By the way, he knows I suspect him. He caught Tina and me snooping around his office. My padrino is not one to let anything interfere with his accumulation of power and wealth. And I turn eighteen next week."

I explain, "She'll inherit the trust he's been managing. Forty percent of the shares. If she asserts her legal rights as a shareholder and swings others to support her, she could sideline her godfather or even remove him altogether."

"As Tzinacan, he's probably furious at the thought of losing power again," Blanca says. "Maybe he wants to use Tina as a pawn to control me."

As if on cue, a knock comes at the door.

"Enter," the DA calls.

Her secretary pokes her head in.

"We just got a call from a park ranger, ma'am." She looks at us pointedly.

The DA waves impatiently. "Don't worry about them. Spit it out."

Taking a deep breath, the secretary continues. "They've found a body at Little Washoe Lake, near Steamboat Creek. A teen girl."

Blanca grips my arm, gasping. "That creek runs to the Truckee River."

A message, I realize. As clear as if he'd signed the corpse.

"Ranger says her body is frozen solid," the secretary adds.

There is a moment of horrified silence as we realize Tzinacan can wield the frigid might of his volcano.

Then Blanca chokes back a sob and rushes out of the office.

Full of sorrow and rage, the rest of us follow.

CHAPTER

32

It's only a twenty-minute drive out to Washoe Lake State Park. Even though Daniela's going as fast as safety allows, it feels like a thousand years have gone by since we got on the road.

I sit, cold and silent, in the back seat of Daniela's SUV, petrified of what we will witness when we finally get there. Greg grips my hand, but I barely register the sensation. Only one thing fills my mind; it's my fault she was targeted, my fault she's gone. The realization eats away at me, corrodes everything good that has happened in the few hours since we remembered our past lives.

All I can do is tremble and weep for Tina, my best friend—*my mother.*

When we get there, Daniela leads the way, but she asks us to stay back before she goes to speak to the officers at the forefront of the investigation.

As expected, there is little commotion around us, so I can't really tell what is going on. It's obvious the investigation is over, because photographers are leaving and the officers around us are all speaking quietly to one another in person or relaying messages on walkie-talkies and phones as they wait by the bulk of a body—*her body,*

Tina's body, my mother's body—covered by a white tarp at the edge of the lake.

Cold tears run down my face, and, in the distance, I hear sirens, wailing their mournful song. But I still wonder why this had to happen to her—*to her!* She only wanted to help me—to protect me, to make sure nothing happened to me—*to me, her best friend, her only daughter.*

"Blanca?" Greg asks, following me as I move closer to the lake, because a convoy of service vehicles has arrived, including EMS and a coroner's van, and I want to be with her when they pick her up and take her away from us.

"Excuse me!" I yell at the men who have put Tina's body into a zippered bag and are now walking with it to the coroner's van. "Where are you taking her?"

"She'll be transported to the county morgue," a female police officer tells me, stepping between me and the coroner's assistants. "Are you family?"

"Can I go with you? Please," I yell after them when they start to close the door on the van. "I have to be with her. She needs me."

"Blanca," Greg whispers as he stands behind me, supporting me. "It's not an ambulance. You can't travel with her."

"I know," I say, turning away from the scene, because watching them drive away with her is making me want to scream, cry out like a lechuza in flight. Instead of letting it all out, I pull away from Greg, turn away from the officers and crews, and walk down the incline, until I am standing on the edge of the lake, peering out at its shimmering, resplendent expanse—trembling with rage.

As I look upon the tranquil body of water, I am transported to another time, and suddenly, I am five years old again.

A dark door opens, and he's there, my padrino, standing in the winter storm with the lightning flashing behind him, outlining his

256

form. My parents are dead, he tells me. They're gone. Gone. He goes down on one knee, reaches for me, but I step away. Again and again and again, I step away from him.

Then I'm out the door, running. Running down the street as fast as I can. Running against the wind and the rain and the sleet. Running from the coldness in my padrino's eyes. Running from the shadow of a snowcapped mountain. Running from the bitterness that is now home. Running from his shadow—and everything he's taken from me.

The sobs wracking my body start to form icicles around my heart, but I don't want to be cold; I want to feel every bit of rage and hurt and woundedness that is making me seize up. I want to pay him back tear for tear, using the same element he's used to kill everyone I love.

As I tremble, trying to hold on to my anger, to dispel the numbness spreading at my core, tiny tendrils of ice start pushing through my fingertips. And because I don't know what else to do with this power, I let it seep out of me to crystalize at my feet and crawl out into the water, freezing it inch by inch, until the wind starts to swirl around me, an ice storm sweeping down the slopes of Mount Rose to help obliterate the scene of Tina's death.

"Blanca! Blanca! What are you doing?" Helpless, Greg rushes toward me, but he can't reach me, and I can't move for the wall of icy rain and sleet swirling around me.

Instead, Greg attempts to protect the people around me. I feel him draw from the magma far beneath my feet to create warm pockets of air for the officers and EMS personnel who are struggling to get free of the unseasonable storm while I stand frozen beside the lake, overwhelmed by my own power.

"You're going to be all right. You hear me? You're all right," he keeps saying, until my horrified despair subsides and we are the only two people left standing in this cold, miserable corner of the world.

When the shield of ice collapses, I hurry to Blanca and embrace her, pushing warmth into her body. The sleet becomes warm drizzle, and the lake starts to creak and pop as its frozen crust melts.

"Here," says Daniela, handing me a silver raincoat. "Get her to my SUV."

Covering her with the raincoat, I guide Blanca away from the lake. No words can console her, but I must propel her forward.

"Come, beloved. Daniela's waiting to drive us home."

"Home?" she whispers, staring absently at the snowcapped mountain that looms over us. "I have no home. I'm an orphan."

I want to insist that I will always be her home, but I respect her grief and lead her to the vehicle, where she collapses into the arms of DA Flowers, sobbing softly before letting herself be helped into the SUV.

"Don't go home," Daniela warns. "You're not safe. Rafael knows three things: he's Tzinacan, you're Popoca, and Blanca—by inference—is Iztac. He didn't kill Tina because she's Maxio, but because she knew too much."

"They should stay at my place," Flowers says as she shuts the back door. "He won't suspect that. And I've got some leftover chicken soup that will ease my daughter's chill."

Blanca leans on me for support as we take the elevator with Daniela and Ms. Flowers to the DA's apartment in the heart of Reno. I get her to eat a little broth from Christina's leftover soup before she gets up and wobbles toward the guest room. I follow and help her get under the covers. After crying softly for a while, she drifts off into a fitful sleep. She clings to me, but I ease out of bed.

Christina Flowers and Daniela are sitting in the living room, drinking coffee in silence. They look up as I enter.

"How is she?" Flowers asks.

"Asleep. But still in shock. Losing her best friend and the mother she never knew at the same time—if she were any weaker, it would break her."

Daniela grimaces. "That must be what Rafael is counting on. If he can obtain a legal declaration of incapacity, he could extend his guardianship beyond her eighteenth birthday."

I drop into a chair across the coffee table from them.

"That makes sense. Rafael wanted to send her to Harvard for a good six to ten years, time enough to maneuver himself into greater control of the company and her assets. I bet he and Ted Caldera were banking on having Blanca marry Jackson. The three of them were willing to gaslight her to prevent her from taking over Montes Realty."

"Do you have a plan?" Flowers asks. "I'll pull whatever strings I can."

"I have a few ideas. Once Blanca's feeling a little better, we can help her decide on the best way forward."

"Better act soon," Daniela warns. "Isn't her birthday next week?"

I rub my hands across my face. "Yeah. But she needs time to grieve. While she's coming to terms with her loss, we can do something else. Where's Tony?"

"At home," Flowers tells me. "Blaming himself for what happened to Tina."

"Maybe I'll hold off on visiting him, then," I say. "Instead, I'm thinking of tracking down the last reincarnated Toltec. Daniela, you entangled their souls. Who else has returned?"

"Tecpancalli," she says.

Flowers's eyes go wide. "My husband? The emperor?"

"That makes sense," I say. "Iztac's father, who didn't stand up against Tzinacan and then was killed by his own rebel son. Our redemption wouldn't be complete without him."

"Maybe he's someone close," the DA suggests. "Someone influenced by Rafael Montes."

Names spin through my mind for a moment. Then I slap my fist against my palm.

"It's got to be Ted Caldera."

Flowers sighs and takes a swig of coffee before adding, "Yeah, I figured he was one of us."

Her phone starts buzzing.

"It's the city attorney," she explains. "I'll put him on speaker. Hello, Mr. Cooper."

"Christina. I'm calling on behalf of the mayor. Would you care to explain why there's a patrol car parked outside the house of Rafael Montes?"

Rolling her eyes, the DA leans toward the phone. "His goddaughter's best friend was murdered. Tina Gorena was like a member of that family, even accompanying them on vacations. We suspect

260

someone is targeting the Montes family. So we're protecting Don Rafael."

"And his goddaughter? Blanca? Lawyers from Montes Realty are all over city hall, demanding answers."

"I'm holding her in protective custody," the DA lies, "at a safe house. She could be in danger at home."

"Please don't tell me you suspect Rafael." Cooper sighs. "He's going to end up suing you for harassment. The city, too."

"Don't worry, Mr. Cooper. It won't come to that. I've got to go, sir. More soon."

She ends the call.

Daniela scoffs. "Big business in Reno *loves* Rafael Montes."

Flowers nods. "Yup. I need to get conclusive evidence that he was involved in Tina's murder."

"Will you have time to go with me tomorrow?" I ask.

"Where?"

"To confront Ted Caldera, the reincarnation of your husband."

All she can do is groan in response.

I smell coffee long before I notice Blanca missing from the bed. She's moving around the kitchen, speaking softly with someone.

I find Daniela and Sofía sitting with her at the table, steaming mugs in front of them. In unison, they inform me, "Christina is in the shower. She'll be out soon."

I shudder. "It's so weird when you all do that. Morning, Blanca."

"Morning, babe," Blanca says, trying to smile. "Want some coffee?"

I raise my hand. "I'll serve myself." I grab a cup. "Did you sleep well?"

"As well as can be expected." She sips her coffee while I serve mine. "Greg, I need to visit her parents. Tina's. I'm sure they're devastated, and it'll . . . help me if I go comfort them."

I sit beside her, across from the two aspects of the goddess.

Taking Blanca's free hand, I kiss it gently.

"Want me to go with you?"

Blanca hesitates, then shakes her head. "No. The Sisters tell me you and Christina Flowers are going to pursue a lead. They'll come along instead."

I look into her dark eyes, swirling with emotions. The Sisters haven't told her that Caldera might be her father. I trust their instincts and say nothing. We'll confirm first.

"Okay. Whatever you need, just let me know."

After breakfast, we head out. As the district attorney drives, I call Ms. Dresch and fill her in. She agrees to meet us later, at the Caldera residence.

The DA and I make our way to the headquarters of Caldera Resorts, on the top floor of their oldest resort, Obsidian Legacy. Caldera's secretary objects, but Flowers threatens to question her as part of the investigation, and we're buzzed in.

Placing his meaty hands on his desk, Ted Caldera thrusts himself to his feet, indignant. At first, his narrowing eyes fall only on Christina.

"Ms. District Attorney," he booms with authority and confidence, "your harassment has reached its limits. My friends with the Department of Justice—"

I step in front of Flowers.

"Will be of no help to you, Emperor. Not against me."

His eyes grow wide.

"Popoca," he mutters. "What are you doing here?"

I cock my head. "You had no idea the others were reincarnated, and their faces are different. But you saw me, unchanged after centuries, at the grand opening of Imperial Silver Casino. Why didn't you contact me once you remembered?"

Ted clasps his hands together in front of him, staring at the district attorney in confusion before bowing his head in shame.

"I was afraid of what this return means. You were unstoppable when you left Tollan with Iztac's body. The gods themselves seemed to protect you. I've hardly slept, wondering why they have allowed me to return."

Taking a deep breath, I release it with a sigh.

"I'm not here for revenge. I need your help to bring Rafael Montes down."

Caldera flinches at the name. "Why would I touch Montes? His business and mine are too intertwined. If he falls, so do I."

I grit my teeth. "That's a price I'm willing to see paid."

His hands tighten into fists as he lifts his chin. "Well, I'm not! I've spent my life building this empire."

It's too much. I rush to his desk and sweep everything to the floor.

"*Screw* your paltry empire! We're not the only ones here, Ted. *All of them are.* Blanca is Lady Iztac. And Rafael Montes is Tzinacan."

The emperor collapses into his chair, overwhelmed.

"Blanca is . . . Rafael is . . . ," he mutters, clutching at the armrests.

"That's right. And he just killed Tina Gorena. She was Maxio, sir."

For a moment, it seems he'll have a heart attack. But I press on.

"You can't let your daughter *also* be destroyed by that monster. This is your chance to get forgiveness from me and everyone else whose destruction you set in motion when you caved to the demands of the Oztohuah clan and gave Iztac in marriage to Tzinacan."

Caldera's pale face has gone red. Tears begin to stream from his harrowed eyes. His gaze flits to the district attorney.

"You said they've all been reborn. Then who is she? She knows what's going on."

Christina, who has kept her composure this whole time, gasps with a strange blend of anguish and relief.

"It's me. The one who avenged your death a hundredfold on the battlefield. Your precious wife."

"Xochitl?" Ted breathes, amazed.

She hurries to him, takes his trembling hands in hers.

"Our daughter needs us. Let's not fail her again."

CHAPTER
34

"Thank you for coming." Tina's mother hugs me tight before she and her husband walk back to their seats in the front pew of El Santuario de Santa Rosa. We are all convened here, in this small Catholic church, because Tina's parents have chosen to lay Tina to rest near her grandparents' gravesite.

The church is a few blocks away from where Tina rolled out on a moving stage, a flatbed, singing her beautiful siren song, celebrating the renewal of this town just a few weeks ago. It is this picture, taken onstage that night, with her bright eyes, wide smile, and flashing hoop earrings, that her parents have selected to place among the flowers and tributes beside her coffin.

My heart aches as we walk down to the cemetery behind the small church after the service. If Ixcuinan were not flanking me, both their arms hooked to mine, I might fall to my knees.

I don't participate much in the funeral. It's a short service, and I spend most of it in tears, weeping for the beautiful girl with hazel eyes whose splendor will never grace the stage again.

"She made the world a better place," I tell Sofía and Daniela when we are back in Greg's car, being driven up to Reno by Stilson.

"She was resplendent," Daniela agrees. "Even in the afterlife, when she became a cihuateotl and accompanied the sun to the western realm, where it sets for the night on the women's side of the world, Empress Maxio was splendid. Unmatched in beauty and fierceness."

"I just wish I'd had more time with her, as my mother," I say, because I can't help it, my human heart is aggrieved, and I can't reconcile my heartbreak.

"I know." Sofía puts her arms around my shoulders and kisses my temple as she hugs me to her.

"It had to be this way," Daniela says as she tightens her grip on my hand. "But I hope you understand. Your mother needed to come back here, to see you before she made her final journey. She needed to let go of her love for you if she was ever going to make it through Mictlan and reach paradise."

I press a tissue against my swollen eyes and take a deep breath. "I do," I tell her. "I also made that treacherous journey. It is not easy letting go of those we hold dear in life."

"But it must be done." Sofía's watery smile echoes my sentiment. "And when it's over, she will live in peaceful eternity, calmly awaiting you and your siblings' ascent to paradise."

"Oh my God—Tony!" I say, because it hits me then, that I have no idea how he is. I've been so aggrieved, so focused on my own pain, that I've failed to ask how my younger brother is doing. "How is he? Where is he?"

"At home," Daniela says. "Blaming himself for the loss."

"No. Can you take me to him?" I ask.

Daniela taps the shoulder of the driver's seat. "Stilson."

"Already rerouting," he says as he presses icons on the navigation system on the console and then speeds up to jump on the highway.

266

When we get to Tony's house, his mother welcomes us inside. "Come in, please," she says, showing us to the family room in the back of the house, where Mr. Alsobrook is sitting with Tony.

We all greet one another with as much enthusiasm as befits the situation. Nobody's really happy to be gathering together under these circumstances. But as brokenhearted as we all are, we are also concerned about Tony.

"My condolences," I say, after I give him a big sisterly hug and sit quietly beside him.

"It was my fault," Tony says. "I left her there. Alone. Like an idiot. I should have stayed until the band showed up. Instead of . . ."

"You can't blame yourself," I say, interrupting his ramblings. "You had no way of knowing this would happen. None of us did."

"I don't understand. Why would they do this to her?" Tony mumbles, raking his fingers forcefully through his hair.

Daniela shakes her head. "She was asking too many questions, trying to make connections between Montes and criminal activity."

It's not the whole truth, but the Alsobrooks don't need to hear about the plot to strip me of my inheritance or the revelation of our reincarnation. They already look utterly overwhelmed with their son's distress. I empathize with them.

"I'm so . . . sorry." Tony's voice falters. Then he breaks down. His shoulders shudder, and he covers his face with his hands. His mother puts her arms around him and hugs him silently. After a moment, Tony looks up at me, tears still glistening in his eyes. "Can you ever forgive me?"

As Tony's mother and I attempt to comfort him, Daniela's phone rings in her pocket.

"Excuse me," she says as she steps out of the room. I can hear her voice moving away as she walks down the hall.

"That was the DA on the phone," she says when she returns. "We've found a vital piece of the puzzle. Tony, would you be willing to come with us, give an official statement, and help us put this together?"

"Can't you take his statement here?" Tony's mother asks.

"I understand your reluctance," Daniela replies, "but Tony just turned eighteen. He can decide for himself if he wants to go with us. He was the last one to see Tina alive. His statement might be critical in helping us find her killer."

The agent waves her hand before Tony's mother's eyes, and suddenly the professor's expression becomes pleasant and carefree. Mr. Alsobrook frowns at the strange occurrence, and Daniela locks eyes with him and repeats the action, making his eyes soften as he smiles at her. "What do you say? We could really use his help."

"What did you do to them?" Tony asks, when he's in Daniela's SUV with us. "Are they going to stay like that forever?"

Daniela laughs. "No. Just for a few hours. You'll see when you come back. Stilson, take us to the Caldera residence. Pronto."

"Caldera?" Tony looks upset. "I don't want anything to do with that guy. He and his son dragged me into gambling."

"I hear you," Daniela says, "but right now you all need to sort things out and join forces. It's the only way to heal and defeat Tzinacan."

I know she's right. We must regroup, speak plainly, let go of the past, and start working toward a better future. If we don't do this, if we don't let go of the ties that bind us to that tragedy, we will go through this lifetime making the same mistakes and the cycle of horror will be repeated. Only one thing bothers me.

"What you say is true," I tell Daniela. "I just don't understand why we have to go to the Caldera residence."

"To meet the last of the Returned," she explains.

"Who?" Tony asks.

"Please don't say Jackson," I beg.

Sofía suppresses a giggle. "No. It's Ted Caldera, Blanca. He's Emperor Tecpancaltzin, your father."

"My father?" Suddenly, I am a knot of conflicted emotions. Anger, rage, woundedness, disappointment, loss—they all rise up inside me, trying to penetrate my cold, icy heart. I close my eyes and slow down my breathing, force myself to be calm.

Once we drive through the gates of St. James Village, we are so close to Tzinacan I can feel his sinister presence. I can almost see him in my mind's eye, sitting at his majestic, mahogany desk in his dark office in the bowels of the house, a seething volcano waiting to claim and consume everything around him.

The Calderas' butler, Santiago, is waiting at the door. He shows us to the expansive living room.

"El Señor Caldera and his other guests will be with you shortly," Santiago tells us.

I glance around the house I've been to so many times before, with Jackson, back when I thought he was worth my time. I had hoped to never set foot in this house again. But it's clear that when we least expect it, the past comes back to haunt us.

"Blanca," a voice says behind me. Christina Flowers. Xochitzin. The only mother I've really ever known. I turn to face her. Beside her stand Greg, Ted Caldera, and Annabel. The wise strength of Tollan's greatest ruler glimmers in his eyes, tempered by grief and regret.

"Emperor. Empress," I say, bowing to my parents.

"Dearest daughter, jewel of our very hearts," Ted Caldera says, opening his arms to me, even as tears stream down his shamed face. "Can you ever forgive us for the disservice we have done to you now and in that former life?"

I want to be mad at him, to open my lips and recriminate him for every moment of pain and suffering, every trauma, he has caused me. But the truth is that I can't. When I see the way his hands tremble, as he waits for me to unleash my wrath, I can only feel sadness, and something else. Something I can only describe as . . . *hope*.

"I watched over you from paradise. And when you went into battle, I prayed for you," I tell him, as a stream of cleansing tears starts to fall from my burning eyes.

"We were so wrong," my father mumbles. "Please, forgive us."

"Forgiveness is not our charge," I tell him. "It is something only the gods can bestow once we cross the Underworld. We have to make amends. That's why we're here, no? To set things right?"

My father's shoulders shake, and he drops to his knees.

"I do not deserve such a daughter," he says, raising his eyes to the heavens beyond the huge skylight in his living room. "I do not deserve such a gift."

I step forward, take my father's hands in mine, and squeeze them tight, vowing never to burden him with reproaches for past sins, past hurts, actions we cannot undo, no matter how hard we try. "Rise, blessed father," I say, as I tug gently on his hands. "Rise and embrace your daughter, the girl who loves you so much she cannot bear the sight of you in such a sorrowful state."

A sort of snorting chuckle escapes my father, as he stands and hugs me to his chest, enveloping me with his strong arms. Never, in our lives together in Tollan, did he deign to give me such a hug, and my soul sings the song of the sweet birds I held in the palms of my hands during my long stay in paradise.

The empress joins us in that eternal hug.

"Blanca, dearest daughter of Tollan." Christina Flowers takes my face in her hands after I pull away from their embrace. "I raised you in that other life, loving you as my own child. And I will be here for you now, loving you with the same motherly heart. Always make your heart known to us, and never again keep your true desires from us. I may not be your biological mother, but I love you as such."

"I know. I waited and waited for you, after you passed," I say, because I really don't know what happened to them after they were killed in battle.

"It was the pain of losing you so savagely, so unnecessarily, that made it impossible for us both to join you in the afterlife," my father admits.

Christina Flowers nods. "After our warrior's death, we accompanied the sun as fallen soldiers do, but because we were unable to move on, we guarded Tonatiuh for twelve centuries—an eternal penance for our unresolved heartaches."

Sofía sighs. "That is a high price to pay for clinging to your earthly pains," she says. "But not as terrible a fate as Tzinacan, who has been forced to wander the earth as a vengeful spirit—cursed for all eternity—never to know the blessedness of eternal peace and love in paradise."

"But you all have been given a second chance," Daniela says, smiling as she looks at us standing together in my father's home, united for the first time since our youth in Tollan. "You may have worked through the worst part of your pain, but this is only the beginning. You should sit together and eat and drink, but don't celebrate yet.

Rest, instead, for soon you must face Tzinacan, defeat him, and be cleansed of sin. This must transpire to restore balance in your lives."

"How do we do that?" I ask, after a few moments of silence.

Greg puts his arm around my shoulders and pulls me in for a side hug. "We have a couple of options," he says as he looks at my father. "But we have to move fast, if we're going to catch Rafael off guard."

CHAPTER
35

That evening, Blanca and I find ourselves alone at last. Now that we've decided on a course of action, each of the Returned has gone off to handle a different task, guarded by one of the Four.

As we're sitting on Christina's sofa, I take one of Blanca's hands. "Something's been bugging me. I understand everything that led to the goddess snarling their souls to yours . . . Except for what happened to you that day. What you felt, saw, or heard that drove you to . . . remove yourself from the world."

Blanca winces but speaks openly.

"Once Tzinacan returned with news that you had died, I was devastated. Father had been fighting off pressure from the traitor's clan for years. Now they insisted that, since Tzinacan had fulfilled the charge father had given *you*, I should marry *him*. All I wanted was to mourn you, to weep the bitterness from my heart while you swept across the sky with the sun."

"But that meant civil war."

"Yes," she admits. "My stepmother tried to convince me. The captains had pledged their loyalty to Tzinacan. Half the council was already allied with his clan."

Tears tremble in her big, brown eyes.

"The empress left my wedding robes in my chambers. I took up the ceremonial scarf and its matching sash. My fingers began to braid. When I looked down at what I'd woven, I found a noose."

"Ah, beloved," I groan. I lean forward to wipe away her tears and kiss her gently on the forehead.

Blanca's bottom lip trembles.

"But I couldn't bring myself to do it. We'd sworn an oath. On the eve of your departure, you'd said, 'Tollan above us both. Should I fail to return, mourn me, but then fulfill your duty.' So I pulled on the robes and wandered the palace gardens, remembering our many moments there, begging the gods for wisdom."

"And that's when you heard Tzinacan and his captains," I interrupt.

"Yes. I turned to flee but felt a hand on my bare shoulder. I'd been discovered. In a flash, I understood. He intended to marry me."

I nod. "It would give his reign a veneer of legitimacy."

"Refusal was unheard of," Blanca continues, "but even if I found a way to reject him, Tzinacan would use the army to attempt a coup. My death was the only leverage I could use to pry my father from his cowardice and force him to protect the empire. I yanked away from Tzinacan's grasp and ran back to my chambers as shouts came from all over the palace. Commending my soul to Ixcuinan and to Tonantzin, the Mother of All, I slipped the noose around my neck . . ."

Sobs begin to shake her, and I pull her close, stroking her raven hair.

After a time, she asks, "Now you tell me—it has been hard, yes? From above, I could not see your human life, just your time as god of the volcano. Have you forever lived with this youthful, handsome face? How did you manage to remain unnoticed?"

I laugh a little. "No, this *handsome* face does indeed age. The cycle was established when I first awakened after death. For fifty-two years, I would search for you, aging normally, growing old. When I appeared to be seventy, I would return to the cavern, where my body would rest and be renewed for another fifty-two years while my soul protected the volcano. Then I would awaken and descend again."

Blanca strokes my cheek. "So many lives you were forced to live, so much loneliness."

My chest clamps around my heart. "This is my thirteenth. But early on, people in the village of Xalitzintla discovered my secret. They swore fealty to me, the god of their mountain, and we built a network to look for signs of your return. Over centuries, these enterprises became businesses, generating all my wealth."

"You had worshippers, employees, but what about friends?" Blanca asks. Then, softly, she adds, "What about other loves?"

Flustered, I take a long drink of water before attempting an answer.

"During my regeneration, my memories got purged. I was allowed by the gods to forget stuff that didn't really matter, as long as it was all recorded in the volumes that now sit—"

Blanca interrupts me. "I wasn't trying to pry, Greg. Let me rephrase that. I'm not mad if you . . . found others. Twelve hundred years is a long time. What I want to know is—how many times did you fall in love?"

"Oh, that's easier," I tell her honestly, raising her hands to my lips to kiss them. "Just once. With you. I have never loved again."

The next five days are a whirlwind of activity. We're all in this battle together, most of us camped out in Christina's apartment, strategizing.

Ted provides crucial information right away.

"Rafael's original plan was to have Jackson marry you, Blanca. The majority of the shares would have been transferred to him through various mechanisms. When you broke off your relationship with the boy"—Ted sighs—"ah, I'm ashamed to say that I devised a solution. Conservatorship."

Anger knits Blanca's brows. "What? Declare me unfit? Take my agency away?"

Ted reaches for her, but she bats away his hand.

"Blanca, I'd never do that to you *now*. You're my daughter!"

"Ah," she snaps, "but you would do it to a stranger? If you could benefit from it?"

Daniela interrupts. "It's a sin, Ted. You'll need to repent. But we can use this. Can't we, Ms. Flowers?"

Christina nods. "Greg, you said there's a wrinkle to calling a shareholders' meeting on Blanca's eighteenth birthday so her new allies can align themselves with Blanca?"

"Yes," I affirm. "How to neutralize Rafael long enough to let the meeting take place."

Daniela turns to Ted. "The petition for conservatorship. What judge was it filed with?"

"Barry Dollinger."

"Boom," Christina says. "Slam dunk. When I show Dollinger the evidence I'm taking before a grand jury—"

"He'll nix my padrino's petition as completely stupid?" Blanca finishes, still fuming.

"He would if I asked. But I don't think we *should* quash it. If we cut off this avenue, he's going to feel backed into a corner, then gods only know what he'll attempt."

Blanca snaps her fingers. "But if we lull him into thinking he's won . . ."

Tony jumps to his feet, excited. "He'll walk right into our noose!"

We all glare at him. After a second, he ducks his head with sheepish regret.

"Oh, my bad. Too soon for that joke, huh?"

Rolling her eyes, Christina sums up. "I show the judge everything I've gathered over the past decade about Rafael's crimes. Realizing that the grand jury will likely indict the man, he'll agree not to grant Rafael status as conservator. That's when I'll suggest our alternate."

Blanca looks at Ted. "Father, yes? It's the only way Rafael is going to buy this."

"There will be a hearing," I point out. "You'll have to act."

Blanca laughs and gestures with her chin at Annabel. "Luckily, I had a great drama coach. I'll trick that snake, beat him at his own game."

The hearing happens two days later. I sit shocked by the list of evidence that Rafael has gathered or manufactured to show Blanca's instability. Security footage from school at key out-of-context moments. Snippets of her phone conversations, which he had been recording in secret. Edited text messages. Recordings of her outbursts at home.

Most damning is what I know are the notes Blanca made as she crafted a one-act play for drama club. It features a conversation between Juliet and Lady Iztac in which the two debate suicide as a solution. The handwritten brainstorming sounds horrifying out of context.

For any outsider, it appears that Blanca is suffering violent mood swings and is considering killing herself.

"Ms. Montes," the judge interjects. "You've run away from home. Your living arrangements are unstable. Your best friend was just murdered, causing you to suffer a breakdown. The court is concerned for your well-being. Yet we'd like to give you an opportunity to weigh in about this proposed conservatorship."

Blanca gets up and stumbles toward Rafael.

"You gaslighting son of a . . . ," she gasps. "You're the one who keeps pushing me, twisting things up, trying to drive me crazy. Suicide? Yes, maybe I've thought about it. But only to escape you!"

She bursts into tears. The bailiff moves toward her, but the judge waves him back.

Slapping her hands on the table in front of him, Blanca suddenly screams in Rafael's face, "But if I go, I'm not going alone, padrino! A ver a cómo nos toca."

Beside Rafael sit his attorney and Ted Caldera, and they both recoil at this threat. Our lawyer hurries to Blanca, drawing her back to our table as Rafael lets the smallest hint of a smile play at the corners of his lips. I reach over to give her comfort, but she shrugs me off. So I stare at my hands as the judge speaks.

"I am going to approve the conservatorship for a period of six months, at which point we will reconvene to assess Blanca's capacity and competence, unless the conservator requests dissolution of this arrangement before then. However, it is my estimation that the ward's state may be worsened by her current guardian. I am therefore appointing a different conservator, one who has known the ward for most of her life and whose business interests intersect with her inheritance in trust. Edward 'Ted' Caldera."

Ted does a great job of appearing shocked and of then regaining his composure enough to reassure Rafael, patting his hand. Our enemy grows calmer and nods, whispering something back.

"What? No!" Blanca exclaims. I turn to her and make a show of trying to calm her down. She grabs me, sobbing into my shoulder.

"Ms. Montes," the judge adds. "You have two days to coordinate your living arrangements with Mr. Caldera, to his satisfaction, understood? If he reports that you are being uncooperative, other measures will be instituted."

Blanca turns red-rimmed eyes to Barry Dollinger and gives a single, defeated nod.

I walk her out of the courthouse. Stilson is waiting.

Inside the car, I begin to applaud.

"That was spectacular. I was nearly convinced!"

She gives a sad little laugh. "That's because half of it was how he's made me feel. The secret to acting. Wrap your lie in the truth."

At Ted's urging, Rafael now agrees to hold a shareholders' meeting. They have to explain the conservatorship so that investors won't turn against Rafael or sell off their shares. The quarterly earnings report is phenomenal, so Ted emphasizes that they can manage any fallout.

Ted tells us that Rafael has repeatedly dropped hints about his true identity, as if trying to see if Ted is more than he appears to be, but the emperor is a veteran of many political battles and boardroom sparring. He doesn't reveal a thing.

On the morning of Blanca's eighteenth birthday, we watch remotely as shareholders begin to fill one of the conference rooms at the Imperial Silver Casino. Once everyone has settled in, Rafael Montes addresses them.

"Thank you all for attending. When you approved the plan for our partnership with Caldera Resorts, I promised you a surge in profits and dividends. Today, friends, I'll share our quarterly report. You will be quite pleased."

There follows a high-tech review of the data on screens on all four walls. Most shareholders are happy and likely wouldn't mind that a chunk of the profits comes from money laundering. Others, those we've made a deal with, take out their phones and finalize our transaction.

Blanca rubs her palms together in anxious anticipation. She and I are watching this unfold on my tablet in the hallway outside. Ted had casino security give us access.

"Finally, before we adjourn," Rafael says, "comes the matter of my daughter's state of mind. You may have heard rumors of a conservatorship. They are true. I'll have Ted speak to the specifics, as he's been appointed Blanca's new guardian. But I want to assure you that while her mental health is our number one priority, we are carefully managing any possible public relations fallout. Ted?"

The emperor stands and approaches the podium.

"Thank you mighty, compadre," he says in his normal car-salesman patter. But his voice changes as he continues speaking. "It's true that Judge Dollinger approved Don Rafael's request to set up a conservatorship for Blanca Montes. But early this morning, I met with the judge and had it dissolved, revealing the bad-faith motivations for the petition and the manipulation of evidence that followed. Blanca Montes has been declared capable and competent. And today she turns eighteen, legally triggering her control of the shares she inherited."

It's our cue. I push open the door, and Blanca strides in, wearing an elegant yet severe white Dior suit with a blue blouse and heels. I follow behind her as she makes her way to the front.

"Good morning, everyone," I announce. "I'm Gregorio Chan of

Grupo Tolchan. Minutes ago, I acquired twelve point five percent of Montes Realty shares. Thanks, former shareholders who were willing to sell at such a strange time. Enjoy your profits."

About a dozen men and women rush out. Rafael Montes turns his eyes on me then, and I can feel his hatred thrust against my heart like shards of ice.

Not just metaphorically. Magically.

Confused, I push back with heat, and he shakes his head as though dazed.

"As major shareholder and heir," Blanca announces from the podium, "I would like to make a motion. The immediate removal of Rafael Montes as CEO and president of the board of directors of Montes Realty."

"Seconded," Ted echoes beside her.

"Submit your votes via the secure app," Blanca says. "The results will be displayed on the screens around us."

Rafael's calm smirk becomes a sneer.

"You fools! You'll destroy the company if you put it in her hands!" His voice begins with a tremble and builds toward a panicked snarl. His face goes purple, his eyes shifting back and forth. "You'll regret more than lost profit. If you turn on me, I'll make you pay! You've no idea the power I wield!"

He scares some. But he doesn't stand a chance. Blanca controls forty percent. Ted seven. And I now own nearly thirteen.

"Let it be entered into the minutes that at eleven forty-eight a.m. on this date, sixty-four percent of shares agreed to dismiss Rafael Montes," Blanca announces, her eyes sparkling as she at last takes leadership. "Padrino, until you find yourself in prison, you may only attend shareholder meetings. You have the rest of the day to clear your office. As per our corporate charter, the CFO and the vice president of the board of directors will serve as interim CEO and president. With that, our meeting is adjourned."

As the remaining stockholders stand, I raise my voice to get their attention.

"There will be a press conference in the lobby in fifteen minutes."

Everyone files out, leaving Blanca, Rafael, Ted, and me. I have just turned to leave as well when the door flies open and Jackson rushes in, a manila folder in his hand. From behind him comes the sound of Tony's shouting.

"Blanca!" Jackson's face twists with rage. "The impostor has really screwed with your head, huh?"

"Impostor?" Blanca demands. "What are you babbling about?"

Jackson lifts the folder and focuses furious eyes on me. "Gregorio Chan. My mom had a shoot in Geneva a couple of weeks ago. So I visited Le Rosey School. Talked to some of your former classmates. An ex-girlfriend. Julie Berger? Ring a bell? Of course not. Because you don't know them. You were never there. I have *proof*! What did you do, find a good plastic surgeon? Did you really think you'd keep fooling every—"

Tony comes barging in, rushing at Jackson. Blanca stops him with a raised hand.

"I can handle this spoiled escuincle. Ah, Jackson. You're a little behind the curve. Everyone here already knows that Greg isn't what you thought he was. Then again, neither is anyone else in this room."

"Whoa." Jackson's eyes widen as he feigns shock. "You really are nuts, aren't you?"

That's when our quarterback snatches the folder from his hand.

"You're messing with forces you can't understand," Tony says. "It's like you're trying to play flag football with a bunch of pros."

Jackson reaches for the folder, but Tony dances away easily.

"Go back to Belgium, Jackson," Blanca advises. "It's safer for you. You may be a jerk, but I'd rather not see you get hurt."

"What the hell?" Jackson says, as he looks at Blanca, Tony, and me. "I heard the news, you crazy ditz! A judge has put you under *my dad's roof.* You think I'm leaving? I have you just where I want you."

"Jackson!"

The voice booming across the conference room, reverberating from every wall, is none other than Ted Caldera, using his emperor's tone as he glares at his mortal son.

"Dad," Jackson whimpers as Ted Caldera comes to stand before him. "Didn't see you. Thank God you're . . ."

Jackson doesn't get to finish his thought, because Caldera slaps him so hard that he stumbles backward.

"Don't you ever talk to her that way again," Ted grits. "From this day on, you will show Blanca the respect she deserves."

"But she's acting like a . . ." Jackson holds his hand to his blazing cheek.

Ted Caldera roars at him, his face flushed. "Treat her like the gift that she is, or I will write you out of my will. Forget living in comfort. Forget Harvard. You'll lose everything!"

Eyes brimming with angry tears, Jackson glances around. His gaze stops, and I follow its focus.

Rafael is at the podium, ominously calm.

"Come, Jackson. Those fools have betrayed us. But this isn't over. If you want your revenge, leave with me now."

Angry and confused, Jackson hurries after Rafael as the man exits the conference room.

Of course he does. Who else would take the coward under their wing but Tzinacan, who strokes the wounded egos of his allies so they'll do his bidding?

Fifteen minutes later, we're in a semicircle around Christina Flowers, who's addressing the reporters in the casino lobby, in front of the decorative curtain of water that falls from several floors above.

"You've heard Mr. Caldera describe the changes to Montes Realty that happened moments ago and the voiding of the falsely obtained conservatorship. Such behavior is a strand in a larger pattern. Moments ago, I notified Rafael Montes and his legal counsel that my office has impaneled a grand jury to review evidence that may lead to his indictment. My hope is that the process will move quickly and that charges will be brought against the defendant soon."

The press corps explodes with questions, eager hands shooting up.

As Christina begins to answer, Blanca shudders beside me.

"Something's wrong, Greg," she whispers.

The air pressure is changing. Humidity is being sucked away.

"It's getting too cold, too fast," she adds.

Suddenly there comes an earsplitting *crack* from above us.

The entire curtain of water is freezing, top to bottom, ice rushing downward like glittering spears. I grab Blanca and Tony and leap toward the reporters. Panic and confusion set in as the knot of people surges in every direction.

The ice slams like a cage around the emperor and empress, then rushes toward us as well. Hauling on my beloved and her brother, I scream with all my might.

"RUN!"

CHAPTER
36

We run with almost supernatural speed, pushing through the throng of reporters and out of the building just in time, followed by the folks who have kept their wits about them. Within seconds, ice encrusts the doors behind us and spreads in every direction along the front of the casino.

Greg's first concern is for me. Standing just outside the casino, he touches my cheek, looks into my eyes, and asks, "You okay?"

"Yes. Yes," I say, though I'm shaking all over. And if I am feeling this vulnerable, this shocked, I can only imagine what my true parents and the others trapped inside are feeling.

Before me, the external wall of thick ice continues to grow, devouring the building. Like an all-consuming white fire, it moves upward from its frosted-over foundation at lightning speed, bringing an unexpected chill to the air. People pull their light coats tight against themselves as they jump back and run across the street, seeking safety. They watch in awe as the building becomes a crystal tower, an iceberg that glistens and glints in the November sunlight.

Unlike the rest of the spectators, watching from the street and beyond, under awnings and from behind cars, I walk over to the building and place my palms against it, gingerly, because I don't know what to expect. The ice is so cold, it feels almost hot to the touch. Its surface is made of shards. Dangerous and sharp, every sliver of ice in that massive wall is jagged, like billions of tiny crude knives fused together to keep us all out. When the frost becomes unbearable, I pull my hands away.

"What's he doing?" I ask, looking up at the top of the frozen building. "Why's he locking us out?"

Two helicopters drop men onto the roof. They repel off the icy, slippery building, but even with all their drilling and mild explosives, they can't find a way through and are soon hauled back up and flown away. On the ground, the same thing. Nothing the cops shoot or throw at that impenetrable wall of ice works.

"It's no use," Daniela says, when we rush up to meet her at the forefront, across the street from the massive iceberg of a casino. "Our weapons are futile against his magic as long as we're out here."

"Then it's time to fight ice with ice," I tell them. "I can send thousands of sharp, icicle arrows to shatter the exterior layers. Greg, you can then use your heat to melt the new ice, until we make a wide enough opening to get inside."

"Out here?" Greg asks. "In broad daylight?"

"Why not?" Sofía asks, pulling her compact out of her halter purse and opening it wide. "I'll cast a spell."

"Work your magic, Little Sister," Daniela says.

"Ma mehua in mixtli, in poctli, in ayahuitl," Sofía begins to chant.

As she intones the ancient spell, a gray sliver of smoke curls from the mirror of her compact. It grows and grows, climbing up into the sky and spreading a gray cloud over everyone around us. Thunder roars in the distance. People pull back, abandoning their places at the barricades and getting back into their vehicles. News teams tap at lenses, peering around themselves, clumsily trying to fix their equipment, while the mist takes over, a quiet, lingering fog that permeates everything within a square block.

At the same time, I feel something manifest itself within the grip of my right hand and sitting on my back. Bringing it up, I see it is my bow and arrow set, the one my father gave me in ancient times. Only this time, I know its power. Looking around, I see that Greg and Tony bear long, obsidian swords, and Annabel is hoisting an assault rifle over her shoulder.

"All magical, I gather?" I ask the goddess, and they nod.

"Time to fly," Greg says, and he takes the lead.

We rush forward. Through either our own magic or Ixcuinan's, we can see what others cannot. Standing in front of the two front doors, I brace myself, one leg forward, one leg back, and throw a strong thread of cold frost from my fingers. Like an icicle forming from rain and frost, a strong arrow of ice starts to form. Then, snarling, I dispense my rage in a hundred bolts of energy, thousands of icy arrows that one by one begin to crack the surface of Tzinacan's frozen fortress.

Greg steps forward, letting his own ire slice through the ice with the force of a red-hot sword he directs. His force is molten lava drawn from the depths of the volcano that has housed his heart throughout so many centuries.

But nothing we do is enough. After the sixth time its glow is quenched, Greg despairs and plunges his glowing fists into the ice I've thinned, screaming as he attempts to hollow out a path to the entrance with his bare hands.

As we exhaust ourselves, pushing through the pain, police and FBI agents continue to try to break into the building. And just as I'm about to give up, when I run up to Greg and put my hand on his shoulder to stop him from harming himself in the attempt, something extraordinary happens.

The ice disappears and the doors open.

Before we can react, Tony and Annabel rush past us, through the entrance.

Greg takes my hand, and we follow.

Somewhere behind us, Daniela yells, "Wait! It's a trap!"

But she's too late. The magic has engulfed us. As we stand side by side in the grand foyer, holding hands, exhausted but shivering with rage, we understand Tzinacan has allowed us in.

And he has sealed the entrance behind us.

CHAPTER
37

My eyes scan the lobby. To our left there's a large cylinder of ice with screaming people inside.

On the floor before us, six dead reporters are trapped in a curling wave of frost.

Beyond the crest of that wintery wave stands Rafael-Tzinacan, eyes wild with power and fury. Beside him, Jackson sneers. Behind them, a smaller, more transparent prison holds the emperor and empress, who are embracing.

"Welcome back, Popoca," Tzinacan says, grinning. "Ready to negotiate?"

"Is that why you've taken hostages?"

He shrugs. "You pushed me into a corner, Commander. Left me with little choice but destruction."

"What do you want?"

"Wealth. Veneration. Power. Why should I allow lesser beings to inherit such lives? I am far more worthy."

I feel heat building in my heart. "So instead of working for your own, you steal ours. But we've stopped you, twice."

"Not twice. I hold all the cards now. Unless you are willing to sacrifice everyone in this room. Believe me, I will kill them all with a smile."

"Not if we kill you first," Blanca says, her tone deadly frigid.

I turn to Tony and Annabel. "Free the reporters. We'll deal with this traitor."

Blanca takes my hand and pulls me to the right while the others go left.

"Get down on the ground!" Annabel shouts as she whips the rifle around. Aiming at the top of the cylinder, she opens fire.

Round after round slams into the ice as she fans the weapon back and forth. Once her clip is emptied, Tony uses his sword to hack away at the hole she's opened, trying to widen it.

Blanca pulls me around the wave. But Tzinacan gestures with crooked fingers and shouts, "Arise! Destroy!"

The frozen floor beside us shudders and cracks as the dead trapped beneath the ice emerge, eyes glowing blue, strange fretworks of gelid power spidering just beneath the skin.

"What the . . . ?" Blanca mutters. "*Ice zombies?*"

Before we can do anything to help, Tzinacan turns toward us, lifting his hands.

"Come no closer, or I'll make zombies of them all."

The pent-up rage of twelve hundred years, of loveless lifetimes endured because of this traitor's greed, triggers my connection with nearby magma, flowing just beneath the surface of southeast Reno.

I fling fire at Tzinacan. He blocks my attacks with shields of ice that regenerate as fast as I can melt them. Gunshots ring out as Annabel and Tony try to keep the ice zombies at bay.

"Help them!" I shout at Blanca, whose attempts at using her power against her padrino seem to strengthen him more. "I can handle him myself!"

As I draw more energy into my flesh, I push forward, slamming heat against Tzinacan's defenses. But the slush around my feet suddenly begins to freeze.

The temperature is dropping.

I take a second to look for Blanca. She is fighting the zombies, but every use of her power makes them stronger and adds more ice to the almost unbearably frigid lobby.

"That's not working, beloved!" I call. "You need to stop! Find another way!"

"No, please keep feeding us," Tzinacan counters, cackling with mad glee. "Once I break your boyfriend with your own power, perhaps you'll bow your head and bend your knee. Or perhaps you won't, and you and I will die again. It makes no difference to me. I'll simply try again in the next life. Chaos has promised to reunite us all again."

"No," I shout, flames rippling on my skin. "This twisted connection gets severed today."

I hurl balls of flame at him, set furniture alight and send it spinning toward him, push shock waves of pure heat in his direction. He blocks it all, but takes step after step backward, till he has almost bumped into the prison of ice that contains Blanca's Toltec parents.

The buckle of the belt holding my sword sheath in place grows unbearably cold and then cracks. The blade clatters to the floor behind me. I shrug.

"I don't need weapons, fool."

"Neither do I." Tzinacan grins as he blasts me with swirling hail.

Then, unexpectedly, the mounting cold slackens.

Blanca gives a loud groan, then a triumphant cry.

"Yes! Who's next?"

I glance her way in time to see her rush up to an ice zombie, wrap her arms around it, and tilt her head back. The animated corpse shudders, and a wave of blue energy passes from its cold flesh into Blanca.

The person collapses to the icy tiles. Breathing. Alive. And Blanca turns around and rushes another frozen zombie.

Now that Blanca is literally defrosting the enemy, Tony and Annabel continue to widen the gap in the ice. As I stave off a new wave of ice energy from Tzinacan, reducing it to steam that makes it difficult to see much of anything, a worrisome thought hits me.

Where is Jackson?

A scraping sound. Running footsteps. Then, from the heart of the mist, a sickening sound like meat being cleaved.

A cry of pain. A thud.

"What have you done?" Tony shouts.

"Sorry, teacher's pet."

Jackson. He must have hurt Annabel.

"Put your cricket bat down, Tony," he mocks. "You're not taking our prisoners anywhere."

A dozen ice daggers come ripping through the fog, aimed right at me. With a violent gesture, I explode them into sleet.

No further attack. I can't see or sense Tzinacan anymore through the dense mist.

Tony spits an inaudible curse.

"Annabel! Huixachin!"

"Yikes, Tony," Jackson quips. "I think I might've hit an important organ. Lots of blood. Time for you to drop your weapon."

"I am Crown Prince Meconetzin. Hundreds fell beneath my blade in battle. I'm more than a match for garbage like you!"

As the clash of their weapons rings out, I reach the cylinder that contains Christina and Ted. I summon enough heat to melt an opening.

"Tony needs your help. Annabel's been wounded. Get the civilians out. I'll take care of Tzinacan."

The former rulers of the Toltec empire rush into the fray. I hear Jackson spit angry words as, together with their son, they subdue him.

"You never have my back!" he screams. "Mom was right. So was Don Rafael!"

"That's enough, you pampered wretch!"

Nearer to me, blue eyes glower in the fog. Then the attack comes, stronger and harder than before, unrelenting, like a gale blowing off a glacier. I plant my feet and send a whirlwind of fire.

Our energies push against each other with ever greater violence. Every time I feel him thrusting past the shield of my heat, I draw more energy into myself.

Unlike the centuries I spent under Iztac's watchful eye, calmed by the gentle winds of heaven every time my fury threatened the world, there is nothing to stop me now. My hatred and grief pull heat into my heart from the torrid veins of the earth.

I become a conflagration, a miniature sun. Above me, railings begin to melt. Windows overlooking the lobby shatter. The distant ceiling catches fire. Humans choke and cough as they fight to reach the exit at last. In the flickering light, I see they're led by Caldera and Flowers, who are dragging Jackson between them. Tony is following with Annabel on his back.

Then Tzinacan answers my escalation with his own.

In an icy transfiguration, he becomes a deadly comet, as frigid as the void of space, shedding steam as he hurtles toward me.

Then Blanca appears, twisting her arms around him and yanking him to a brutal stop.

"Hola, padrino," she says, voice impossibly loud amid the din of destruction. "To paraphrase you, why should I allow a lesser being to wield such power? Especially when I can just take it from you."

Her eyes flash blue as she tilts back her head. Wave after wave of energy bursts from him, slamming into her flesh.

Unlike with the zombies, the cold that pours into her makes her shudder and moan.

Tzinacan howls with laughter.

"You like that? Here's more, you greedy cihuachichi!"

He closes his eyes and grimaces. Energy pulses faster and faster, as if he is pulling all the icy might of the Nevado de Toluca through his body and into her flesh.

"Iztac . . . Blanca . . . you've served your purpose, the only reason I let you live! You can't withstand the blizzard in my heart. It will destroy you, just like it did your parents a dozen years ago. Prepare to join them!"

"Nooo!" Her face twisting in a paroxysm of fury and grief, Blanca *thrusts her icicle fingers into his chest, howling*!

The last wave of gelid power rips free of Tzinacan and slams into Blanca. And she begins to transform. A blue glow surrounds and fills her. Her flesh becomes transparent. Pure ice.

Then, with a harrowing snap, the connection between our enemy and his volcano is severed. Blanca shudders, letting her padrino go.

She has become a crystal in which swirls the blue cold of the ages. I shudder at the sight.

"I feel them both, Popoca." Her voice is a swirling blizzard of sound. "Two volcanoes, filling me with absolute, eternal cold. I could plunge the world into darkness if I wanted. But I can't touch him without returning the gift Chaos once gave him. It falls to you."

At that moment, all barriers to my power dissolve. No one is pushing back.

Blanca steps away from Rafael Montes, from Tzinacan of House Oztohuah.

Her smile is like sunlight, glinting off freshly fallen snow.

"End this, beloved," she tells me. "Destroy him and let the gods' will be done."

Hot tears of shimmering lava dribble down my cheeks. I am no longer certain there is a way back from our transformations. We have wielded power like mountain gods. Can we ever be mortal once more?

We have waited so long to be reunited. But can a being of pure flame ever hope to embrace one of pure ice? Can hearts of fire and snow ever beat as one?

As always, we will put duty first, family first, community first.

With impossible hope, I channel the unquenchable blaze of the hidden volcano into Tzinacan's traitorous flesh.

He is obliterated. Not burned up or melted. No. My touch makes him burst into molecules that are consumed by supernatural heat into their constituent atoms.

Nothing but a soft haze remains, fading into the smoke and fog all around or drawn into the swirling vortex of flame that now wreathes me.

Parts of the building have begun to collapse. Blanca and I stand in the midst of the destruction, staring at each other. She too is garlanded, by a blizzard that whips round and round, a twister full of sleet and snow.

The air between us swirls and snarls, caught between two extremes of temperature, frantic and frenzied.

I take a step toward Blanca, but the air crackles with static and clouds blossom. Thunder rumbles. I shrug off condensation with more flame.

"That's enough, my child!" Ixcuinan demands, stepping in the maelstrom forming between us. "You must stop!"

My voice is the roaring of a furnace, the crackling blaze of a forest fire.

"I. DO. NOT. KNOW. HOW!"

"Let go of your rage. The casino is on fire. Lava is pouring from Steamboat Springs!"

I imagine the red-and-black flows, rippling hot and deadly toward the city.

But I am a howling whirlwind of fire. Blanca's cold caress can no longer reach me.

A laughing voice fills my mind, some dark part of me or Chaos itself.

It has all been a ruse. The gods never intended for you to have her again. You are merely a tool for the punishment of the wicked.

Reason fades, replaced by an all-consuming and raging need to devour.

I hunger for destruction. Tzinacan's death is just a taste. I should leave this casino, this city, this state, this *country* in smoking ruins.

Long have I suffered. Long has my heart ached with unquenchable sorrow and rage.

If I cannot have Blanca, cannot get close enough to even touch her, then let me extinguish myself on the world.

It deserves to burn.

Ixcuinan's pleading recedes as my vision goes red.

I cannot be reasoned with any longer.

Burn.

Burn.

Burn!

CHAPTER

38

I am cold. Colder and more dazed than I've ever been before. It is a relief to be numb with power. To feel nothing—nothing threatening me, nothing capable of penetrating my heart again, nothing capable of wounding me—for I have been wounded. Tzinacan's affront on my beloved, his cold disposal of my kind parents, his violence against Tina, his destruction of everything and everyone I've ever loved is too much, and I never want to feel again.

There is a peacefulness that comes with this chill, this frost; it gives me respite. But my heart still aches, so I close my eyes and try to thaw out of this icy vestige, to relieve myself of this frozen morbidity that wants to pull me away from this place, this moment of exhaustion.

"Blanca!" Little Sister's voice seeps into the coldness that surrounds me. She taps my icy cheeks. "Wake up, Blanca!"

"Tzinacan?" I ask, unable to keep my eyes open even one more second. "He is . . . defeated?"

"Blanca, listen to me!" Little Sister puts her hands on my shoulders and shakes me. "Look at me. Can you open your eyes, please?"

"I am . . . so tired," I tell her, keen to lie down, to let the numbness take me to another place, another time, to my palace in paradise . . .

Little Sister puts her hand on my back and pulls me up into her arms. "You can't lie down," she reminds me. "Stay with us, Blanca. The world is not yet safe. Your job is not yet done."

I open my eyes and see him, my beloved. Only he is no longer Greg, the handsome young man who stole my heart when I was nothing more than a human teenager. But he isn't Popoca, the courageous general who lost so much to Tzinacan, either. No. My beloved has been transformed into a fire that burns and blusters in a vacuum. His fierce features are barely recognizable to me, encased as they are by a giant flame that twists and roils and wraps itself around a liquid body made of volcanic lava. He is deadly and bright and out of his mind with rage and rancor and a rabid hunger that makes my chilled heart tighten in my chest.

"Beloved!" I cry out, clinging to Sofía as I struggle to stand up. "What is wrong with him?"

"He is being consumed," Big Sister says, standing on the other side of me. "Chaos has hold of his heart."

I step forward, refuse to let the fiery flames that lick at my icy exterior keep me from the one I love. "Popoca! Can you hear me?" I call to him.

The miniature storm brewing between our extremes of heat and cold shoves me back, but I push forward, turning the condensation to jewels of ice that cling to my frigid limbs.

Greg turns as I approach; his volcanic exterior swirls and whirls. I can see his face hidden behind the flames. He looks tortured, tormented by his own desires to burn everything in his wake, to be done with this bloody curse, this undeserved penance.

"If only there were a way to lift this curse," Little Sister wails. "To release the hold it has on his heart!"

"The hold Chaos has on his heart . . . ," I whisper, as I look down at my frozen hands.

Suddenly, I am there again, in that moment, at the altar, listening to Tzinacan's lies. I was broken, devastated to learn of Popoca's death. It turned my heart to ice. I felt nothing then as I feel nothing now. But I cannot relive that mistake. I cannot lose him again. He is fire. I am ice. Together, we are one. We are Balance. We are Order.

Chaos cannot consume Love.

I lift my chin and look straight into the liquid fiery-red eyes of my beloved. "Let it go," I whisper to him. "Release your pain."

And with those words, I freeze the swirling mist between us and smash my way through. Then I plunge my frozen hand into his blazing chest. There is pain in it, a cold, searing agony that makes me cry out like a wounded wolf. But I don't let it stop me. Instead, I use that profound pain to push my hand the rest of the way into my beloved's torso and wrap my fingers around the volcanic rock that has been burning inside his heart.

I tear it out of his blazing chest, ripping the flaming network of volcanic veins protecting it. The lava threads lie limp, seething, before cooling down and frosting over around my wrist and forearm. As the volcanic rock seethes and sparks, I tremble at its power. One thousand years of torment blusters and hums in my frozen hand.

I squeeze, and the connection to the volcanic field dissipates, releasing Greg.

"There is one more thing you must do. You must release yourself as well." Big Sister takes my forearm and guides me as I thrust that burning coal into myself, unfreezing my flesh and breaking my connection to the dormant volcanoes. At the same time, another weight falls away from my soul, and I realize that the tangled thread that has bound the fates of my family and friends to mine has now unraveled forever.

I feel the coldness leave my limbs, slowly, gently, and I shudder as the silvery, magical skein that connects all our fates thins, then breaks, dissipating into nothingness. My entire body flushes at the same time the fire dies around Greg, and when he is standing there, as human as we once were, so long ago, I throw my arms around him.

"It's over," I whisper as I hug him tight.

"Over?" he asks, confused.

Holding his face in my hands, I look deeply into his confounded eyes. "Yes, beloved. Over."

"The curse is revoked." Big Sister nods.

Greg's lips lift at the corners as I press my forehead to his. "It's done with?"

"We are restored," I tell him, and he wraps his arms around my waist and kisses me. Deeply, passionately, taking my breath away.

Greg's smile, when he pulls away to look down at me, is beautiful and bright and full of life. "I can feel it. I am mortal again, my love. Do you know what this means?"

"That we can live the rest of our lives as the gods intended," I tell him.

Greg caresses my cheek with his fingertips, sending a sensual warmth into my body. It inches down, to the very center of me. "Yes," he whispers. "Loving each other, raising children, growing old together."

"A normal life, yes. That's what I want, too."

Before all the gods of both Chaos and Order, I sigh and kiss him again.

EPILOGUE

Six months later, on a magnificent morning in May, Greg and Blanca stand at the foot of Popocatepetl in Santiago Xalitzintla, happy among the throng of villagers who have risen early and prepared delicious food for a feast.

There are fireworks displays, and music and other entertainment fill the streets nonstop. It's now dawn on the third day of the pilgrimage. Mayor Genoveva Cadena de la Rosa stands before them, flanked on either side by Roberto Chan and Dolores Ihpotok, who have played the roles of Greg's parents with diligence, as did multiple couples from this town down the centuries.

"Just as, with the help of Ixcuinan, our beloved Popocatzin and Iztactzin have severed the divine strands that bound them to the volcanoes," the mayor says, "so do I stand here to help Goyo release my people from their centuries-long service. The curse is broken; the commander and his princess are reunited. Gregorio Chan Ihpotok and Blanca Rosa Montes, please say the words."

Disguised, we Four stand and watch amid the throng of children, elders, and friends as Greg falls to his knees, pressing his head against that volcanic soil. Blanca does the same.

"Tlazohcamati huel miyac." Greg sits back and speaks to our people. "I thank you from the depths of my soul. Hear me now. I am no longer a god. You are no longer my followers. When I rise, I rise as one of you. Until the day of my death."

Blanca's voice breaks as she repeats the final phrases. "I rise as one of you. Until the day of my death."

Cheers, applause, embraces, and praise are the gifts of Santiago Xalitzintla as they stand. Thereafter, the lovers shoulder packs and join the villagers. It takes three hours to carry offerings of food to the summit of Iztaccihuatl. Young and old wend their way up the worn path, through the dense pine forests and along bubbling brooks.

They reach a small waterfall. Beside it, an alcove has been carved into the bare rock of the volcano. There, the people of Santiago Xalitzintla long ago erected an altar to our beloved Popoca while Iztac watched from the paradise of Tamoanchan.

Amid worship and prayers, the abundant bouquets of red-and-white carnations, the papayas and watermelons elaborately carved to resemble a fragrant bouquet of their own, are all laid on the stone altar.

Though it is the Day of the Holy Cross, all have come to beseech the guardian of Iztaccihuatl—for a new goddess inhabits these slopes—to protect them, to bring good rain, and provide a hearty harvest. As a well-respected curandera burns incense, they chant along, light votive candles, and set them at the feet of the statue in the alcove.

Afterward, Greg leans in and kisses Blanca's temple, and they leave the altar to sit on a flat rock a bit away from the villagers who have started to prepare food over an open fire.

"So, what's next?" Greg asks.

She takes his hand and kisses it. "It's hard to imagine anything more important than this."

"I know," Greg says. "But we should think about our future, because this is only the beginning."

"We'll graduate, of course," she tells him, her voice trailing off. "I'll get an MBA, at Nevada, and start working with organizations that matter to me."

"And after that?" Greg prompts. "Or perhaps while you're working on these things . . ."

She giggles. "We'll marry, of course."

"And start a family?" he asks. "We had always agreed on that."

Blanca grins. "I think the universe is aligned with this part of the plan. But that's not all the gods want from us."

"Of course," Greg says. "We'll do much more."

"We'll start a foundation to preserve water, and replace lead pipes across the country, helping other communities with water issues."

Excited by the prospect, Greg snaps his fingers. "I'll buy up the corporations that have been polluting natural water sources and reform them."

"We'll return rights and whatever land we can to the Native peoples and other communities to whom they rightfully belong," she insists.

"Yes," he agrees. "And we'll teach our children and their children to do the same—to care for others as they care for their own."

Blanca hugs him. "We'll change the world."

"Yes." Greg lifts her hand and kisses her fingertips. "And we'll do it together. Always."

———————————

We pull back from the lovers and the mass of faithful who kneel not far from the very gods to whom they once prayed, now happily and wholly human.

Are your hearts as moved as ours? Are you not awed by our ineffable design?

We peer along the strands of their intertwined fates, far into their futures, and this is what we see, dear children.

Ted Caldera and Christina Flowers wield their wealth and influence over Reno during the next several decades, making a veritable center of the arts that also manages to lift the standard of living for every one of its residents. A Mexican reporter refers to it as a modern Tollan. The nickname sticks.

After graduating and spending five years abroad, Tony Alsobrook returns to Reno. He and Annabel Dresch become best friends and business partners, establishing a series of community-based schools that center the particular identities and cultures of students with great respect, drawing on local funds of knowledge to create a new generation of capable geniuses.

Even Jackson Caldera, when the time is right, will bend the knee to us, begging that his sins be devoured, that he be given a second chance.

We are always willing to help our children change. All you have to do is ask with a penitent heart. We are listening. We tempt you, but we can also help you heal.

And our protagonists? Commander Popoca and Lady Iztac?

They live long, joyous lives. They have children, and grandchildren, and great-grandchildren, all of them blessed by the love and wisdom of Greg and Blanca, old souls who do indeed carry out their shared vision despite a society resistant to change.

And after many fulfilling years together, the two die side by side in their old age.

Peacefully. Smiles on their faces. Accepting the shared fate of every living thing.

Moving beyond. To the Unknowable Realm that awaits even gods at the end.

This time, there is no need for us to erect mountains in their honor.

Together, Greg and Blanca have reshaped the world.

And it forever remembers them.

ACKNOWLEDGMENTS

I have to start by recognizing my hermana del alma and literary partner, Guadalupe García McCall, who recommended that our second book draw on a pre-invasion Nahua legend. Thanks for putting up with my dogged determination to tie the story to real people and places in the past and present. As always, you brought beautiful poignancy and playfulness to the project while inspiring me with your willingness to kill your darlings . . . and boy, did we slaughter about twenty thousand beloved words!

Any measure of success I have, I owe to the wonderful work of editorial teams like the fine folks at Bloomsbury, especially Mary Kate Castellani; to the wise guidance of my agent, Taylor Martindale Kean at Full Circle Literary; and to the continued support of my family, especially my grandson Coyo, whose impish smile has lifted my spirits again and again.

Finally, I owe a debt of gratitude to all the unnamed storytellers—Indigenous and Mestizo—who have retold the legend of Popoca and Iztac down the long centuries, as well as to the poets and painters who have in recent times tried their hand at reframing that tragedy. Most notably, my respect goes out to the untold hundreds of Chicane artists who kept the image of the star-crossed lovers alive in the barrios where I grew up on the border—silkscreened on T-shirts, airbrushed on lowriders and vans, or tattooed on their flesh.

> *Esta leyenda es nuestra. Una tragedia, sí, pero también una promesa.*
> *El amor verdadero nuna muere.*
>
> —DB

Primeramente, I want to acknowledge and thank my best friend, mi hermano del alma, David Bowles, who continues to join me on this journey and who, like me, gets swept away in the stories of our antepasados, la buena gente whose DNA we share and whose loving spirit lives and breathes in us. I owe you so much, hermanito. Your compassion, empathy, and devotion to our stories is so special, so genuine, so unique, son cosas engendradas y nacidas en el corazón. These are things for which I can never repay you, but I promise to continue to feed you taquitos and true friendship to show my gratitude. Likewise, I am thankful for the devoted, caring team of people without whose hard work, devotion, and staunch support publication of this book would not be possible, my wonderful agent at Transatlantic, Andrea Cascardi, and the fantastic team at Bloomsbury, especially our dear editor, Mary Kate Castellani.

I am also ever so grateful for the support of my beautiful family, whose love and care feed my soul and in turn my writing. I could not do this work, give this much of myself to my craft, if my sweet husband, Jim McCall Jr., was not right there, urging me to move forward, to write the next story, to believe in myself, and know that I am worthy of this dream, this life that feeds my soul. I adore you, darling boy. Your love keeps me strong, and our children, James, Carelyn,

Steven, Jeremy, Jason, Sara, and especially our loving, gentle, funny granddaughter, Julie, give my life meaning and purpose and fill me with hope. Thank you all for forming a protective, loving circle around me and surrounding me with such powerful joy. I am blessed, blessed, blessed and though I can't bring down the stars and lay them down at your feet as you so well deserve, I will continue to make you calditos and sopitas de fideo to reciprocate your warmth! Y también le doy gracias a mi diocito lindo, for He keeps me, and helps me, and protects me, always and forever in His grace.

Last, but not least, I am grateful for our antepasados who, through oral tradition, passed down to us their sacred knowledge and wisdom. I am so very grateful for the cuentistas y artistas, the storytellers and artists, who through the epochs and up to this very day and age have always looked at the world as a reflection of the human heart with its unrelenting spirit and unwavering strength. Their work continues to keep our stories alive in the world.

Este cuento es mas que nuestro linaje, es el latido de nuestro corazón.

—GGM